EMMIS

A SMALL TOWN IN MINNESOTA 1938

By Cecil Wade

To Tom & Paige —
If you hunt hard Enough
through the story you'll
find your old friend
Jake McGuire
Cecil Wade 2/11/09

ACKNOWLEDGEMENT

This novel is dedicated to my husband, Milo Wade, my son, Martin Wade, my friends, Jean Birk, Denise Remick and Laurel Batson, who thought I could write a novel, to the Benton County News for allowing me to keep my pencil sharp.

It would have been impossible for my novel to have found its way to publication without the talent, enthusiasm and hard work of Greg Harren and Nat Stensland. Greg, who transformed it to a bound book and Nat, who advised me on technical issues when I reluctantly laid down my pen and who designed the cover for EMMIS, gave me invaluable assistance.

My number one proofreader, Danny Dziuk, most kindly rid my manuscript of many errors, although I may have included several more when his job was done. Old habits die hard.

Cecil Dziuk Wade has published poetry and short stories; EMMIS is her first novel.

Writing a weekly column for Benton County News, published in Foley, MN the writer of this novel is reminded that the life of everyone is a complicated story: even tales of characters in a work of fiction set at a certain time in history tell us something about the larger world.

Living two miles from where she was born, the authour created EMMIS as an antidote to the often heard criticism of friends and family who charge that living in the same town for seventy-five years erodes one's power to enjoy a larger landscape.

Creating a town with no history, giving life to people who never lived, enjoying the freedom to allow anonymous people to do good and bad things... a writer need not stray far from home to arrive at another place for the time given to its whimsical development.

For the author of this brief novel, EMMIS is that place.

CHAPTER I

This morning, Cy slid the coffee pot to a spot just above the firebox of the kitchen range. The fire had been lit an hour ago and the kitchen was warm: he hung his sweater on the back of a chair near the table.

Bert had gone earlier than usual to school, happy to have Christmas behind her, anxious to get back to teaching at Emmis High.

Thea had left even earlier, before anyone else in the Kennedy house was awake, to get the Advocate office and pressroom ready for her small crew's arrival: a fire in the big heating stove, window shades raised, the coal buckets filled for the day.

Gladdie Olson, housekeeper at the Kennedy farm, wouldn't be back from her sister's place in St. Paul until the third week in January. This was a custom that began at Cy's insistence when Bert and Thea were ten. Cy feared she would tire of caring for the house and the twins unless she had a decent reprieve from her responsibilities. Her month in St. Paul, these many years later, was welcomed by Cy as a pleasant rite in the long Minnesota winter. He grinned as he looked out the window beside the kitchen table.

It was nice to be alone.

A sliver of the moon, nearly spent, cast a sheen across the farmyard that was most visible from the window. Cy wondered if he would ever have known this sense of place and time if he'd chosen to live somewhere else. The shadow of the windmill cast dark shapes across snow that was stippled with the luster of thin-layered ice.

Marking the edge of the field nearest the house was evidence of last year's vegetation, frost-dead stems and seed-heads standing in tufted wisps above the snow. Clearly visible, a snowy owl, patient and unafraid, sat in the bare branches of a vase-shaped elm, ready to pursue whatever moved below.

Turning from the window, Cy remembered that he'd better close the damper on the stove before all the heat escaped through the chimney: Gladdie's most frequently offered criticism of her employer's domestic ventures. Gladdie, who had a small house at the edge of Cy's east field, fretted about him and his daughters, he was sure: her shrewd eyes, her pursed lips, the set of her shoulders as she darted about the household chores.

But there was no doubt that Gladdie regarded the Kennedy house as the center of her life, a life, by her own choice, she would never surrender.

Gus and Gladdie Olson had married less than a year before Ayma and Cy's marriage. Gus, a railroad section hand, had purchased an acre of ground from Cy just on the southeast corner of one of Cy's largest fields.

Gus had worked for Cy a couple of years but he didn't like farming and when he signed on with the railroad crew he bravely asked Cy to sell him enough land to build a small house and a shed for a horse and buggy, maybe a nice garden. Cy couldn't say no.

His brothers helping him, Gus built in a few weeks the snug, modest home where Gladdie continued to live after Gus was killed a few miles north of Emmis ten months later, steel rails being unloaded from a flat car twisting when a chain slipped, one of the long rails breaking Gus' back.

A few months later, Ayma, in the midst of a difficult pregnancy, was persuaded by Cy to ask Gladdie to help with the work in the big Kennedy farmhouse. Cy worried that the reserved, often aloof Ayma might be too arduous a taskmistress for the young widow but within days after Gladdie's appearance on their doorstep, his worries were laid aside.

The friendship between the two women was spontaneous and never wavered. Gladdie was at the farm every day except Thursdays, and even then if something unexpected occurred at Ayma's house or on the days when harvest crews needed to be fed. On Thursdays she did chores her own house and garden required.

Cy told Gladdie, just once, that she was welcome to live at the farmhouse; a buyer for her own house could be easily found. Gladdie refused, near tears, and they never spoke of the possibility again.

Often, late on a Thursday afternoon, Ayma and the small twins would walk over to the Olson house where Gladdie would guide them through her flower beds and allow them to examine the pieces of embroidery she fashioned in the evenings, alone in the lamplight of her front room.

When Bert and Thea were five and Ayma died in childbirth, along with her stillborn son, Cy, numb with disbelief and nearly helpless with pain, knew that his own grief was no more genuine than Gladdie's. He heard her speak directly of her feelings just once.

A few days after Ayma's burial, he found Gladdie in the kitchen, her forehead pressed against the window pane through which the last rays of sun filtered, casting a glow on the thin curtain.

Sensing someone behind her, Gladdie turned, her face wet with tears. She held both arms stiffly, clenching her hands, the knuckles outlined like white marbles. "If I love them, they always die!"

Cy moved toward her and she backed away against the pantry door as though by distancing herself from the possibility of his reach he might think someone else had spoken.

Years later, dressed almost always in the cotton dresses she sewed, wearing a full apron until she left the Kennedy house at the end of each day, her small feet encased in black kidskin shoes tied tightly, and her once dark hair held back from her face with the imitation pearl set of combs the twins bought her years ago: anyone who had ever known Gladdie Olson would recognize her instantly.

Cy knew that the least happy years Gladdie had spent on the Kennedy farm were those when the twins were at St. Mary's College, when sometimes they didn't return home for several weeks.

Born only twelve minutes apart, the closeness of the space they had shared within their mother's womb seemed to be the only commonality that marked Alberta Rose and Althea Summer as twinborn sisters.

Their genetic heritage absolute, Cy sometimes in a fanciful moment wondered if the girls might have made a pact prior to their entrance into the world to be nothing, think nothing alike.

The twins' persistent loyalty to each other often appeared to be no more than the common unmitigated regard observed in quite ordinary human alliances but Cy could not imagine that anything or anyone could weaken the attachment between Bert and Thea.

Especially in their childhood years, disagreements so resolute they seemed beyond the possibility of civil reconciliation ended by means of a raised eyebrow or a slightly theatrical glance of exasperation by one, almost always by the sudden laughter of both girls.

Thea, nearly six inches taller than her twin by the time they left Emmis to enroll in college, was regarded by their friends to be the decision maker and was most often the speaker for the Kennedy twins. Cy knew better, and his perception of the truth was shared by Gladdie and Shorty, Cy's longtime foreman in charge of most of the Kennedy farm operation.

Thea, who more closely resembled her father and carried his unspoken authoritarian manner, was more willing than Bert to take risks. Bert, hesitant to let her feelings be known and seeming to weigh all options carefully had the gift, according to Gladdie, of knowing when to bide her time.

Shorty and Gladdie felt that they'd never been given permission or the responsibility to report to Cy their observations of his daughters, and took it for granted that Cy heard what they heard, saw what they saw and that they need only to keep watch insofar as the twins would be kept from physical harm. And if by chance they did comment to Cy on something regarding the girls' behavior, both Gladdie and Shorty knew that their words were appreciated by Cy and most often discarded.

Gladdie found great delight in Bert's movements, quick and synchronized with whatever purpose was at hand, and the seemingly unplanned organization that led directly to the conclusion of her plans. In Bert, Gladdie saw daily reminders of Ayma, the willingness to give comfort and ease to all, the self contained confidence so humanized by a sense of shyness and mystery, the woman now, whose presence in Gladdie's life had become a persisting symbol of the friendship she had shared with Ayma.

Bert's dark hair, worn in what Gladdie called a sensible bob, framed a heart shaped face remarkably lit by eyes more violet colored than blue. Smaller than many of the students she taught, no one in Emmis could recall an instance when anyone had intimidated Bert Kennedy.

If the twins were aware of the town of Emmis watching them or making judgments of their lives, the girls never seemed to give any substantial credence to what might be said or thought.

Thea's yellow Chrysler coupe, usually driven a tad past the speed limit, didn't draw many more comments than Bert's Ford Model A coupe or Cy's Terraplane pickup truck.

Thea, eight years after she became editor and publisher of the Emmis Advocate, had relinquished the frequent thoughts she'd entertained as a college student, dreams of living in some other part of the country, preferably in an area where the winter months didn't dominate the landscape and the lives of everyone living there.

Those vague schemes to abandon Emmis and the farm were lost now; the popularity of her newspaper provided her with the same feeling of success that Bert found in teaching. While the twins had never made a conscious effort to befriend the town, they were trusted and admired by most of Sutton County.

During the thirty years in which Earl Graham owned and edited the Advocate, his desk had been in a corner of the press room, surrounded by machinery, rolls and reams of paper, overflowing wastebaskets, all the furnishings blending together under the cover of ink stains. The week before Thea began her work in the town's "news office", she and Shorty dragged the big scarred desk to the spot where it sat now just inside the doorway and close to the large window. For most of every day she had Emmis in her sight, and the passersby who nodded or waved as they glanced through the plate glass window expected and received her swift response to their greeting.

Thea's hair, like Bert's, had a natural wave and Bert trimmed her sister's hair every few weeks. Everyone in the Kennedy household, even Shorty, knew that Thea detested the reddish tone that showed in her dark hair and remembered what she said when an early classmate called her "Red": that she couldn't wait to be as bald as Shorty or maybe gray like Gladdie.

Her skin was as fair as Bert's but Bert was spared the freckles that were evident on Thea's face and arms. Gladdie told her, when Thea was small, that the spots that grew darker in the hot sun of summer were angels' kisses. Thea, who loved the sun and wanted nothing to do with angels, became enraged.

Taller than most women, Thea's slimness was worrying to Gladdie, who asked Cy when the girls came home from St. Mary's the first time if he wasn't worried that Thea "never filled out".

"I thought by now she'd be a regular size woman. Maybe it's those cigarettes."

Absently, from the chair where he was reading the paper, Cy seemed to agree. "Could be, Gladdie. Could be."

When the twins were younger Cy was aware that his housekeeper seldom found fault with Bert and he attributed Gladdie's fondness for his smaller daughter to her nature and appearance, reminders of Ayma. He recalled that once, when the girls were small, Gladdie made one small complaint about the laxness of his authority when Thea often "bent the rules". Cy knew it had taken a certain courage for Gladdie to confront him and she wasn't satisfied when he told her that both girls were allowed to bend the rules now and then, but Bert chose not to.

Gladdie stared at him for a few seconds and said, "For that, you should thank your lucky stars, Cy Kennedy."

Before the girls left Emmis to attend college, Shorty seldom saw Bert unless she was in the kitchen when he stopped to see Cy, or when she was trailing behind Gladdie in the garden. The girl's resemblance to Ayma was unmistakable and he felt the same oddly cool distance between himself and Bert that he had experienced with her mother's presence, a distance not initiated by either Bert or Ayma but by his own inhibition.

Shorty was less reserved with Thea. She regarded him as an authority on every phase of the farm's operation and he was amazed at the ease he felt, talking to her.

"Why are those bees hanging around the buckwheat field?"

"Why didn't our steers go to St. Paul when Johnsons and Bradys shipped theirs?"

"How come you plowed that sweet clover right back in the ground?"

For Shorty, the satisfaction of being well regarded by Thea ... the skinny twin...was secondary to the unfolding revelation that Cy appreciated the friendship between his hired man and his restless, inquisitive daughter.

Gladdie hinted that Thea spent too much time down at the barns and sheds and Cy, aware of Gladdie's scorn for most of the barn and field help, told Thea as they sat down at the kitchen table, "Gladdie's worried you're down there with Shorty, bothering him and keeping him from getting his work done. Don't get in his way and you'd better shake the hayseeds out of your shoes before you come in the house. And don't pick up a lot of bad talk from those fellas down there."

Coming through the doorway of the pantry, Gladdie knew she should have kept her worries to herself.

Cy was pleased to sense the satisfaction of both Shorty and Gladdie when the twins returned to Emmis and were praised for their work at the school and at the news office.

He knew that Gladdie had struggled to take the place of their mother when the girls were small and he knew she'd deny it if he told her he knew the reason for her endless effort, that she'd shrug her shoulders. "It's just my job, Cy, like everybody's got a job of some kind."

Just once Gladdie had conveyed in words her instinct to preserve Ayma's memory in the lives of the twins. When Thea took over the Advocate, she ordered from Dolly

Marchant, the most popular seamstress in Emmis, a half dozen pairs of pants. Cy overheard Gladdie, when she confronted Thea, telling her that Ayma would be disgraced to know that her daughter wore trousers to work, right on the main street of Emmis.

Cy hid his grin behind his newspaper and when Thea left the room, Cy aked Gladdie to sit with him a few minutes.

"Gladdie, there's not a day somebody doesn't tell me I was always lucky to have you running the house and overseeing the girls. I've told myself that a million times. Nobody's going to think you fell down on the job if the girls do things different than you or different than me or different than Ayma. Ayma had spunk and you've got spunk and I see that in both girls."

As Gladdie began setting the table Cy added, "I see when I drove past your house today that fence at the front of your flowers is leaning. I'll send Shorty down tomorrow."

A month later, when Thea was showing Bert the pants she'd picked up at Dolly's, Cy heard Gladdie say, "I like the dark ones best, but the gray pair is nice, too."

When the twins were in high school and running around with friends, Cy never considered the possibility that either of them would not marry; he hoped they'd finish college first. He wondered now if each was waiting for the other to make a break from home first. Why would they feel that way?

Thea's involvement with Ralph Stewart didn't seem to be moving closer to marriage but Bert's friendship with the high school principal, Davis Mader, was evidently gaining momentum, according to Shorty. In an uncommonly candid moment, Shorty had recently asked Cy, "Wouldn't you think a guy like that Mader fella would up and say, *"Let's get married?"*

Amused and surprised, Cy answered, "Well, when he comes around again, I'll tell him you're worried."

After a moment, Shorty replied, "Well, I maybe spoke out of turn, but Bert's a good girl."

CHAPTER 2

So. 1938.

The twins were thirty years old, both working within a couple of miles from the farm. Gladdie insisted she needed no extra help in the house, Shorty had talked Cy into selling off the hogs and increasing the herd of Shorthorn cattle; the long drought had ended. None of the men who rented the smaller farms Cy had purchased for speculation, except for Hank Kootseema, were behind in paying rent. Farm market prices were not high, but stable or advancing slowly.

Some of the farmers had taken the government up on the new forty year loans at 3% interest. Cy and the twins talked a little at the supper table about Japan moving across China and Hitler pushing across Europe.

Gladdie passed the bowls and plates from place to place, confident that none of those foreign trouble makers from Japan or Germany would make any difference in the lives of anyone in Emmis.

Now, Cy pulled the window curtain further to the side. Had someone just walked past, toward the door of the back porch? None of the men working in the barn would be scurrying around in the half-light, Cy was sure, and if Shorty wanted to see him, he knew Cy would stop down at the shop before he began his morning trip to Emmis.

Furtive rapping at the porch door brought Cy to his feet and he pushed the switch to light the porch as he opened the kitchen door.

Amelia Kootseema, a babushka covering nearly all her unkempt, straying hair, stared at him with red rimmed, puzzled eyes. Her long, once-black coat was unbuttoned above her waist, revealing layers of God knows what; sweaters, Cy supposed.

Cy stepped aside, motioning for her to step inside.

Amelia, her bony feet in men's mud rubbers held tight to her feet by encircling rubber jar rings, shuffled past him into the warm kitchen where she dropped to a chair at the side of the table.

For a few seconds, bereft of words or motion, Cy stared at the haggard woman. Although Kootseemas hadn't paid rent for two years, Cy had not confronted them, mostly to not have the confrontation that he knew was unfolding in his early morning kitchen.

Cy took a second cup from the cupboard near the stove and filled it with scalding coffee, then refilled his own. He sat across from the silent woman and asked, "Amelia, how've you been this winter?"

The question hung in the kitchen. Was the wall clock still ticking, was the gentle sound of wood settling and burning in the stove suddenly on hold?

Amelia ignored the steaming cup before her, wrapped her arms across her breasts, the slack lines of her mouth suddenly pulled straight. She shifted in her chair slightly and peered out the window.

Cy thought, "Good God! This woman was good looking and well liked in Emmis! This bag of bones, this smashed down creature, how much closer to the ground can she crawl?"

Suddenly, she shifted her gaze to Cy.

"Hank and me, we can't make it with just those few cows. After Matt died you took the papers on our place, we can't get no more money off the bank. Mabel, just because Hank gave her and Glory a place to stay, she takes the egg money for her and the girl."

She fell silent once again and Cy felt a familiar pain fleeing across his chest. He looked at her eyes, wide open now, begging. Begging for favors.

He cleared his throat.

"Times are tough, Amelia. We both know that. Hank's not much of a cow man, and you're like me, getting a little old for a string of chores every day." He tried to catch her eye with a smile but she turned to look through the window again.

"I haven't got tough about the back rent, Amelia, and I don't intend to get tough unless something changes for the worse. You folks hardly put up enough feed for the herd you've got, Hank sells the calves as soon as they're old enough to stand. You can't build a herd that way, Amelia. I understand Mabel feeds all of you with her garden and her hens and as far as your place goes, Eli sold it to me when you never paid the mortgage off.

"Hank needs to feed his cows and sell the cream, use the skim milk to keep a few hogs."

Cy knew he had gone too far. Amelia leaned across the table, her coat sleeve dragging inches from his cup.

"Don't you tell me about money! You can hold off on the rent and all that, but don't you tell me how we could do as you do and be something better!"

Cy leaned back in his chair, thinking, "Good God, having a fight with an old woman in my own kitchen!"

"Amelia, what can I do? I'm not saying Hank couldn't make a go of anything, but he doesn't get the hang of farming, you must know that! Even men who are born to farm have had a hard ten years. He was hired on the road gang, he quit. He put in a month at the feed mill and walked off. He went with the section crew less than a week and didn't show up again. I can't carry Hank, Amelia, and neither can you."

Suddenly, Amelia's hands quit twisting and she sat upright in the chair. Her voice was no longer ranting, her eyes, fixed on Cy, were illuminated by something Cy hadn'd known she possessed.

"But I did carry him, didn't I?"

Cy's breath caught, he stared back at her.

Once this woman, Amelia Jako, had been the best liked waitress and barmaid in Emmis. The birth of her son, Hank, her marriage to Matt Kootseema when Hank was a child, her never-ending alliance with alcohol, her descent into abject, bottomless poverty had transformed the free spirited young woman whom Cy had barely known into this beggar whose kindest critics, now, considered a lost soul.

Aware suddenly of the waves of pity coursing through his body, Cy began to reach across the table, to cover her hands with his.

Amelia quickly folded her hands together in her lap, scraping the legs of her chair away from the table. The look in her eyes shifted from the hollow, half-dead expression she commonly wore to one of nearly fearful delight, as though the risk of coming here might be rewarded, after all.

She began to stand and Cy commanded, "Sit! God damn it, Amelia, what in hell can I do for you? I'm not going to pay for you and Hank to go on living on my property, what kind of sense does that make?"

He could barely hear her reply. "I'll see we do better. It ain't so easy, but we could try more, I guess."

She stared at Cy as he unbuttoned his shirt pocket. pulling out his wallet and placing a few bills on the table. He slid them over to where she sat and said, "You folks should be looking for another place to stop, Amelia.

"Matt let the place go to hell when he was working for your dad and that's not your fault. Mabel seems to be a good worker. Don't come to me for more money, Amelia. To tell the truth, if you and Mabel shook loose of Hank, you might all do better."

Unsmiling and with a dismissive air, Amelia folded the money in one hand and, bracing herself with the other, stood beside the table. Glancing at the smeared floor, the snow that had melted from her castoff footwear, she said, "You got a mess here. I guess I got Gladdie's floor dirty."

As she shuffled through the door, Cy saw the half-smirk on her face. He emptied both cups in the sink and closed the dampers on the stove. He hoped for an early spring.

. . . .

Glancing out the window of the newspaper office, Thea smiled and nodded when Wes Carey tapped on the frosty glass, motioning with his thumb toward Pavlik's saloon, a few buildings south of the Advocate.

There was a coffee pot half filled on the coal stove that heated her building and she was behind in this morning's work but Thea could nearly always fit in a few minutes time to catch up on the gossip that floated through Pavlik's. It didn't bother her that she was almost always the only woman among at least a dozen men...mostly farmers... who gathered there nearly every day.

Today it was only about an hour until noon when Thea joined Wes at the far end of the bar, and the morning crowd had thinned out. Wes, who owned Emmis Hardware and Furniture, sat at the bar, a beer bottle beside the dollar bill he'd laid there. Clyde, behind the bar, brought Thea a scarred mug filled with coffee that had been heated several times throughout the morning.

John Pavlik, the owner of the saloon, was talking to a liquor salesman behind the bar and shook his head as Thea lifted the mug to sip the molten mixture. He pointed to a bottle of brandy, open on the back bar, and looked at Thea. She waved it away and John shrugged, shaking his head.

The dimness of the light in Pavlik's, Thea had long ago decided, was part of the narrow building's charm, but even on a day like today when the town was lit by brilliant winter sunlight, the darkness in here meant that from her stool she could barely see the few men seated and standing near the bar in the front part of the saloon.

She asked Wes if he thought the windows in Pavlik's had ever been cleaned.

"If they were, " he said, "they didn't buy the buckets and brushes from me."

Clyde came back to the end of the bar where they sat, to see if Wes wanted another beer and asked Thea, "Cy ain't lost a steer or a couple of veal calves, has he? Your neighbor to the north just laid a twenty dollar bill on the bar."

Squinting, Thea recognized Hank Kootseema among the small knot of men near the door. She and Wes walked past Hank a few minutes later as they left Pavlik's, and Hank reached for her arm. She turned in surprise and saw his usually sullen face twisted with an odd look of secret triumph.

"I'll buy you a drink, he said. "Top shelf if you want it."

Thea backed away from him, bumping into Wes. "Why don't you go home and take care of your family?" She was sorry at once for answering

Hank and filled with quick regret when she heard her own voice, filled with anger.

On the sidewalk, she breathed deeply and Wes watched her. "I get so damned mad! My dad could put Kootseemas off that place in a minute, sometimes I think he gives Hank more slack than Bert and I ever had!"

Wes laughed, punching her arm. "I doubt it, Miss Kennedy. And anyhow, who are you mad at, Hank or Cy?"

Thea looked at Wes and said nothing. When they reached the door of the Advocate she said, "See you soon, go sell some nails."

Sheriff Frank Keefe was waiting for Thea, inside her office, leafing through the auction bills hung on the wall across from her desk. "More than half of these sales are foreclosures; things are loosening up a little but I don't think Sutton County's gonna see many millionaires milking cows and slopping hogs."

He sat down abruptly across the desk from Thea. He laid his hat on the corner of the desk and fidgeted for a minute, getting himself into a comfortable position. He flexed his fingers scratched an ear, then stared at Thea.

"Any chance, you think, of getting your old man to throw Hank and his miserable bunch off that place? I can't keep up with them and the stuff they pull..."

Thea laughed. "I was discussing this quandary with Wes five minutes ago. I take it you want them out of the county...I just want them out of the neighborhood. My reason is simple, they drive me crazy. I suppose your reason is the same, really, you don't want to see them or hear about them.

"Bert and I...and Gladdie... know it's no use to argue anymore. If one of Dad's other renters lets a fence post lean in his pasture, Dad drives over to talk to him. Hank pulls a corn crib down for firewood...well, Frank, I wish I could help you but I don't know how."

Frank settled deeper in the chair.

"I've run out of ways to deal with them, nothing ever works, anyhow. Amelia's been blacklisted at Pavlik's for five years, never sets foot in the saloon which is the only place in town to buy whiskey and she gets drunk as hell every time she comes to Emmis.

"Right now, the village council is telling me she stopped at Ollie Jenson's woodshed the other day, used it for a toilet and lit out when Ollie hollered at her."

"Mabel, skinny as an old crow, doing the best she can. And Glory, the girl, hasn't been in school since the middle of November. How in the name of God, Mabel ever saw fit to drag herself and that poor little girl to Kootseema's farm for a hook-up with Hank is beyond all sense."

Frank paused for a minute, looking at the floor.

"Well, they got cut off relief money last spring, except some little check for Amelia, some kind of widow's deal. Shorty told me a while ago Cy sent some stove wood up there or they'd freeze to death. Hank owes everybody that's dumb enough to let him in the door, he buys gas a gallon at a time, probably swipes Mabel's egg money."

Thea chewed on the end of her pencil, watching Frank, waiting for him to wind down, wondering what she was really being told. The sheriff had sat in this office often but his exasperation had never been so visible.

"Frank, you know Bert and I can't tell Dad what to do with that darned farm! We've heard Gladdie and Shorty giving him hell about it, and they never get heated up by anything else he does. He admits he hasn't seen a nickel of Kootseema's money in two years. One day I think he's going to go up there and torch the whole place and the next day I hear he's putting a new roof on the house."

Frank stood and zipped his mackinaw, taking his hat from the desk.

"The thing about Cy, he doesn't do very well, being a man better off than most. The thing is, he could do a lot better having a little of his brother Tom's ways. That's a man never looked to the good of anyone but himself."

Thea stared at Frank and motioned for him to sit down.

"We've wondered, Bert and I, why our dad never talks about Tom. If he were alive and walked through the door I wouldn't know who he was. Gladdie, Shorty...you all knew him. Why so quiet? Bank robber? Hold up man? Killed somebody?"

"Two different people, Tom and your Dad. Both set in different ways. Tom was my age but I lost track of him long before he died. It's dumb to bring his name up."

As he opened the door, Frank smiled at Thea. "Don't tell Cy I was asking after his renter. I'll get it all figured out somehow."

Bert Kennedy parked her Ford coupe near the west entrance of the high school, carefully positioning it so it wouldn't be in the way of either school bus when they arrived with the farm kids who attended Emmis High.

She loved walking through the silent building in the early morning on the way to her big classroom on the second floor, near the library. Guy Ronning, the school custodian, had already unlocked the rooms that would soon be filled with the noise of three hundred students.

The blackboards had been washed during Christmas vacation, the shades fastened to the tall windows adjusted to let in the light of the winter sun. The dictionaries and reference books in the glass-fronted shelves near her desk were upright; she knew without a glance that Guy had wiped the inside of the pencil sharpener with fine oil.

The students' desks stood in five straight rows, aligned with the narrow maple flooring that had been brightly polished during the two week absence of students and faculty.

In the Kennedy house, Gladdie had always been a compulsive maker of good order, as Thea referred to the housekeeper the twins had known all their lives. Bert wondered again if her own habit of watching Gladdie sort bottles and jars and cans in the pantry, carefully placing big bowls to the left of smaller bowls, straightening kitchenware two or three times a week, had initiated her own love for the symmetry found in common spaces, little jobs.

Fitting her handbag and gloves into the second drawer of her desk, Bert smiled, remembering the twins' eighth birthday when Gladdie announced that Cy had at last agreed that each of the girls might have her own room.

Thea knew that Gladdie and Bert were highly critical of her careless, slipshod use of space in the room she shared with her sister and she wasn't surprised that Bert wished to be emancipated from a room in which half the space was often buried in chaos. But Thea was surprisingly reluctant to accept even this minor step toward being divided from Bert. She felt her sister and Gladdie had conspired against her and that Cy was oblivious to the unfair standards which put herself across the hall from her twin.

But, almost overnight, Thea found there was unexpected freedom in her young life; an end to the dark looks and frequent complaints about scattered books, strewn clothing; a pleasant surprise that outweighed the silence of her lone occupancy of another bedroom.

Bert, too, valued the privacy of her unshared space and smiled now, recalling hearing Gladdie tell Shorty, as they drank coffee on the back porch, that it was no harder for him to clean the colt pen than it was for her to pick up after Thea.

Just this morning, on the road to Emmis, Bert wondered as she passed Gladdie's little house how much longer the Kennedys could count on the daily presence of the woman who had held their lives together when the girls were small.

She and Thea seldom spoke of the inevitable changes which would occur in their lives and in the life of Cy if Gladdie chose to leave the job she'd shaped around Ayma's family.

Shorty and Gladdie were aware that each of them were owners of special accounts in Eli Kanter's bank. Their wages were increased annually and neither of them spent as much as they earned. When Cy explained to the twins the finances surrounding the two, he had called Shorty and Gladdie "friends of the family".

When Thea and Bert returned to Emmis as college graduates, they left behind classmates disappointed by the difficulty of finding jobs. The Great Depression had settled in. Emmis High School had two positions open and Cy convinced the twins that if Mayme Kraemer and Alice Harding had kept their teaching jobs there for thirty years, Bert and Thea could teach at least one term.

Thea was restless and dissatisfied but Bert felt that even if her options were not dictated by hard times, she was happy to teach in Emmis.

Sutton County's official newspaper, the Advocate, was for sale and Cy asked Thea to meet him in the old building located as close to the center of Emmis as it could possibly be.

Thea didn't renew her teaching contract, she kept the staff that had worked for Mr. Graham and in two years, doubled the circulation of the Advocate.

When Thea and Bert had been home a few months, Gladdie wrote her sister, "All is fine here at Emmis. Nicer than if the girls was gone."

Out in the hallway, Bert heard footsteps coming from beyond the library. She was unable to hide her smile as Davis Mader stepped into her classroom.

His smile was broader than her own.

Laughing, he clasped Bert's hand. "Well, I see you made it through the holidays!"

And then, before Bert could speak, "Well, I guess that's as trite as anything I could say to someone who quotes Tennyson and Shakespeare. I mean, Bert, God it's good to see you again! Two weeks in Iowa with my mother and sisters is two weeks quite far from heaven, believe me."

She pulled her hand from his and sat on the edge of her desk. She hadn't noticed until now the gray in his carefully trimmed hair; he'd confided early this term that his fortieth birthday was just around the corner.

The most neatly dressed of the men who taught at Emmis High, Bert overheard often in the faculty lounge and the lunchroom the comments by the younger women on the faculty about his nearly always flawless appearance.

Davis Mader's voice, surprisingly deep, made him a natural arbitrator among the students. Like Bert, he was less tall than many of the older students in school, but his slight stature seemed to have no bearing on the measures of discipline he exhibited from time to time.

She told him now, "I had a great vacation. Thea and I spent a few days together, one day we went back to St. Mary's to see the nuns. Thea likes to go back once in awhile, probably so they can see the nicotine stains on her fingers. Dad and Shorty took a load of steers to St. Paul. Sadly, Thea and I were given the job of buying a new coat for Gladdie's Christmas gift and she nearly killed us."

Bert laughed and Davis asked, "Why? Wrong color?"

"With Gladdie, it's not the color of the coat, it's the color of money! 'You girls, you should know I can get another five years out of the one I wear now!'"

They were laughing when the rush of feet in the hallways reminded them that the first bus had arrived.

Davis backed out of Bert's classroom as she promised to save a chair for him in the lunchroom if she was there first.

When the students began wandering into the room before the first bell sounded, they nodded at their teacher. It felt a little like the first day of the school year, but actually, it was just the first day of classes in 1938.

Most of them had heard in the lower grades that Miss Kennedy could be an old crab, even a tyrant. Judging by the pleased look on her face this morning, they didn't think they'd have to worry today.

That evening, helping to clear the table after supper, Thea told Bert about seeing Hank at Pavlik's. Cy, smoking a cigarette in the chair near the north kitchen window, stared across the field to where the dim lamplight marked the Kootseema house.

"Dad, did you hear me tell Bert that I saw Hank this morning and for once, he seemed to have a little money?"

"I heard you," he replied. "I ran across Amelia this morning, too. Hank should share with his mother."

Bert asked, "I wonder where he gets his money? He's not working, is he?"

Cy stood up and threw his cigarette in the kitchen stove. "Probably some damn fool just handed him some cash."

The girls laughed.

CHAPTER 3

January, that winter, was the hard month it's nearly always known to be. There was little talk about the possibility of a January thaw. Fences were buried in snow, the cold so intense the little skating rink near the court house was closed and soon the rink itself was buried beneath the snow.

Outside Emmis, township roads were blocked and those plowed open by the county highway department were narrow. Cy, his farm just two miles from Emmis, managed to drive to town every day; sometimes he saw no one on the streets and sidewalks.

But during the last week in January the thaw came in. A southwest wind moved across Sutton County for three days. The changed weather was so unexpected that John Pavlik poured a free drink for anyone who stopped at the saloon, and Wes, at the hardware store, dug around in the basement among his off-season merchandise and brought a carton of fly swatters upstairs, handing them out to perplexed customers.

When the fly swatters were gone Wes went back in pursuit of the kites that had not sold last spring, but Delphine, his part time bookkeeper, slid the box of kites under her desk and told Wes to grow up.

"You haven't even paid for them yet, you hopeless idiot."

After a week, cold weather returned, but the wind and the temperatures were less severe and on the farms around Emmis loose hay was brought to the farmyards from meadow stacks. Diminished snow and still-frozen ground allowed load after load of manure to be spread on corn and grain fields.

Farm papers predicted an early spring and when February was still quite new, the soft winds and bright skies found only the old-timers in Sutton County wary of the changed appearance of the land.

Gladdie told the twins, "You wait and see, Shorty's goin' to be bustin' his britches, hounding your Dad to get the grain in. Same thing, every spring."

Shorty came to the house for supper, and reminded Cy that three years ago, in '35, they'd seeded more than two hundred acres in March. Cy answered, "The two of us are going to the southern part of the state to that big machinery auction next week. Forget planting." Gladdie winked at Bert and Thea and they laughed.

Then the hope for an exceptionally early spring wavered among the weather watchers. Cy wasn't worried at all about the ordinary February weather that stalled the field work but he was concerned about the grain and livestock markets, faltering again and bringing anxiety to his neighbors. The rumbling sounds in Europe were met with grim faces; some of Cy's best friends had served in the Great War just twenty years ago.

Disheartened, he was glad when Bert asked him to stop at the creamery in Emmis and bring the ice cream she'd ordered for the school's Valentine's Day party. He was there at eleven o'clock and carried the cartons to the gymnasium, where tables were lined up and dozens of cakes brought by the students were watched over by a few teachers.

Bert had told him last night she'd not likely be free this morning and Cy had visited briefly with a couple of her friends in the gym. Then, as he walked through the hall to leave the school, he saw a slight figure in the distance, coming closer, her face lit with a smile, the slight swing of her arms...Ayma!

Behind him, long rows of children were pressing to be first in line as they entered the gym; their voices were suddenly deafening. Cy leaned against the wall and, pulling his handkerchief from his pocket, wiped his eyeglasses, then his forehead.

Bert tugged at his arm. "Dad! Are you alright?"

Cy looked at her, smiling, and gently removed her hand from his arm. "You better get in there before those kids get the bellyache."

He'd been thinking of Ayma lately, more than he had for a long time.

It was 1905, Cy was twenty-four and the sheds and barns on the land he'd chosen as his farmstead were built. More than one hundred acres of field ground had been cleared and Cy spent long days traveling to St. Paul and Minneapolis, learning which pieces of farm machinery he could use in Sutton County. Planting and harvesting, deep furrows and fenced pastureland became his life.

He knew he was on tilting ground. Cy's father, Timothy, never iron-handed, offered as much support as a man could give someone who insisted on reaching for the unknown when the surety of the known was close at hand.

Cy's mother, Bridget had no confidence that the same land from which a lumber empire could rise might lend itself to the pursuit of any other kind of prosperity. Her father had farmed in Ireland, she had cousins yet in Galway who farmed and were all but starving, she reminded Cy often. No one but a perfect fool would follow plowshares.

Cy dismissed the disfavor of his mother with an open mind; he had no hope of pleasing her and had great hope that, in the end, his farm would please himself. He hired Shorty Brill, a Sutton County man, away from Timothy's sawmill and knew he'd never find anyone who would do a better job holding together the young men hired to work in the fields and barns.

His father asked, "How did you sneak away Shorty? Twice the pay?"

"Same pay, but no sawdust down his neck."

Shorty, who knew no more about farm animals than Cy, was sent to talk to farmers who had established successful herds of cattle. Both men knew something about the draft horses hauling logs and lumber in the woods and around the sawmills, and the teams that Cy purchased to work the farm were better horseflesh than anyone around Emmis had in their barns.

Until his farmhouse was built, Cy often stayed at his old home in Emmis overnight, leaving his Morgan mare, Lady Rose, in the livery barn near Timothy's house. Cy knew he had paid too much for Lady Rose, sweet tempered and easily managed, when any horse he owned would have taken him to anyplace in Sutton County.

He knew, too, that the beauty and the grace of his mount might brand him as a too-proud farmer. Well, so be it. He chose her, he fed her, he owned her, the finest looking horse who passed into and out of Emmis.

The night watchman at the barn grumbled, "Just like a circus in here if the word gets out that young Kennedy's mare is in a stall."

One early morning, in April, before he left Emmis to return to the farm, Cy walked up to Callahan's Store to buy leather mitts and gloves for the men who were picking rock from the fields that were plowed last fall.

Clothing was sold in one end of the long mercantile, shelves and tables for menswear on one side of the aisle and a larger area displaying women's shoes and clothing and wide bolts of fabric nearer the large door at the front of the store.

Neither Mike Callahan nor Mike Murphy, the old man who waited on customers, was in sight and Cy searched until he found the bins where bundles of horsehide mittens were bound together. He hunted on the crowded shelves for gloves, the only light the sun filtered through the big windows looking out on the dusty streets of Emmis.

He thought he heard a voice, and turning, saw a diminutive girl talking to a woman, the sun coming through the clouded windows pooling around them in the half-dark store. The woman, describing something, gestured with her hands and laughed, the young woman (not a mere girl, Cy thought) laughed with her and busied herself tying twine around a package.

One eye on the women, Cy, impatient to finish his own shopping, searched for the gloves he needed, annoyed that the largest store in Emmis gave its customers so little help.

He found the gloves at last and gathered them up with the mittens; good God, now even the clerk on the women's side had disappeared. Cy walked to where he'd seen her a few minutes before and heard somone humming, close to the wall where big packing boxes were stored.

She was reaching carefully into one of the boxes and lining up a row of colorful hats and bonnets on a long table, folding with care the sheets of tissue in which they'd been packed. She studied each, tilting her head and smiling as she examined the hats; she seemed enchanted by the beads and ribbons on those which were most ornate.

Her arms appeared to be too short to reach the hats in the bottom of the box, and Cy cleared his throat. "Let me help you."

She spun around to face him and Cy heard the quick intake of her breath.

"I'm not here for any kind of harm, I've just got a little buying to do."

She stared for a moment, then laughed. "I'm supposed to be doing a little selling, so you have no need to apologize."

Cy reached past her and carefully finished lifting the hats from the deep box.

Explaining that her uncle, Mike Callahan, wanted the money from each side of the clothing areas kept separate, she helped Cy carry the purchases he meant to make back to where he'd found them, then wrapped them in paper.

When Cy left the store he was surprised that he knew so much about her; there were twelve shiny buttons on the front of her dark dress, two on each cuff, three combs in her dark hair, each with four small stones. She wore no rings. Given the size of her neck he thought the chain on her locket was probably about a foot and a half long. He judged her feet to be about eighty percent as long as his mother's.

On the sidewalk, he remembered Timothy telling him that it's surprising what you can learn by paying attention.

At the livery barn he backed Lady Rose out of the stall before he thought to put the bridle over her head and had Lady Rose on the street before he remembered he hadn't paid for her overnight keep.

Three days later, Cy was back in Emmis and walked into Callahan's in late morning. He watched as she sold some buttons and thread to an older woman, then approached her.

"Easter's next week and I need a hat for my mother."

She looked up at Cy. He was unsettled, seeing the laughter in her eyes. She led him to the wire racks where hats were displayed, waited for him to select one. He faltered. "I guess that blue one, the feathers are nice. That ribbon...it's like for under the chin?"

She nodded.

The transaction took far less time than Cy had hoped. He said, "I need one for somebody else, too, the woman who works for my mother."

She smiled more openly. "What color?"

"I don't know. You pick one."

She laid a lavender bonnet beside the blue hat. "It should be a nice surprise for someone you've probably not paid any mind, until today."

Cy felt the heat rising in his face. He hated the way his fingers fumbled the catch on his small pocket purse; the leather felt clammy in his unsteady hands.

He picked up the neatly wrapped parcels and took a half dozen steps, then wheeled.

"What's your name?"

"Ayma. Ayma Flaherty. My aunt is married to Mr. Callahan."

"Ayma. I never heard that name before. Irish?"

"I really couldn't say. I think it means 'someone who sells hats to a man who really doesn't want hats.'"

Fleeing the store, Cy swore he'd never return to Callahan's.

But he did.

Cy was glad that Bert looked so much like Ayma and he realized that the twins, in just two years, would be the age Ayma was when she died. My God, My God!

Suddenly, sitting in the alley behind the school in his Terraplane truck, Cy laughed out loud, recalling that his mother had told him later that she'd given the blue hat to the wife of the farmer who delivered milk to the homes in Emmis.

Cy drove his pickup into the shed and stopped near the machine shed to talk to Shorty, who lamented in detail the weather forecast. "We'll never get that rye seeded!"

"For God's sake, Shorty! It's not late! We've had good grain that wasn't seeded until May!"

Shorty hesitated. "I know, but I didn't figure on the snow that's in the forecast."

"How much are they talking about?"

"I don't know. I just caught it when they said snow."

Cy looked at him. "Shorty, there's a pint of Wilkens Family in the toolbox of the corn binder. Bring the damn thing in and we'll have a drink tonight."

In the kitchen, Gladdie told Cy, "Shorty, he seems sad all day. Didn't come in for coffee, either."

"Shorty's the best man I know but he's got to let the weather come and go as it will."

Gladdie nodded and said, "Well, you can't blame him. Winter gets old after awhile."

She eyed Cy carefully. "When do you think I should get those baby chicks? I don't want to run the stove in the brooder house for two months if it's real cold."

"Ask Shorty. He's the weatherman around here."

Cy laughed and Gladdie shot him a dark look. What was so funny about asking a question about chickens?

Snow mixed with sleet fell thickly all morning, and just as the noon hour slid past, the watery sun disappeared behind the curtains of gritty white.

Sparrows were gathered on the hard packed snow near the granary door, busy picking over the kernels of barley and oats spilled there, and even working at the chaff that hadn't been blown away by the wind. Their tails were turned toward the wind and each had an eye measuring the distance to the sheltering pines behind the barns.

Cy headed across the yard, thinking that next summer he was going to build a shed nearer the house for his pickup and the twins' cars. "Get a northwest wind, and we might as well walk to Emmis as to the damn shed."

Close to the granary he saw the group of sparrows as they spied him, too. They lifted away and sat nearer the horse barn, watching him. Cy veered to the granary and reached into the nearest bin where a small pail rested on the clover seed Shorty cleaned a week ago. He tossed a shower of seeds across the spot where the birds had been eating.

Bert had explained to him once, in detail, how birds' small bodies and string feet survive in colder climates and Cy didn't feel any great waves of compassion for them, anyhow. But the seed wasn't worth a whole lot and too much cold, too much wind, too little sun didn't do anyone good, even these small birds.

Backing his truck from the shed, Cy tried to recall exactly what Frank Keefe said when he phoned this morning, something about a conversation Frank's wife had with Loretta Swanson, Mabel Kootseema's sister.

Cy knew that Loretta had asked members of the county welfare board to help Mabel and Glory survive and he supposed she was worried that the two were in danger of starving to death. Why would she think the sheriff could influence the board?

Last fall, Elof Elofson, who rented from Cy eighty acres east of Emmis, had paid part of his rent by delivering several cords of stove wood to the Kennedy farm. Cy, over the protests of Shorty and the twins, had sent four cords up to Kootseemas. Unless Hank had sold it, the woodpile should last until spring.

Frank stood in the doorway of his office as Cy walked down the familiar hall in the courthouse. The sheriff stood aside so his old friend could enter and Cy saw the anxiety in his glance. He felt the apprehension that always floated near the surface when the Kootseema family was under scrutiny.

Throughout the Prohibition years, Sutton County's lawmen had little interest in anything but maintaining their own positions and the money they earned by breaking the law themselves. When Frank Keefe hinted that he could be persuaded to seek the vote in the sheriff's race, Cy became his strongest supporter.

The Keefe family had been in Emmis as long as the Kennedys had lived there but Frank and Cy had barely known each other until fifteen years ago. Frank, younger than Cy, had been a friend of Tom, Cy's younger brother.

As close as Cy and Frank were now, Frank had never said why, when he was sixteen, his friendship with Tom had ended.

Frank's father owned the dray business in Emmis and one summer evening Frank helped his father sort the freight that had arrived at the train depot late in the day. By the time the dray wagon was loaded, Frank was too hot and tired to join his friends down at Balder's Bridge.

Tom and two other boys took one of Timothy's buggies and Bridget's small gray mare from the livery barn, leaving Emmis soon after supper. Two dozen young people from Emmis and the neighboring area came to dance, the next night the moon would be full and never brighter, ever, than on this night when fiddles and banjos were heard as far away as Old Man Balder's house.

Near midnight, Tom and his friends took three young women into the deeply wooded place furthest from the narrow stream which ran beneath the bridge.

The music ended about midnight, also, and later, some said that as they headed home they heard cries from the woods. Some said they heard sounds like birds or animals fighting, or maybe something caught in a trap. By then, the moon was beneath the scudding clouds.

The next day, the father of one of the girls who had entered the woods appeared in Emmis; his farm was five miles south of town. A recent immigrant, he explained haltingly to the men in the barn that his daughter Clara, fifteen, had been dropped off near the mailbox at the end of the lane leading to his farm. Bruised and bleeding, she would describe only the small horse pulling the shiny buggy.

Frank's father was at the livery barn delivering freight when Clara's father pointed to the trim mare that belonged to the Kennedys. Both men who worked in the barn fidgeted and looked at the straw littered floor; the constable, Jack Sawyer, looked doubtful.

Keefe turned his dray wagon around, still half loaded, and drove to the sawmill. Timothy was in his office, where two-thirds of all the commerce in Emmis was documented. Seated at his desk, he looked inquiringly at Keefe, who said, "We both have boys. You have this big job, I have a job not so big. But you should know this."

Delivering freight two days later with his father, Frank saw Tom sitting on the front porch of the Kennedy house with his mother. His face was covered with welts.

Neither waved at the other, ever again.

At the next meeting of the Rosary Society Bridget refused to speak to Frank's mother. But Frank had an even stronger memory of a related incident; his father, late the next autumn, planned to build a new box for his dray wagon, one that could be transferred to his sled for the winter months.

Timothy heard that Keefe had priced the building material at the mill and requested the widest, knot-free pine in stock. Timothy told his shop foreman to tell Keefe that he could build the wagon box in the mill shop, out of the weather, and that two carpenters would help him.

A week later the box was finished and after the first big snow, when Keefe's sled was pulled up and down the streets of Emmis, the freshly painted sides were clearly lettered, "KEEFE'S DRAY LINE • EMMIS, MINNESOTA".

Timothy charged Frank's father for the lumber but refused to accept money for the carpentry. "My men needed the experience."

Now, Frank swept a couple of newspaper sheets from the chair near his desk and Cy sat there, waiting for Frank to stop opening and closing drawers, rearranging the papers that nearly covered the ink stained blotter.

"I see the twins now and then, Cy. They're great girls, by God, it must make you feel pretty good, no one saying anything bad about your kids...half the people in Emmis..."

Cy interrupted him, "That's not exactly true, Frank. Just last night I heard Gladdie tell Thea there was a mort of dust under her bed and she gave Bert hell for not turning the light off in the kitchen when nobody's there."

Frank laughed. "Getting hell from Gladdie is kinda like getting bit by a butterfly, I'd say."

"Well, the three of them squabble pretty regular but nobody seems to get hurt. Latest thing is, since the electric poles started going up in Warren Township, Gladdie thinks I'm going broke every time we snap on a light or turn on the radio. Hell, that old Delco plant cost more to keep in shape than my electric bill runs."

Both men knew they were delaying speaking of the problem for which Frank thought he needed Cy's advice.

Frank pushed his chair back, opened a top drawer and put one foot on it. He laced his fingers across his stomach and looked at Cy.

"Last month I stopped to see Thea, asked if she thought you'd ever push Hank and the rest of the trash off the place; between the two of us we figured it wouldn't happen anytime soon. I'm not sure I could toss those women off, either. But Cy, it's not just us worried, half the town's ready to kill that fool Hank."

Cy waited and Frank didn't go on. "Hell, Frank, I thought you wanted me to stop off here so you could tell me I've got good kids. Or that maybe you were going to say your wages were bumped down so I'd pay less taxes. I didn't think you had anything against my neighbor."

"Cy, Midge Corrigan, teacher out at District 9, she told Esther last week that Mabel's girl, that Glory, well you know what I'm trying to say, Cy. Midge, she thinks the kid is having a bad time at home, the way she talks, her head hanging down, marks on her arms, you know what I'm saying here." Frank hesitated.

Cy didn't answer.

"Whether it's a beating she gets or something worse,I don't know, but Mabel's sister, Bud Swanson's wife, she stopped Esther yesterday, in the shoe shop, and told her that she hates to let her kids near this Glory, or whatever her name is. Talks tough, got secrets."

"Cy, she says the damn kid doesn't wear underwear half the time. Good God, Cy, what a rat's nest."

Cy asked, "So it's my fault, for giving them the roof over those women's pitiful heads? How is pushing them off going to make things better?"

"I don't know, Cy, but couldn't you shake up that son of a bitch and tell him if things don't get better he's off the place?"

Cy laughed. "Frank, you're not telling me this so I get mad enough to go up there and kill him, are you? I tell you what. Work at it from another angle. Get the relief people upstairs here to find a home for Mabel and Glory, and we can let Hank and Amelia rot up there. Shorty's probably right, he wants me to sell the Kootseema place to someone else, then Hank would have to clear off. Two things, though. I *want* Matt's farm and if they got scattered when somebody else came on the place, where the hell would the women go? I wish to hell Hank would rob a bank, you could put him in jail."

Frank shook his head. "You know, when I came into this office it wasn't hard times yet. A lot of bad liquor, a little trouble all the time. But that damned...."

Cy said, "Frank, I don't want to hear his name again today. Glory and Mabel are sad cases, but I'm out of thoughts, I guess. Last summer, Bert asked Gladdie to use Glory around the house, just little stuff, and Gladdie gave in because Bert asked her. It was one scrambled mess, I tell you. The kid hated being there, Gladdie hated having her around and Bert hated having set the arrangement up.

"Well, three weeks later Bert took Glory to St. Cloud, bought her some school clothes and shoes and a good coat. Gave her thirty bucks for her wages.

"School starts and Loretta Swanson stops in to see Thea and says Mabel tried to sell her Glory's new clothes for Loretta's kids and said Hank took the thirty dollars. Thea told Bert and Bert hung her head. I can't rectify anything going on up there, Frank, I would if I could. You should sure as hell know that."

The two walked out the side door of the court house and stood near the flag pole. Frank said, "I never told anybody this, Cy, but last summer when I went up to Hank's after his dogs tore up Mac Dever's sheep, Mabel had the young dog tied up to the corner of the porch, the old hound was sleeping in the shade by the water tank.

"When I jumped Hank and told him next time those two got in trouble I was taking the dogs, he reached up under the porch roof and brought down that old .410. In a half second he shot the one laying there loose and walked up to the one tied and blew his head apart. That kid, Glory, ten feet away, never said a word.

"And then Hank hollered at Mabel, 'Get your hand cart and haul this shit out to the stone pile. They'll draw flies, laying here.' And, by God, Mabel did it.

"Mac, barely getting by, he never even tried to collect for the sheep. Hank's not got a dime, nothing. Living as close to him as you do, Cy, you must see it's getting worse up at Kootseemas, crazier every day."

Cy answered, "I know, Frank, it's wearing on me, too. I look across the field, and I see what old Gottfried did there; he was about the same age as my Dad. His times were tougher than Matt's, worse off than Hank's. Dad said neither Gottfried nor Annie said a sentence in English when they came over here; they worked the clock around. Matt was slow, but not a bad kid. That damn Jako made a fool of Matt and then pushed Amelia on him. And I stood there like a wooden-legged jackass and let him do it. Well, we're all paying for it now."

CHAPTER 4

Cy felt stricken, cornered, when the talk at the supper table that night turned to the Kootseemas.

Thea said, "I went down to the basement beneath the office today to look through Earl's newspapers from the Twenties. I wanted to find out who built the band shelter next to the tracks, it's going to be painted again in a couple of weeks.

"I ran into the story of Matt Kootseema getting killed. No one ever told me he was running moonshine at the time. God, that family's just a long line of ignorant fools! No wonder Hank's so shiftless. Matt was no better."

Bert looked at Thea, ready to say something, when Gladdie laid her fork across her plate and folded her hands in her lap. She said, "I think both you girls are to the place in your lives when you know better than to speak bad of the dead."

Thea and Bert looked at each other, wanting to laugh, when Cy pushed his plate away and stood up. He picked up the newspaper from the small table near the door, folded it under his arm and walked into the living room.

Gladdie began clearing the table although Bert or Thea usually did the after-supper chores.

Bert began running hot water in the sink and Thea told Gladdie she'd drive her home, the temperature was not too far above freezing. Gladdie said, "I got my boots and anyhow, fresh air is healthy."

Hanging the dish towel on a rack near the stove, Bert asked, "What was all that about?"

Thea answered, "A conspiracy. Dad and Gladdie are getting ready to send us to an orphanage. This is just the start. They're going to rent our rooms to Hank and Mabel and Gladdie's going to convert Amelia to the Swedish Lutheran Church."

The next afternoon, Cy drove over to the country schoolhouse where Midge had taught for at least twenty years. The chairman of the District 9 school board, Cy looked at this small frame building as a quintessential gift of his neighborhood to the children who lived in the district.

A town child, Cy's school years had been spent in the square brick building between the courthouse and St. Mark's. Ayma, when the girls were almost old enough to start school, made Cy promise that they'd be sent to the school in Emmis, too. Small for her age, Ayma, at a country school, had suffered at the hands of the older children who chased her, and she admitted to Cy that her childhood had been nearly unbearable; she had been told by her parents to not complain and by her tormentors to run fast or else.

The girls' first school year began months after Ayma's death, and Cy was torn by the knowledge of what his neighbors would think about his kids going to the school in Emmis. Gladdie, showing him in late August the dresses she'd sewn for the twins said, "Ayma would be glad we didn't forget her ideas, Shorty and me. I got everything ready I could think of, and Shorty said he'll one hundred percent be ready to take them and fetch them from school when you can't."

Cy, one of the small dresses in his hand, looked startled.

"Thanks, Gladdie. Takes a load off my mind."

The students had been gone from the schoolyard for nearly fifteen minutes when Midge stepped out, locking the door behind her. She waved at Cy, who waited near her old car.

They talked about buying better wood for the school next year; Midge complaining that the pile they'd bought from Jim Hart had been two thirds ashes and one third smoke. Cy knew Midge was in a hurry to get home and he told her about his visit with Frank. "I hear you have an idea that Mabel's girl might need help."

Midge leaned against the hood of her car and adjusted her head scarf, setting her big purse on the fender. Cy said, "Let's get in my truck, I've had the heater running for a half hour." He took her elbow and walked her to the Terraplane; the heat, when he opened the door for Midge, felt good.

Midge was about sixty and Cy had always thought she looked young for her age. Today, she looked old.

"Well, you know as well as I do that poor Glory needs help, all kinds of help. There's not enough help in the world to change her past and maybe none to make a difference now. But yes, I think there's more wrong now than there was when she was younger, more than even what I saw about the time she quit coming, late last fall."

Midge stopped, looking out the side window of the truck, wishing that Cy would help her. He was silent, and she went on.

"She told me once a few years ago that Old Amelia locks the doors sometimes, leaving Glory outside in the dark. Mabel's scared of Amelia; no help, no mercy there.

"We have the same mailman as Kootseemas and he told me a week ago Saturday that Glory is bruised, her arms, her shins, sometimes her neck, and I don't think the damage is coming from the old lady. Art, the mail carrier, he's not the kind of man who reads True Detective magazines or looks for trouble. One side of Glory's neck, he said, was black and blue two weeks ago and he asked her about it. She said she fell, bringing in an armload of wood.

"Well, Cy, I don't believe it.

"Art said she stands by the box most days, waiting for the mail and they never get much of anything. He's started taking her the farm magazines he's read."

Cy looked at her and saw the tears in her eyes. He gave her the handkerchief from his pocket and she twisted it in her hands, looking away.

"Roy tells me to mind my business, which is teaching school, and put Kootseemas out of my mind."

"Pretty good advice, I'd say", Cy told her.

"I don't mean to get so involved, Cy, but Glory was such a sweet little kid in first grade! My aunt knows Mabel's family and thinks Mabel's life was a lot like Glory's. This should have been the year Glory finished the eighth grade, maybe she even had a chance to go to high school, or at least, to take some little job, get ahead. I just don't know where things can go from here."

They talked for a minute about having a bigger chimney built in the school house before next term, and Cy walked to her car with her.

She smiled at him, shyly, as though she wished she hadn't been so candid, talking to the chairman of the board. She and Roy hoped that she could teach five more years. As Midge drove out of the school yard, Cy knocked a little snow off his boots before he got back in the truck.

No help, no mercy for Glory, and not a lot of help and mercy for Midge, either.

He smiled wryly as he turned the truck toward home. Seemed he was feeling sorry for a lot of folks lately. He thought about Timothy's reaction when Cy had apologized for some small childhood infraction, "I'm glad to hear it, but sorry is never enough."

Shorty Brill, just a year younger than Cy, was protective of everything on the Kennedy farm but Rowdy. Cy refused to have more dogs than one at any time, and the day that old Gyp, a fine cattle dog died when the twins were college students, Cy told his top hired man he could choose the farm's next dog.

Laboriously, patiently, Shorty scanned the ads in at least two newspapers. He knew Cy would pay whatever it cost to get a good young dog, one that could be trained to take Gyp's place.

He had narrowed the possibilities to two or three when, driving home from college one Friday evening, Bert spied a small dog nearly in the ditch, a dozen miles from Emmis. Thea was persuaded to drive back and get the dog.

Shorty blamed himself for not standing firm, for not reminding Cy that the place needed a farm dog, not a mutt that he declared early on was a half breed: fifty percent mixed dog and the other fifty percent, God only knows.

Cy, unable to deny the girls the pleasure of their discovery, semi-welcomed Rowdy, and Gladdie perversely doted on him. Cy told Shorty, "Go ahead and get a dog you want, hell, what does it matter?"

Shorty answered, "For thirty years you said, 'One farm, one dog.' Somebody else's memory may be fading, but it ain't mine."

He continued spurning Rowdy's friendly advances and complained about the dog every day.

Della Janson, Shorty's only sister, lived seven miles from Emmis, a widow with three grown sons who farmed the place where they were born.

Last week, Gladdie asked Cy, "Did you forget Sunday is Shorty's birthday? If you'd be here I thought maybe I'd be here, too, Sunday or not. Church can wait a week. His sister Della don't live too far, maybe her and the boys can come. And Bert and Thea."

Gathered around the table Della and Shorty told the three young men stories they'd never heard before and Cy watched his daughters helping Gladdie serve dinner, laughing about their childhood memories, the years when they thought Shorty's authority was equal to Cy's. Leonard, Della's youngest son, asked Shorty if he had any use for a nice collie pup; he could have his pick of the litter. Shorty replied, "Old Rowdy's as good a dog as a fella could need."

Bert looked at Thea, Thea set her coffee cup carefully in its saucer. Both looked at Cy. He pretended he was deaf.

The poignancy of the day, the lack of desperate acts, the time of the year...surely all of winter would end soon...such thoughts engulfed Cy as he sat in the dark living room. He was sure that no one but himself recalled that twenty-five years ago today, Ayma died. Or maybe Gladdie had remembered and this gathering of kind and reasonable souls was meant to be in honor, also, of some old memory Gladdie kept silent, locked inside her heart.

He rolled the last cigarette he'd smoke today as Thea called from the doorway, "Bert and I are taking Gladdie home, then I have to check something at the news office. You might be asleep before we get home so I'll say goodnight now."

How could all of this sweet life, all the days not so much different than today, occur here and never fly over the rusted barbed wire that ran between this farm and old Gottfried's?

He'd go one step more, tomorrow, trying to get things fixed for Mabel and her daughter. Hank and Amelia?

Cy twisted his cigarette in the ash tray and bent to loosen his shoe strings. "If there's any fix for those two, it won't be found in anything I've done."

When he was a young man living in Chicago with his parents and a younger sister, Eli Kanter dreamed of becoming strong enough to conquer any obstacle that might prevent him from becoming the greatest baseball player in America.

It was more than coincidental that his parents, Rudolf and Hilda, dreamed that one day Eli would replace Rudolf as an officer in one of the grand banks on North Randolph Street.

The dream that was cosseted by his parents ended when, in 1907, the Financial Panic caused that large, impressive bank to fail and Rudolf lost his position. Eli's dream had succumbed earlier, when, at seventeen, he'd been thrown from an automobile driven by his sister, his left knee crushed so badly that one doctor suggested that there might be no answer but the amputation of his leg. His leg, saved, was stiff now and prone to aching much of the time.

After working as an accountant at a Chicago meat packing plant for two years years Eli was convinced by his father that surely the Federal Reserve Act of 1913 meant that no more American banks could fail even if the stock market went to hell again, so help him God, and when Eli came to Emmis in 1923 to head the National Bank, he believed his father.

In 1929, he lost that belief.

The town's other bank went under three years after the Crash and for two years Eli didn't sleep more than three or four hours at night, worrying about the fate of First National. And he found that he liked living in Emmis.

This morning, walking from the vault to his office, he glanced at the few men in the lobby and saw Cy Kennedy talking with Jule Hobart, the mechanic at the Ford Garage. Eli stopped a moment, watching them. He remembered what Einar Johnson, the former bank president, said about Cy. "That son of a gun could talk to the Pope and then to the guy who cleans the elephant pen at the circus and you'd find out he said the same thing to both. Cy doesn't look much for the difference in people."

He remembered, too, that he had learned how headstrong and uncompromising Cy could be.

It was a summer day, and Cy strode into the bank a few minutes before it closed at three o'clock. Eli had just closed the vault and Mary Luchek, his assistant, was pulling the shades on the windows that overlooked the sidewalk.

Cy nodded at Mary and followed Eli into the office, his smile somehow seemed forced as he dropped into a chair close to Eli's desk.

"Eli, I wonder if you've ever thought of putting Jack Casey's boy out to pasture?"

Eli felt ambushed and stared at Cy. "Morgan Casey? Why would I let him go? He's been in that teller cage for six years. In easier times, I'd have pushed him upward already, he'd be sitting just outside the door to this office."

Cy crossed his legs, the faded denim of his overalls looked nearly white against the black felt hat he cradled on his lap. "Frieda Bolansky came over today, a neighbor gave her a ride on his way to town. Here's what she said.

"She sold that long strip of grass there by the creek to Fred Loomis, got seven hundred for it. Best field ground on her place. Says she kept out two hundred to pay some bills and brought the rest in here Tuesday, to put away to bury herself.

"Frieda never handled that much cash and she felt scared until she handed it over, and Morgan never gave her a receipt or an account number or a damn thing. She never banked before but she says she felt funny about it and the next day she hooked a ride here with the mailman and asked Morgan for something so she'd know where her money was.

"Morgan told her he remembered her asking about bringing the money in but she never handed it over."

Eli was silent, looking past Cy at a picture of Ben Franklin, a portrait Eli had seen often in his father's office when he was a child; his mother asked him to hang it in his own office here. Mary stood in the doorway of the office, her hand pressed against her face. "Mary", Eli smiled, "It's past quitting time, you can go."

"No", said Cy, "Mary's part of the bank, too. Let's get this rounded up."

"Eli, any business you do yourself is as straight as a hard rain with no wind. The whole town knows it. You don't need to take any blame."

Then Cy's anger showed plainly when Eli said, "Morgan is due in at nine tomorrow morning, I'll see what I can do."

Cy leaned forward in the chair, his hat held tightly in one hand. "No, this isn't about seeing what you can do tomorrow. It's about doing it now...Frieda doesn't lie."

Eli glanced at Mary, he seemed to be looking for help, than looked at Cy. "What do you want?"

"I don't care what goes on between you and Morgan. You can figure that out for yourself. I want five hundred dollars in a savings account with Frieda's name on it and I want it set up at three percent more interest than the sign outside says you're paying. And

I want you to make sure that when I stop in here tomorrow to pick up Frieda's savings book, that God-damned Morgan Casey is out of a job."

He turned to Mary. "And I want you to make sure that anytime Frieda Bolansky steps in the bank she's treated like she was the queen of England."

Eli hated recalling the trembling in his hands that day as he took his hat from the brass hook near his desk. He told Mary, "I'm going out to John Casey's. Give me anything in Morgan's desk that belongs to him."

It was almost noon the next day when Cy appeared at the bank carrying two small wooden boxes of strawberries. "What I like about a berry patch is that it gives a man something to share with his friends."

He handed the boxes to Eli and Mary and pocketed the envelope Eli handed him, then left the bank after greeting a couple of friends in the bank's lobby.

Now that the worst of the drought was behind them and the farm markets, still weak and sometimes dipping lower than they were last year, gave a little hope to those who'd withstood the mid-depression years, both Cy and Eli were guardedly optimistic.

As he walked toward Eli this morning, Cy didn't look like he'd stopped in to discuss the economic upturn in Sutton County, and Eli waited for his friend to close the office door and sit beside the desk.

Cy usually wasted no time when he'd come to visit, and Eli was surprised when Cy inquired about the health of Eli's wife and son and commented on the new public drinking fountain installed on the bank corner. "It's good for the town", he remarked.

Eli waited. He was surprised that he felt faintly amused, sensing Cy's unease. He wasn't so surprised when Cy abruptly began to question him. Serving his second term as a Sutton County commissioner, Eli was also chairman of the county's welfare board. He was resigned to hearing questions for which he seldom had answers.

"What's the chance of getting that girl of Mabel Kootseema's away from Mabel and maybe into some kind of home or something where she could maybe get ahead on her own?"

Eli sighed. "I'd say about the same chance you have of looking in the mirror and seeing a twenty year old man. It's not going to happen, Cy. Every county in the state looks at those situations all the time and, believe me, we get to know the meaning of "hopeless" pretty quick.

"For starters, that girl must be almost grown, isn't she? She probably likes her mother, doesn't realize she's living in a shack, she maybe guesses she's different than most others and she doesn't know what to do about it. Mabel thinks, I'm sure, that everything in her life and in her kid's life is already figured out and in the works and she'll fight to keep her daughter. She gets a few cents for her eggs, Amelia gets twenty dollars the first of the month until the county goes broke and Hank chisels whatever he can from both women. Bud Swanson's married to Mabel's sister and I get the lowdown on the Kootsemas every time he's in the bank."

"Yeah", Cy answered. "Loretta stops in to see Thea at the news office, she says Mabel doesn't even have much of a garden anymore, the cows are all over the yard. Seems I've taken enough barbed wire up there to keep Hitler out of Austria. Trouble is, wire doesn't string itself between the posts and Hank doesn't, either, at least in the last ten years."

Cy watched Eli tapping a pencil on an open ledger and he knew the banker was anxious to get back to work.

Eli continued, "You can come next Monday evening to the board meeting, Cy, but I don't see that we can do anything. I wish we could. God, Cy, I wish I'd never steered you toward buying that sixty acres. I knew it joined your place and you wanted it, but it looks like you're joined tighter to your renters than to the farm."

Cy stared searchingly at Eli and the banker wondered why. It was true, wasn't it? Hadn't the same thought ever occurred to Cy?

Eli reached across the desk and shook Cy's hand. "Keep your eyes open, and maybe that damned Hank will do something that'll put him in jail. Then all three of those women can sort out their lives and move on."

CHAPTER 5

In 1937,when rural electricity became available in Warren Township, Cy paid for the lines to run to the Kennedy place, to Gladdie's house and to three of the small farms he rented to other farmers. The buildings on those three farms were in fairly good shape and the families who lived there would be able to pay the bill, each month, to the power company.

Cy was quite certain his other renters, the men whose buildings were in worse shape, would be less than cordial when they saw the poles and wire strung across the fieldsof their more fortunate neighbors. He doubted that they'd leave the land they were renting but he knew they were nearly buried in work that didn't bring much money and he saw the despair, sometimes, in their eyes.

It was customary for his renters to pay half the annual rent in June, the other half at the end of the year. The farms had been purchased for speculation and Cy knew that sooner or later they'd be worth more than he paid for them.

Last spring, Cy decided there had to be some way he could maintain the land and salvage the old buildings on the small farms and he'd floated the proposition before the families who lived there: he'd buy the lumber, shingles, concrete and hardware and his renters would provide the labor for repairs in lieu of half the yearly rent.

Since Kootseemas could be said, for all practical purposes, to already live rent free, Hank was not approached by Cy. A year went by and Cy was pleased by the improvements that were made on his other properties.

This morning the February sky had, Shorty said, a spring cast to it, meaning, Cy guessed, that it didn't have any hint of snow. Gladdie was peeved that Cy hadn't warned her that Shorty had been asked to stop in for breakfast so he and Cy could discuss whether this would be the year part of the pasture would be turned into meadowland.

Cy knew he'd hear from Gladdie some time today. "I didn't put on a fresh apron today, I was going to scrub the porch floor, and then you brought company!" Cy knew, too, how the complaint would end after he pointed out that Shorty wasn't exactly company.

Gladdie would look at him with all the reproachfulness she could summon and say, "Well, some look at things different than others."

Before Shorty left the kitchen, Cy looked at him and said, "Those homemade haircuts you've been treating yourself to all winter aren't panning out too well, I'm scared to say. I'm going in to Emmis in an hour or so, I'll stop at the shop before I leave and you hop in, I've got to get a haircut today, too."

Shorty grinned sheepishly. "Yeah, I know. It ain't the thirty-five cents Myron charges, I just hate everybody walking by and seein' me in the chair, feet off the floor, no hat, it don't feel good to me."

Cy laughed. "There's another barber, down there by the post office. Maybe he can trim your hair while you're wearing your hat."

Shorty laughed, too. "I don't need a ride, though, Cy. I ain't had my car on the road for six months. I need a couple of belts and a battery and I'll stop at the filling station; need gas, too."

Shorty's car was the 1929 Chevrolet sedan he'd bought six years ago when both twins had rejected it and Cy was about to trade in the car he'd driven for a few years.

Not a dent nor a scrape of a blemish of any kind marred the sedan, the green paint as shiny as the paint on a new car.

"When you've got your ears lowered, stop off at Pavlik's", Cy told Shorty. "I'll see you there."

When Cy asked Shorty, long ago, to come to the farm and help him set up a crew of men to work there, the two of them sat at the bar in Martha's Hotel. Cy signaled for drinks and asked Shorty, "You a whiskey or a brandy man?"

Shorty said, "Whiskey, but not much."

It was true; Cy learned that Shorty always had a bottle in his small living space at the back of the shop, and he occasionally asked Cy to bring him another; Thea said a couple of years ago, that maybe Shorty used whiskey to clean machine parts.

Thea was shocked when Shorty pushed open the door near her desk, laughing when he saw the surprise on her face.

When he removed his hat, she said, "Shorty! What's going on here? New shirt, short hair, you're not taking off for some strange land, are you?"

"Nah, I had a little fixin' needed doin' on my car, too early for field work. Thought I'd stop by, ain't been here since I helped move things around here when you took over." He sat on the edge of a chair.

His eyes swept the office and stopped when he saw the framed pictures on the shelf behind her desk. He grinned, one of the photos, taken by Gladdie, was of himself and the twins sitting side by side on a hay rack; Thea and Bert were in their first year at St. Mary's College.

He shook his head when Thea pointed at the coffee pot on the wood stove. "I was wondering, where can a fella buy that peppermint candy, that hard kind Gladdie likes? She put buttons on my summer shirts..."

"At the drug store", Thea replied. "I'm stopping there on my way home, do you want...?"

He broke in, "No, no. I'm going there, anyhow. Razor blades, you know. I'm on my way now, down the street to see your dad, and then pretty quick, home."

Thea sat there a minute, not quite recalling what she'd been doing when Shorty had come through the door. Then she pulled her thoughts together, discarding some and reserving some for later contemplation, and went back to work.

Cy had been in the saloon twenty minutes before Shorty appeared and he didn't notice his hired man's presence right away. John Pavlik and George Presley were arguing about the town's decision to finance a community band, and, half listening to them, Cy was turned away from the door.

He hadn't been surprised to see Hank Kootseema nursing a nickel glass of beer, sitting apart from a half dozen men along the bar.

Now, as Shorty walked past Hank, headed for the stool where he saw Cy seated, Hank called out, "Hey, Shorty, whatcha doin' in Emmis? You ain't here lookin' for women, you got your pick of three out at Cy's place!"

No one was talking, now, and Cy stiffened as his feet hit the floor. Shorty turned toward Hank and reached for his head, driving Hanks face into the curved rim at the edge of the bar; Shorty pulled Hank's head back quickly and smashed it again against the sharp mahogany surface. Hank's hat fell behind the bar, Clyde, who had been polishing beer glasses, sailed over the bar, his apron flying, and pulled Hank from the stool.

As Clyde marched the struggling Hank to the door, Pavlik appeared at Shorty's elbow. "Here, here now. We can't have anything like this!"

Shorty, breathing hard, said, "Well, ya got it anyhow, ain't ya? Sorry."

Clyde righted the fallen stool where Hank had been sitting and everyone turned away in disgust as the white towels Clyde swiped across the bar turned crimson. Then talking among the men resumed and everyone watched, covertly, the stools where Cy and Shorty sat.

Clyde came back to his place behind the bar and walked toward Shorty, asking him what he wanted to drink. As he reached for the bottle of Four Roses, he said, over his shoulder, "So, what's this, Shorty? You don't like our Hank?"

Laughter rippled in the dim light, and Shorty pulled his wallet from his shirt pocket. John Pavlik craned his neck from the other side of Cy's stool and said, "Put it away, Shorty. I hate trouble, but by God, I'm with you. I hate Hank worse."

Clyde, behind the bar, felt something beneath his feet. Stooping, he straightened up then and held Hank's hat high. "Anybody want a nice felt hat?"

John growled, "Wash your hands, you damn fool, and shut up."

Cy knew that Thea would probably hear about the incident before the day was done, and he didn't care. Cy would say nothing to Bert or Gladdie; if Thea chose to tell, it would be okay.

At the supper table, when they had finished eating, Gladdie carried the candy dish from the cupboard to the table; taking off the lid, she passed the dish around, the white lozenges heaped inside. "Shorty brought us this treat, today, from Emmis."

Then, glancing toward Cy, she said, "And I hope we don't complain about his haircuts and such around here. We should be thankful for the nice things he does for this farm."

Cy ducked his head, as though he's suddenly seen a spider on the tablecloth, and Bert, looking puzzled, passed the candy dish to Thea. Thea, the cool taste of peppermint on her tongue, said, "Amen, Gladdie. Amen!"

None of the Kennedys were surprised on the first day of March when Gladdie reminded them that the soft spring air, the elegant lift of the sun and the sight of a few early robins were all signs of bad things to come later this month.

"In like a lamb, out like a lion" was just one of the homely myths the twins had heard from their caretaker when they were young and which, by reason of their own young wisdom, had never called upon her to prove.

Bert and Thea had risen early this Saturday, having planned a month ago to drive to St. Paul and spend the weekend with two classmates from St. Mary's. Peg and Mary Ellen were both housewives; Bert considered them contented and fulfilled women, Thea regarded them as lost souls, much too dependent on their husbands, but kindly kept her opinion hidden even from Bert.

Cy had asked Shorty to stop by this morning for breakfast and the two of them sat at the table, Cy making notes as his hired man listed the purchases of seed, fertilizer and supplies that would be necessary when the winter's break-up occurred.

The argument, not heated but persistent, about planting corn with the horse planter occurred each spring and Shorty knew that as long as old Bill Mehr could drive the team and keep the rows straight Cy wasn't going to switch over to a tractor planter.

Shorty would like to see all six of Cy's horses gone from the farm but he doubted the Kennedy place would ever be without a team or two. All winter they stood in the barn; Buster and Prince nipped along pulling the corn planter for a couple of weeks in May, and in early June the three teams were turned out of the barn and spent the time until the next winter in the big pasture, chasing calves, reaching over the line fences and crowding the cattle away from the water troughs near the barn.

Shorty made it plain to Cy how he felt about the horses and Cy looked thoughtful as he listened to each spring's recital by his top hired hand and thanked him for his opinion.

For most of the year, Bill was the farm's handyman but his best days of the year were the golden days in May when he sat behind the old team, traveling back and forth across the tilled fields, the tick of the corn planter dropping seed in the faultlessly straight rows, the click of the planter the only sound except for the soft steps of Buster and Prince as they plodded north to south, east to west.

When Shorty had thanked Gladdie for breakfast and made his way back to the machine shed where he'd begun a week ago the repair of the farm tractors, and when Thea's car had sped down the driveway, Cy sat in the living room, realizing once again that March was for him the month that had paid him the most regret; first the death of his parents in mid-March and so few years later, at the end of another March, when Ayma had died.

Among his farming friends the common thought was that if one made it into March, the chances of surviving another year in the country were bright. For Cy, moving himself safely to the end of March without being buried in great waves of regret had never ceased to signal his entry into springtime.

Today, he lifted his eyes to study the picture of his parents, taken more than sixty years ago; Ayma had carried it from their house to this house the day after his parents had been buried in St. Mark's cemetery.

Timothy, a man content with the mark he had made in Canada and then in Minnesota; Bridget, never as happy as she might have been; a child in Ireland whose family had fled to America and found a surprisingly good life.

It was impossible for Cy to remember his parents without bringing to mind his brother, Thomas; four years younger than Cy and with even less interest in Timothy's lumber business than Cy had shown. No picture of Tom on the wall; no photograph of him in this house. Sometimes Cy thought his decision to put all memories of Tom ouside the lives of the twins ...they had been just five years old when he died...was unfair to Tom and to the girls.

Well, Tom didn't know he was profoundly absent from his brother's family, and Thea and Bert had shown little interest in either the life or the death of their uncle.

Both of these truths, as unfortunate as Cy thought they might be, made his life easier.

When Timothy and Bridget had died so close to home and so violently, Cy was already near despair; Ayma's health was uncertain and little remained of the carefree woman he had married, bringing her to this farm. In the days following the death of their parents, Tom, always at odds with Timothy and having alienated himself from nearly everyone in Emmis, was no comfort to Cy, nor Cy to his brother.

Thea asked early last winter, as she sat next to him in Pavlik's, if he was ever going to tell her and Bert anything about the history of the Kennedys.

"We know you came into a lot of money and we've heard around town that Tom Kennedy was a pain in the neck, but we're curious. Well, I am, but Bert's the kind of girl who minds her own business...paddles along and doesn't look back."

Cy grinned. "You'd better paddle back across the street to the Advocate. Too bad the paper wasn't set up earlier, you could get Tom's story in print. Remind me when you girls have an hour some time and I might tell you what you're wondering about."

He added, "And maybe not."

Finishing her drink, Thea slid to her feet and laughed. "When we were going to St. Mary's we asked Gladdie some questions and she told us that if we were still going to school when we were twenty, we should be smart enough to figure things out for ourselves."

Shortly after the first of March, in 1908, the snow in Warren County had disappeared, even the drifts which had piled along the fence lines and behind barns and sheds was gone. Mud lay in the cartways and roads running between farms and villages, and on the farms grain drills were pulled from sheds; the chains and sprockets on fanning mills were checked and the best oats and barley and rye was cleaned for seeding a new crop.

Early seeding of small grains was welcome. The fields were still too wet and the winter's manure piles still frozen but fieldwork would be welcome after a winter that, even for Minnesota, was long and cold.

On the sixteenth of March a sweet morning breeze coming from the southeast turned by noon to a raging blast from the west/ northwest and the temperature began to fall.

Mayme Mulaney, who lived with her husband on a farm south of Emmis, had recently been chosen leader of the Daughters of Erin group at St. Mark's, and was hosting the annual St. Patrick's Day dinner in her dining room the following day.

Purely Irish, Mayme watched the gathering clouds from her kitchen window and asked God for permission to curse the weather, being careful to not implicate the Lord in any way for the timing of the return of this wintry cold and snow.

On the morning of the 17th no one doubted that at least a small blizzard was passing through Sutton Township.

Coming downstairs, Timothy found Bridget at the kitchen window, staring at the the sullen landscape, through the bare branches of the maples which lined the boulevard near their house.

Bridget was in the habit of seldom speaking these days, Timothy's harsh judgment of Thomas stood between them like an immovable barrier. But moments ago, he had seen her favorite woolen dress, its long skirt trimmed with green braid, laid carefully across the bench in their bedroom.

On a tray beneath the mirror of her dresser the gold watch Timothy had bought her when Tom was born lay next to her best combs and the square locket, engraved with a bird in flight and enclosing, he remembered, a picture of each of their sons. He opened the watch and was surprised to hear the slight ticking noise...Bridget had not worn it for years. How was today so different?

Glancing at himself in Bridget's mirror, Timothy wondered: is some of the trouble in this house going to be mended some day? He seldom thought any more about the part of their lives that had ended before they reached middle age. He knew that his harsh judgment of Thomas lay between himself and Bridget like an immovable barrier.

Downstairs in the kitchen, Timothy could hardly bear the disappointment Bridget's silence and resolute scrutiny of the storm outside betrayed. He pulled on the heavy boots he had thought last week he should put away until another winter. Buttoning his long coat, he touched her arm as she turned to stare at his leaving.

"I won't be long, you stay inside."

Walking through the downtown streets of Emmis leading to St. Mark's, he wondered why he'd cautioned Bridget about going out in today's weather: except to attend Mass, she had hardly left the house in weeks.

Father Cavanaugh answered Timothy's knock at the door of the rectory, he must have just returned from early Mass; the wet marks on the floor were clearly caused by melting snow.

The priest laughed when Timothy asked him if the dinner at Mulaney's would likely be held today; had anyone attending Mass today said something about a change of plans?

"Who among the members of this parish would dare guide Mayme and twenty other Irish women in such a decision? I think we'll leave that chore to God! I'd say the smoke was rolling out of Mulaney's kitchen chimney since long before dawn, and is this weather so much different from any winter day in Emmis?"

Heartened but still vaguely skeptical, Timothy walked briskly through the alley to the livery barn and asked the boy forking clean straw in the stalls to bring his big bay and the cutter around to the house in two hours, the horse in Timothy's best harness, and all the blankets in the wooden box outside the stall piled behind the seat of the little cutter.

At home, he cautioned Bridget to wear her warmest hat and, upstairs, pulled her sealskin coat from the back of the closet. Bridget knew she looked especially fine today, she had checked herself several times in the mirror, and was disappointed when Timothy carried her least stylish coat down the steps and helped her slip her arms into the smooth lining.

Glancing at his wife several times as the cutter sped across the miles to Mulaney's farm, Timothy was pleased to see the look of anticipation, surprised delight, perhaps a hint of memories that had grown cold for both of them, the bit of laughter in her voice as she answered when he spoke above the sound of the wind.

A watery sun showed through the gusting snowfall now and then but Timothy was sure the worst weather was behind them and as he helped Bridget from the cutter stopped near Mayme's front door he promised to return no later than three o'clock. He was speechless when, on the bottom step leading to the farmhouse door, Bridget reached up her mittened hand and pulled his face close to hers. He felt her lips on his cold face and drew back his head to see her smiling eyes. Mayme threw open the door and behind her were the voices of several women.

On the return trip to Emmis, Timothy's earnest face broke into a smile as he raised the collar of his coat against the wind.

Timothy thought about running out to Cy's farm while he had the horse and cutter out of the barn, then decided that perhaps tomorrow he'd persuade Bridget to go there with him. She hadn't seen Ayma since Christmas Day.

Instead, he drove to the livery barn and asked that his horse be fed and watered and left in harness; Martha's Hotel was just a few feet away and he'd stop there for his noon meal.

Martha was surprised to see him and amazed when he told her to serve a drink to each customer who ventured in today, telling them it was a treat from St. Paddy. Timothy would stop here early tomorrow and settle up.

Several of the dozen or so men grouped around the big table in the center of the hotel's dining room nodded at Timothy...most of them had been on the payroll of his mill when they were younger, but he chose to sit at a small table where he could watch the street running east and west through Emmis.

He loved this town more than any place he had ever lived, even more than he loved Ireland, a place that he found was more and more on his mind since he'd seen so much of his old father in Thomas.

Ah, well, today's return to winter wouldn't last long. He and Bridget would soon have a grandchild and the mill would be running two shifts when the farmers began building their barns in the long summer days.

Timothy paid for his dinner and walked in the new snow to the livery barn. He didn't want Bridget to think he had forgotten her.

Before they'd driven five hundred feet from Mulaney's farm yard, Timothy knew that something had changed, something in the speed of the gritty pellets that quickly covered the rump of the horse and turned his own horsehide mittens holding the reins into ice covered blocks. He turned toward Bridget, the laughter and unexpected serenity of this morning gone, she burrowed deep into her coat and he felt her eyes watching him, judging his concern for their safe return to Emmis.

A mile and a half south of town, Timothy decided to send the horse and cutter into the field running next to the icy roadway, less snow lay in the spaces there and the route would be slightly shorter if he bypassed the curve where the sawmills were clustered at the edge of Emmis.

He knew they were making good time and noticed the horse shaking his head now and then, his large eyes filling with the driven sleet that covered the landscape from the hard-packed field clear to the sky. He saw no one else traveling to Emmis or away from the village and his cutter's solitary dash through the late afternoon unnerved him. In Ontario, Timothy, skidding logs across a frozen lake, had fallen into the ice filled water. He had been struck by falling timbers when his first mill in Emmis had burned to the ground. Good men had pulled him from the lake, from the fire. Now he felt he too old to fight some fights but then, this was a battle that would end in a few minutes, as soon as he reached the street running past his mill.

The sleet now was joined by flakes as big as quarters. The wind had picked up as he left the field and crossed the shallow ditch that separated the snow and ice covered roadway from the farmland, and suddenly Timothy turned his head and stared at Bridget, who was nearly hidden in the folds of her coat and the heavy blankets he had heaped around her for the journey home.

Although Bridget was close beside him, he felt hopelessly imprisoned by the swirling ice and snow; there had to be some sound...the laboring breath of his horse, the sliding of the runners beneath the cutter, even the wind as it cut through the blinding curtains of white that formed vaporous walls around himself and Bridget.

Emmis

He heard nothing; he knew he had lost the way to Emmis.

It should have been so simple, a few dozen houses, the yards of stacked lumber, the big mill, the smaller shed where shingles and barrels were made, the railroad tracks, the roof line of St. Mark's.

Where there should have been at least dark shapes visible, there wasn't anything at all.

And no more visible was the fast moving train whose engineer and crew had been plagued all day by bad weather that had only worsened as night grew nearer. Heading east, no stops in Emmis, the engineer had already warned the section boss that the crossings would need clearing as soon as the wind died down.

Timothy's prize bay had nearly crossed the rails and the cutter was squarely on the track for a few seconds, and in less than a half minute the only evidence of the horse, the cutter and its occupants was a steaming heap of blood, flesh, bone and tangled wood and metal.

CHAPTER 6

Cy had never been able to separate the sorrow he felt for his parents' death from the anger he felt toward his brother, who must have known that his rank indifference had changed the course of Timothy and Bridget's last years.

He didn't mind at all to tell the twins everything he knew about his parents, but in doing so, he would have to speak of Thomas, too.

Cy wasn't sure he had the right words for that story.

Cy remembered Timothy telling him when it became apparent that Tom's nature would not likely change, that Timothy's father, Seamus Kennedy, "had fathered nine children and fed none".

"The priest in our parish told me that sometimes a man couldn't rise above the damnation and bedevilment of poverty. I've always figured that something worse than being poor, something in his blood or in his bones was at the heart of my father's nature. That might be what your brother carries. Who can say? I left my mother, I left my sisters to get far from the sad footing of nearly everyone I knew.

"I knew even before I left Ireland that having nothing is not the only curse that pushes a man into shame. My father could never climb out of the place where he had nothing. Your brother, is he climbing, is he falling? You tell me."

The bright sheen so visible in Timothy's eyes, the shaking of the old man's fingers as he tried to light his pipe overwhelmed Cy; wild anger toward his brother, waves of compassion for Timothy, sudden shame that he, of all people, had neglected knowing the depths of his father's pain.

With daytime temperatures already climbing toward the heat of early summer, Thea saw on the faces of nearly everyone who walked past the window of the news office refections of how she, too, reacted to the balmiest April in memory.

Everyone agreed that it was unlikely they'd seen the death of winter but there was a constant flow of folks who stepped over the threshold of her office to report to Thea the sighting of meadowlarks and scarlet tanagers, the disappearance of all the ice from Stony Brook, the flight of geese headed north, nesting robins, frogs in pursuit of early flies, spiders fashioning webs in barn windows which had been covered with frost just two weeks ago.

Bert told Thea just this morning that if the Advocate continued to treat these sightings as major front page news, she'd cancel her subscription. Thea reminded her sister that no one in the Kenendy household ever paid for the paper and Gladdie said she'd never known two girls who fought more over every little thing like it was the end of the world.

Cy, who was heading outside to see Shorty, said that if Gladdie hadn't stopped him from disciplining the twins when they were small there'd be a lot more peace in the world.

Thea, seated at her desk, saw Loretta Swanson walk nearly past the front window of the news office, then hesitate and retrace her steps. Bert and Thea had always liked Loretta; outspoken, often smiling, her character and temperament so unlike her sister, Mabel Kootseema. Once, when the twins spoke of Loretta, Bert said "charisma in a feed sack dress". Thea laughed aloud and Bert said, "No, I mean it! And I'm not laughing at Loretta, I could easily abide a world filled with people like Loretta."

Today, as Loretta stepped inside and laid her old white pocketbook on the window ledge, Thea saw the strain in her face, heard it in her voice, as though Loretta was intent on delivering words she feared or wasn't sure she should deliver. The leather of her brown oxford shoes, cracked but well polished, her cotton housedress ironed, her arms colored by the sun, she sat on the edge of the chair and chose her words carefully.

"Mabel wasn't home yesterday when I stopped just before supper with some lard I rendered Tuesday and some parsnips I dug so Bud could plow the garden. She ain't there again this morning. Glory, she's there but run off when I drove up and Hank was around, I guess, at least the car was by the shed. I never run after Glory when she took off, she won't give up anything in front of Hank, anyhow. Those two are close."

Loretta paused, as though she wondered if her words were reaching Thea.

"In town, here, I went up to the courthouse to see Frank Keefe but that big deputy there, he said Frank's gone til tomorrow. I can't get help from Bud, him and his brother is spearing suckers up at the lake and he don't want nothing to do with Kootseemas anyhow."

What sounded like a simple explanation for the dread and worry that laid across Loretta was, Thea could tell, an unconscious apology for allowing Mabel to live so grievous a life.

She went on, "Last fall, when it was already cold, Hank locked her in the chicken house overnight, just that once that I know about. He don't hardly let me out of my car or I'd look around up there, myself."

Wondering what Loretta wanted to hear from her, Thea wasn't surprised when Loretta, pretending to have suddenly come to a possible solution, said, "Being as how it's Cy's farm, maybe he could take a gander up there before Frank comes back to Emmis."

Often, in the eyes of the people who called at her office, Thea saw a multitude of uncommon thoughts and fears and she looked away for a second from the despair in Loretta's glance.

"I'm going home at noon today, I'll see what I can do."

The sight of Hank leaning against the corner of the granary filled Cy with disgust, some of it directed inward. The unreasonable waves of regret and loathing he felt every time he had anything to do with the Kootseema family sometimes woke him in the night, and in the dark, he imagined that Hank knew that Cy was not his landlord, but his keeper, someone whose dual onus it was to somehow contain Hank's indifferent capriciousness and, even more strangely, to protect this man he clearly did not like from an increasingly wrathful world.

Hank threw his cigarette to the ground but didn't move to meet Cy. There was never a reason to offer a greeting to Hank, who almost never exchanged a word or a smile and Cy decided to get the search for Mabel underway at once.

"I've got some fellas coming by tomorrow to whitewash my milkhouse and Gladdie's hen coop, and I'm sending them up here. Right now, I'm here to look over the shed back of the house and Mabel's chicken house, might as well get them spruced up, too."

Hank stared straight at him and Cy didn't drop his eyes.

"Use your sense! Ain't no use to fix anything up here. Matt, he never give a lick o' care to anything. Nothin' here", Hank waved his arm in an arc, "Nothin' on this place can fall much closer to the ground. Barn leaks so bad can't store no hay up there...".

Cy controlled his anger, both men knew the barn roof was tight; it had been replaced three years ago. And both men and all of Warren township knew that Hank's few cattle had used the farm's meadowland for summer pasture this year and last, leaving no hay to be harvested for winter feeding.

Cy walked rapidly to the small, squat building that had served as Gottfried and Annie's woodshed. Hank hurried to Cy's side.

"Listen, now. I got enough to do around here, I ain't gonna haul out all the stuff in here so you can slop some paint on the walls. One good windstorm and the whole thing'll be flat on the ground, anyhow."

Cy stared at Hank. "Okay, now. You hold steady. You've got a nasty habit of forgetting who holds the deed here."

Hank stepped back and Cy almost laughed as his renter shifted gears, his voice no longer rough, but pleading for a reasonable chance to be heard.

"I mean, why you wanna sink any more money in a pile of junk like this? Same thing with that old henhouse. Mable ain't got but sixty hens and they won't notice the color of the walls!"

Cy opened the door of the old shed and peered inside, the tangle of rubble and debris higher than himself, and closed the door quickly.

"Let's take a look at the chicken house."

Hank sat down hard on an old broken kitchen chair near the wash line. He looked up, beseechingly, and Cy was nearly vanquished by an ancient memory stored in the back of his heart, that look on another face, the memory of an old fear, a hatred and helplessness in a time almost beyond recall.

He turned his back on Hank and hurried toward the narrow unventilated building where both doors were closed.

The henhouse door was shut so tightly that Cy was forced to rip it almost off its hinges, and dozens of hens frightened by the intrusion fanned the dust laden air. Suddenly, Cy could see nothing. There was no light from the windows and the reality of walls, floor and ceiling could not be proven until the hens escaped in a frenzy above his head, through the open door. It took a couple of minutes for the dust to settle back to the floor.

Cy had stumbled backward and grabbed at the door jamb during the frightened passage of the squawking hens and now he stepped carefully over the sill.

Mabel was against the center post which was bolted to the roof and the cement floor beneath, her ankles tied with twine, a man's leather belt knotted around her waist, binding her to the pole. Her upper body sagged and her arms were wrapped in the skirt of her apron.

"For God's sake, woman, stand still and I'll turn you loose. Easy, now. Your feet haven't got a lot of feeling, I don't suppose. I'll get you some water when we're out of here...that damned son of a bitch!"

Shaking with anger, Cy realized he wasn't much steadier on his feet than Mabel was on her own. Outside the door, she stumbled on the cement step and disappeared when she saw Hank leaning against the hood of his car.

Choking with dust and dirt, old feathers on his boots and overalls and he knew, on his hat, Cy advanced toward Hank. He wished he'd thought to put a wrench in his pocket before he left the pickup.

Hank looked at him, another cigarette in the corner of his mouth. "Well, you found what you came up here snoopin' for, I'll say that. Thing is, they can haul my ass off the place for awhile but when I'm out and back here

I'm still the head of this place just like you're the boss of yours. Mabel don't like it, she can go. I been here longer than her."

Cy felt weak; he hated feeling that something inside himself, not Hank's words, had beaten him. He stood more straight when he saw the amused light in Hank's eyes.

"I haven't decided how far I'm taking this, Hank, but you know this isn't the end. You're done beating Mabel on my land and within the week, Frank Keefe will be looking you up."

Hank spat on the ground, near one of Cy's boots. The screen door slammed as Glory came down the porch steps; the barn cats ran toward her, looking for something to eat. She knelt down to them in the dirt near the pump, oblivious to anything but their soft cries.

Cy stopped at his mailbox and as he climbed from the truck he felt winded and half dizzy. A long trail of dust, uncommon in April, billowed from beneath the pickup as he drove to a spot near the horse barn. Gladdie, shaking rugs on the walk beside the kitchen door, saw Cy sitting behind the wheel and heard the ping of the engine as it cooled.

She walked to the dining room several times, pulled back the curtain hanging in the west window and wondered if she should walk down to the shop to ask Shorty to check on Cy, there in the truck.

Maybe he was just resting, an early spring like this made everything kind of happen at once, almost too much to think about.

It wasn't just that Hank was beating Cy's property to hell, Gottfried and Annie Kootseema's sixty acre farm, fifty years ago, had caught the attention of everyone near Emmis.

When Gottfried emigrated to America his destination was the farm of a friend who had left Europe ten years earlier and sent letters back home, describing his new life in Minnesota. That a man could in so brief a span of time own his farm was unthinkable in the country where they had been boys and Gottfried, on the train from Chicago to Emmis, felt waves of fatigue balanced with a reckless, whimsical excitement that tugged at his mind.

As the train raced through the miles to the town his friend Enoch had described in his infrequent letters, Gottfried wondered if his old friend would still be willing to hire him as a farmhand; could he be sure he knew enough about farming in America to really earn his keep and be able to save his earnings to buy land of his own?

Four years later Gottfried was married to Enoch's daughter, Annie, and purchased sixty acres from the railroad. West of Emmis, the soil of the farm was rich, dark loam and a small creek ran through a stand of trees. With the help of Enoch and Annie's two grown brothers, a small frame house and a well-framed barn were built in a few months. Annie asked for a chicken house with windows facing south and Gottfried built fences and corrals and a wooden walk to the buggy shed not far from the house.

He asked McNeal, the photographer in Emmis, to take a picture of his farmstead and make up twenty postcards he could mail back to his family and friends in the old country.

Life could not be sweeter.

The young couple, who began each day at five o'clock, had plans for a large family but their son, Matt, was their lone child.

Matt was slow moving and looked to Gottfried and Annie for directions for every task he was given, but he worked hard and asked for little. His face, far less attractive than either of his parents, carried an image of contentment and submission. At the tiny school a mile from the Kootseema farm, Matt was a good student and Annie, especially, was relieved.

Matt would keep up the farm when she and Gottfried were unable to work.

America was good, Emmis was good, their farm was very good.

By the time Matt was twenty-seven, both Annie and Gottfried were dead; Gottfried the victim of less than robust strength and his self-appointed servitude to the farm. Annie, boastful of the tall apple trees she had planted as seedlings, braced a ladder within the branches of the highest tree and fell to the ground, breaking her neck.

Neighbors on either side of the Kootseema farm were happy, at first, to see Matt taking care of the land and the farmyard, keeping the cattle and hogs well fed and productive.

Cy noticed, the third year that Matt was alone on the farm, that things were changing. Matt's cows were thin, he had stopped milking them and the calves ran freely with the herd. His hogs, unlike the purebred Durocs that Gottfried raised, walked stiffly and grew shanky in the pens where the wire was no longer held tight against the posts. Weeds choked the fields, not all of which were plowed and planted.

When Cy, who was about the same age as Matt, approached his neighbor and offered to send his hired men to help, Matt asked him into the cluttered house but refused Cy's offer. "I get a little behind, but things will work out."

Cy noticed Annie's red pocketbook hanging on the back of a kitchen chair, Gottfried's barn boots in a corner of the kitchen. Last year's calendar hung by the window, two rosaries on a tray in the center of the table with a dusty prayer book, the words on the cover written in some language other than English.

"I tell you, Matt, you get in a pinch, stop down. I always got a man or two I can lend you and Shorty can help you with anything that needs fixing. I noticed your black mare is limping; let her rest and take a team from me for awhile."

Matt sat, studying his hands. "Sid Jako, up the road, he stops by now and then. I might let things here slide a little and work for Sid."

Suddenly embarrassed, he said, "Sid, he kinda keeps an eye on me."

Cy felt a groan pass through himself and thought, "That son of a bitch Jako, he's keeping an eye on Gottfried and Annie's farm."

His hands on the steering wheel as he sat in the shade of the barn, Cy wondered how in hell he'd let the Kootseema farm become such a springboard to grief in his own life. He knew how it all began, but for God's sake, hadn't there been a time he might have seen the handwriting on the wall?

Cy already owned more than fourteen hundred acres in Sutton County when he bought Kootseema's sixty. The day fifteen or sixteen years ago when he and Shorty has stood at the site of the crash that killed Matt, the day Cy knew with dead certainty that in time he could own the Kootseema farm, seemed now to mark a time when reason had escaped from his life.

He knew now it wasn't only his own lamentable desire to possess old Gottfried's farm that transferred the farm to him, it was the irrational belief that he could expiate by being a protective landlord the collective crimes that trapped Matt and Amelia and the boy, none of them really knowing why they were assembled together in misery. Cy became a self-appointed caretaker who seldom visited the farm where Kootseema's lived; their darkness breaching Cy's dreams, even in the best nights.

Cy felt cold although the air, all day, had felt more like a day in early June than in the month of April. He thought about Sid Jako's Lincoln half submerged in the swollen creek, Matt's hat swept against the shore by the current, remembering that when he saw the body ready to be taken back to Emmis, he saw that the abject apprehension and self doubt of a lifetime were gone from Matt's face, replaced by a core of dignity hitherto unseen, or worse, plainly ignored by those who should have known the signs.

1922. Prohibition had been enforced for only two years but already Matt was aware there were serious reasons to believe the Volstead Act might not remain a permanent part of the nation's Constitution.

He'd let Sid Jako worry about that.

Matt didn't worry very often, either, about what was happening to the Kootseema farm, he knew that someday he'd have to let it go and then, he'd make a trip down to Kennedy's. Matt was convinced that even if the paper was Cy's, he'd somehow be allowed to stay.

Sometimes he did wonder, though, how a piece of land and the buildings his father had put together over thirty or forty years could be so changed in a few year's time.

What did Gottfried have that was absent in himself?

Although he had no feelings for Amelia, he didn't blame her, either, for the poverty and waste that negated the years of toil by his parents. Drinking so steadily now that Sid would no longer allow her to even wash the bottles and jugs his business demanded, she had done no work on the farm for years.

And Matt may have wondered why her father continued to supply his only daughter with whiskey but he never inquired of Amelia or Sid, he sensed no affection in either of them for anyone, certainly not for each other.

Matt did worry about Hank, but he worried in a way he couldn't verbalize. He couldn't recall meeting anyone like Hank, now fourteen. Matt had never known any person so consumed with meanness, someone so detached, whose eyes were filled with endless scorn. Hank refused to herd the few cows now when sections of fence lay flat beside rotted posts, destroying the marked perimeter of the pasture. Some days he sat on the stone pile halfway across the meadow, Matt's old .410 Winchester across his bony knees, watching for hawks or crows and occasionally aiming at the woodchucks and gophers moving in the grass nearby.

Matt knew Hank wasted most of the shells he shot; he never seemed to improve his marksmanship, but what was more puzzling was Hank's lack of interest when a hawk dropped or a gopher's slim body lifted in shock, spiraling upward and fell to the grass. Hank never examined his fallen prey, he brought no evidence of his skill back to the buildings. Never receptive, always aloof to Matt's earlier attempts to be to Hank what Gottfried had been to his only son, Matt now seldom spoke to Hank, even though he knew he should coax him to return to school, to finish the eighth grade.

Last spring, Matt asked Sid to let Hank help fill the jugs, keep the crates repaired, keep the inside and the outside of the Lincoln clean. Sid didn't agree.

"Hank, he makes me wonder, that set of his mouth, those eyes that don't quit roving probably even in the dark. He don't listen, he don't care, Hank's better chorin' up at your place, keepin' his ma company. We got us a business here calls for differnt kind of help than him."

Matt knew that he wouldn't want to live anywhere but the farm where he and Gottfried and Annie had worked together and he knew, too, that the only contentment he knew now was found on the road, alone, and if he had to haul Sid's whiskey while taking pleasure in the hum of the motor, the comfort of the car's fugitive seclusion from his confused unhappiness at home, Matt knew he could carry on.

He preferred the runs that covered many miles. So odd, he knew, to feel that the danger of being pursued by federal agents seemed less perilous than witnessing the decay and collapse of his parents' farmstead. And he felt a justification for that contentment as he sped over the backroads of three counties, giving quick scrutiny to every small turn-off where someone might wait in the dark for Sid's car to sail past. The dust that whirled beneath the car and lifted in the wake of its passage marked Matt's affiliation with an unknown world.

Sid Jako trusted Matt implicitly to never miss a delivery or to ever make a delivery late and, most importantly, he trusted Matt to bring back the little green bag always closed carefully with a brass zipper, the bills inside rolled tightly, encircled with a rubber band.

Sid was surprised that he was fond of Matt, and not bothering with a sense of fairness or questions of morality, he guessed his feelings about his son-in-law were what some men might feel toward a favorite son or brother.

Sid knew that Matt found no joy in anything on the Kootseema farm and that he cared nothing for Amelia. Sid was not blind to the obvious pleasure Matt felt, driving the Lincoln purchased when the salesman in Minneapolis convinced Sid, "You want get-away power, forget false ceilings, double gas tanks, that jazz is for amateurs."

Sid Jako made some changes in the Lincoln at once; the back seat was removed, a search light beside the driver's window added to the safety of this large automobile that traveled mostly in the hours between dusk and dawn.

Matt, as the driver of the new car changed, too, as the sleek steering wheel became more familiar beneath his big hands. With the car safely hidden most days in the lean-to of a barn near Jako's oldest still, Matt drove his old Plymouth coupe to Emmis every two weeks, where Fred Blau, the young barber, trimmed his hair. He carried a bundle of his pants and shirts and underwear to Fred's wife, who had a small laundry set up next door to the barber shop.

At home, he fitted a wooden box with his shaving mug and soap and a can of oil for his boots. He kept a comb in the pocket of his shirt. He drove a long nail in the wall of the back porch and hung his new fedora there; he instructed a momentarily stunned Amelia and an unconcerned Hank to keep their hands away from what belonged to him.

Before he began a run, near or far, in Sid's Lincoln, Matt carefully slipped a clean white handkerchief in the back pocket of his trousers, moleskin cloth, blue and sharply pressed.

Beulah Blau told Fred that Matt had more changes of clothes than anyone else who brought their laundry to her. Rueben Schultz, who stopped at Kootseema's when he was hunting his runaway farm dog, reported the next day in Pavlik's that none of Matt's civilized ways were rubbing off on Amelia. She was more wild than ever.

But on this Saturday night, Matt felt a certain dread as he got ready to deliver a large order of moonshine to Len Henschel's country store, nearly thirty miles from Emmis. Len had scheduled a bowery dance next to the store; it had been raining for three days and Matt knew he'd have a hard time driving on the mud-slick roads.

Sid had warned him, and Matt knew it was true, the damn feds were more likely to patrol on a weekend. Len was a good customer, Matt was a good driver. He could actually start out in daylight with the less conspicuous Chevy coach Sid kept for his own use, but it had little power and not much speed. And maybe, anyhow, the rain might end before dark and the bright lights on the Lincoln would help him pick out the worst ruts and washouts. He'd made tougher runs.

Amelia had slept on the cot in the side porch until noon and Hank was somewhere around, Matt wasn't sure where. Sid had stopped in early today to tell him that Sheriff Walz had brought some good news yesterday: the Feds were going to be watching mostly the Twin Cities area from now until after the 4th of July, leaving these rural roads unwatched for a few days. The sheriff's agreement to share such news with Sid cost something, it was true, but it would be dangerous to operate this business without it.

Sid kept the sheriff in whiskey and a few envelopes of money slid into the sheriff's office now and then, and Matt hoped the news about the Fed's weekend plans was true. Every time Sid heard someone would maybe run against Marcus Walz in the next election, Matt saw the agony in Sid's face, the anger and the fear.

Matt needed a few hours of sleep but he had no place to lie down in the house, no place that would provide a decent rest. The sheets on his parents' old bed, where he and Amelia used to sleep, hadn't been changed this summer. Matt had been sleeping upstairs in the store room, on an old cot, but he'd taken the bedding to Beulah Blau's laundry and not picked it up yet. His childhood bed was now Hank's and he hadn't looked inside that small room for years. He feared how it would feel to turn the knob and step inside.

He decided, when it was nearly mid-afternoon, to drive his coupe over to Sid's and sleep in it until it was time to leave for Len's, nearer dark.

At Kootseema's, the farmyard and unkempt lawn were so drenched it was difficult to reach the gravel road and there, only slightly better footing could be felt beneath the narrow tires.

As Matt turned north to Jako's he looked through the side window at the farmstead that had been a provenance of immense pride in the lives of his parents. He was sure that he'd seen Amelia headed to the granary where, beneath a pile of burlap sacks, he'd hidden the half gallon jug Sid had sent yesterday.

The jugs he hid there were emptied sooner than they were a year ago; Matt knew that of the three who lived there, only he cared nothing for Sid's "Varnish", as his customers referred to the booze Matt delivered. He wondered why Sid didn't care about Amelia and Hank; come to that, he wondered why he didn't, himself.

That's not how life is supposed to be.

The gravel was rutted and occasionally there were marks in the mud showing the wheel tracks of a car or truck that had nearly slid into a shallow ditch bordering the road.

Matt, in the small car but more accustomed now to the weight and safety of Sid's Lincoln, drove carefully, his foot pressed lightly on the gas pedal, his speed barely twenty miles an hour. In the east, a band of light was illuminated further by a brief burst of weak lightning, and Matt was given hope that the rain was about to end.

Maybe his freshly starched and ironed shirt would not be ruined, maybe it wasn't so foolish, after all, that he'd carefully oiled his shoes. With one hand, he laid his hat on the seat beside him and smoothed back his hair.

He wished Gottfried could see him, he thought he could remember hearing his father say once that after all, farming wasn't for everybody.

Jako's farm buildings were on a slight hill and just as Matt turned in the driveway, a cautious sun slid through the clouds which had hidden it for days. Sid Jako owned three stills, two of them located twenty miles north of Emmis, and Matt wondered if the load he was scheduled to deliver tonight was already loaded or if at least part of it was still in the small barrels in the back of Sid's truck, the barrels hidden beneath a couple of cords of stove-length wood.

As Matt climbed from his car, Sid came from the house, grinning as Matt reached back inside the car to get his hat. It would be damned hard to replace the man who made most of the deliveries that were making Sid a good living. It still surprised Sid that Matt refused to take even a sip of the whiskey he hauled and that this blundering slow-foot who stayed with that stupid, worthless Amelia had succeeded more than once to outsmart and evade the agents who patrolled the roads in Sutton and nearby counties.

He told Matt to come inside; the car was loaded and Sid's housekeeper was preparing supper. Instead, Matt sat in a chair inside the enclosed porch and slept until Sid touched his shoulder; suppertime.

After they'd eaten, Matt was reluctant to get back on the road when it was still daylight, but the sky had clouded over again and thunder rumbled in the west. If more rain fell, some of the roads between here and Bud's would be almost impassible.

One way or the other, he'd better get going.

Sid followed Matt to the door and Matt stopped to lift his hat from the chair where he'd slept. "I ain't feeling the best about these runs you set up for the half-light hours. Drivin' in the dark, that's more safe."

Sid didn't feel he had to explain to Matt anything about his business but said, "Len's wife has been visiting her sister and she's comin' home tonight...Len wants to meet the train."

Matt considered Sid for a second, then stepped outside. As though he'd just thought of it, Sid said,

"Say, Matt, if something ever happens to you, Amelia, she'll go through that place of yours in less than a year. Just to be safe, we oughta see the guy does such business for me, and see that her and Hank don't get the place direct. I'd be the natural one to look out for them two."

Matt stared at him and Sid dropped his eyes. "Why would anything happen to me?"

Then, with both feet on the ground, he said, "And I ain't the fool you take me for, neither."

Sid, almost never embarrassed, felt the blood rise to the top of his face. Through the screen door, he watched as Matt slowly backed the big car down the driveway and onto the road."

Squinting his eyes, shaking his head slowly, he said, "Son of a bitch!"

Emmis

A crack of lightning and then dozens of flashing streaks within and between the suddenly darkened clouds followed deep-pitched rolls of thunder, and then the rain began.

Gusting against the wide windshield, the raindrops were so wild and numerous they became a curtain enclosing Matt, separating him from this stretch of landscape he'd known for years.

He wondered why, now of all times, he recalled the summer storms when he was a child, the house lovingly cared for, the barn straight, rafter after rafter, the safety he felt as, seated between his parents, he had watched skies like this from the deep porch, his back pressed against the walls of the house built by his father.

In some places, now, as the sudden rain subsided, he saw grass-choked ditches overflowing, sending water over the roadway, some of these seldom traveled roads little more than cartways.

Matt remembered that when he'd driven this road two weeks ago a farmer was grading and graveling a crossing to his fields and he slowed the Lincoln even more and with the spot light on the side of the car, searched for that small stretch of higher ground.

When he spotted it he swung the car carefully off the road and rested, both hands still gripping the steering wheel.

Forty minutes later, Matt was slowly inching the car toward Len Henschel's store, the unpainted bowery bathed by the gleam of his headlights.

More rain had fallen here than anywhere Matt had been today, and now the sun, low in the west, was scarlet, the light spreading along the horizon in tiny peaks and shallow valleys. Matt smelled the sweat on his own body, and he knew that no matter where he parked the car, he'd alight in mud. The dirt, the mud, the effort to be clean...he pulled his hat over his damp hair, unlocking the wide box fitted behind his seat. Twelve gallons unbroken, two wooden cases of quart bottles. He wished he didn't have to take back the empties from the last delivery; if he was stopped, they'd be as damning as these jugs and bottles filled with moonshine.

Len was waiting; he'd watched the sky toward Emmis all day and knew the storms had been widespread. The two men carried the delivery into the small dirt cellar beneath the store and Len replaced the table which hid the cellar door in the floor behind the scales.

Len was always surprised that Sid demanded full payment for each delivery in cash, handed to this fellow who looked like he couldn't find his way out of a burning outhouse in broad daylight.

The system seemed to work, though, and when Len handed the envelope to Matt, he knew Matt would sort the bills on the hood of the car, count them carefully, then nod as he rolled them tight again, and headed back.

Tonight, Matt told Len he'd had enough of township roads today...some of them nothing but cow trails...and on the way back to Sid's, he'd stay, instead on safer county roads.

Matt knew Sid would not be alarmed if he took a longer road back to the Jako farm. Although this route was less familiar, the surface wasn't starred with pools of standing water. He felt unexpectedly relaxed as he sat back in the car's comfortable seat, the window at each end of the long seat opened to the night, the air surprisingly free of any hint of moisture.

When he saw the headlights of a car a half mile behind the Lincoln twenty minutes after leaving Len's, he realized he'd not seen another motorist since he'd driven from his own place five hours ago. He could suddenly hear the rattle of the bottles he was hauling back to Sid's, "It's not against the law to haul empty bottles in a wooden box", he thought, but, God, he wished he hadn't picked them up tonight. It would be hell to be stopped, especially with that cash in his shirt pocket.

He stuffed the money beneath the seat, and looking back, saw the lights were no longer there.

It had been a hell of a rain, but not such a bad night. He had a few chores in the barn that would have to wait until morning. His clothes were damp and he felt exhausted; he wished Amelia and Hank would be gone when he got home but he knew they'd be there. Hank, God knows where, but Amelia, she'd be in his mother's rocking chair, crumbs and dirty plates on the table, the water pail empty and ashes sifting from the kitchen stove.

He didn't wish them dead, he just wanted them, as long as they were living, somewhere else. What was it his dad had told him about the childhood friends who came to America?

"They pulled out for places unknown."

Just as Sid crossed into Sutton County he saw headlights coming toward him on the dark road, traveling fast. He pulled to the side of the road, not nearly as narrow as some roads he'd driven, but it was better to be careful.

The car, a new looking Chevrolet, Matt was quite sure, slowed and drove past. Men in the front seat and at least one in the back.

Matt pulled back into the right lane and in less than a minute, the back of his car was swept with golden light. Shocked, Matt stepped on the gas pedal, and for the first time ever, failed to scan the road before his headlights. He'd forgotten that Sutton County had rebuilt the bridge across Hayley Creek, making the roadway more narrow.

He missed smashing into the guard post, and the snapping and crackling of the bridge rails outside his window, rolled down because the night air had been so welcome, seemed louder than the whining of the engine and the scrape of metal meeting metal. The sound didn't end until Matt, propelled through the air, his fedora already floating near the edge of the creek, disappeared in the muddy water, its course rushing and swollen by the heavy rain.

Sid's Lincoln, only the hood completely covered by Hayley Creek, had been chained to a huge Brockway truck, and Sid stood, tight lipped, near the driver of the truck.

Sheriff Walz stood nearby, looking past the scene to a line of trees growing near the edge of the water.

Shorty, who had arrived with Cy, stood between the sheriff and Cy, heard the sharp intake of Cy's breath as he looked at Matt's body, stretched out on the bank of the creek.

Young Doc Dennison pulled a blanket over Matt's body and said to the sheriff, "That's the thing about cooking moon, you know. Some make quite a lot of money, some die. That's something a fellow in your position might do well to ponder."

Sid walked toward Cy and Shorty but before he reached them Cy spoke to Doc and turned away.

Shorty hoped to God that no one would ever hate him as much as he knew Cy Kennedy hated Sid Jako and the Sutton County sheriff.

CHAPTER 7

In the early evening of the day after Matt's death, Cy walked down to the shop and into the Shorty's living space. Shorty, his evening meal finished and his kitchen put to rights, was surprised to see Cy and more surprised when Cy sat down in the chair beneath the lamp, the spot where Shorty usually took off his boots, tuned in his table radio and sat until bedtime.

Cy leaned forward and reached for the slim bottle in his hind pocket, placing it carefully beside the radio.

"Shorty, about everybody we know seems to be pretending something. The sheriff pretends he don't know Sid Jako, Sid pretends he has no idea why Matt was borrowing his big car, the county engineer says he figured his crew had put up signs to draw attention to the bridge makeover. Let's you and me pretend we're members of the God damned Wilkens Family and have a drink."

Bemused, Shorty went to a small cupboard and returned with a couple of glasses.

Bands of cirrus clouds drifted across the moonlit eastern sky like the tails of a hundred white stallions sliding quickly through the high winds overhead.

Driving home from Emmis in the late evening, having attended a school board meeting, Bert was angry that she had failed to convince the board that the 1926 encyclopedias in the school library were hopeless tools for her students.

The men on the board were well known to the Kennedys and much respected tradesmen of the town, admired especially by Cy. Earlier at the supper table tonight Bert had expressed her misgivings about standing before them, trying to wheedle money from a budget that was already stretched beyond the means of the taxpayers.

"I could cough up the money myself, but darn it, that's not how a school is supposed to be run!"

Bert was angered by Thea's reply. "Well, how *is* a public school supposed to run when the public's out of cash? Everyone sell everything they own, live in a tent? You and the rest of the the teachers in this district have already taken two salary cuts in the last three years! Hard times, Sister, hard times!"

Cy had spoken then. "Hey, you two! We don't need to rail about hard times at the table, not as long as we've got Gladdie cooking for us. Bert, you're right to try to persuade the board but don't be surprised if you get turned down. Every man on the board is mortgaged to the hilt and trying to keep things together for the people working for him."

Changing gears, he said, "Thea, I notice in the Advocate you're giving a lot of free ink to Chamberlin and Hitler and Munich. You better move the Depression further down the line before you knock us over with stories about the war."

Thea, pouring coffee for everyone, said, "Tell it to Adolf."

Gladdie seldom entered into anything but easy conversation at the table but tonight she looked at Bert and said, "When I was in school, we made do with one or two books and we learned everything in them and we got out of school the same as kids do today."

Thea, sensing a sharp response from Bert that might linger in the air for a day or two, turned to Gladdie and said, "But Gladdie, look at yourself!

What good did school do you? You'll be taking care of Cy Kennedy's idiot children when they're old women!"

Gladdie took Thea's comeback as a compliment and an acknowledgment of their feelings for her, and Thea winked at Bert, who grinned. Cy smiled. It wasn't hard to be a happy man among this group.

Almost home, Bert decided that her meeting with the board was not a lost mission; she felt oddly buoyed by the apologies offered by the members who, Bert knew, denied her request for the most valid of reasons; there *was* too little money. When times were better she'd ask again.

The twins knew that each year, on the anniversary of Ayma's death, Cy mailed a generous check to Father McKee. Bert wondered if her dad might consider a gift, instead, to the school. Neither she nor Thea had ever attempted to pressure Cy to share their interest in anything, but she knew he had strong feelings about the increasing number of students, especially farm kids, who stayed four years in high school and wished for more schooling away from Emmis.

Her car safely in the shed, Bert walked on the path which led to the screened porch. Somehow, she hadn't noticed, at least had not given much thought to the sudden absence of snow on the lawn except for tiny patches of greying, crusted snow beneath the evergreens where cascading limbs resting nearly on the ground sheltered the ground from the longer hours of spring's sunlight.

At St. Mary's, she and Thea had been regarded as true farm girls, ever mindful of the sky and wind, irrefutable weather watchers.

Bert heard behind herself the nickering of horses in their stalls, the barn doors open, partly, to admit the air warmed by the sun and in the dark, now, still carrying the mystery of winter. As she adjusted the window shades in her bedroom and heard, unconsciously, the familiar night sounds in the farmhouse, she recalled the pleasure she'd felt today when she and Davis had walked together to the lunchroom.

Would she like to see the spring production of a three act play at St. Mary's? Davis had already ordered tickets.

She and Thea had received a note from their college, reminding them that opening night would be Saturday. She asked, "Three tickets? Thea, too?"

Davis shook his head, holding up two fingers. "Two, just for us."

Bert had given Gladdie a ride home on her way to the meeting tonight in Emmis.

Gladdie said, "I went in your room before supper to shut the window. I seen you took your red dress outa the closet, there on the chair. I'll press it tomorrow."

She waited for Bert to speak; Bert was remembering Thea's question when the girls were in high school, "Is Gladdie a prophet or just a nosy old Swede?"

"Davis and I are going out Saturday night, Gladdie. The dress is fine, it doesn't need pressing."

"You'll see it does when you hold it up to the light. I already looked"

Twisting in the seat to open the car door, Gladdie said, "That Davis is a good man, quiet. Gus, he never said much, either."

Thea seldom was at the news office all day on Saturdays but today there were several things that required her attention. She had decided earlier in the week she would drive to St. Paul next week where she'd meet Ralph Stewart; he was attending a business meeting there.

Three days of absence from the office of the Advocate, none of them on a weekend...Thea couldn't recall being away from her desk for that many days.

Ralph, who represented a major seed house in Shenandoah, Iowa, had first come to Emmis two years ago, looking for meadows and pastureland from which june grass seed could be harvested. The farmers from whom Ralph bought the seed were happy to have an unexpected cash crop, although the amount of money exchanging hands was not much. With the rock bottom prices paid for all farm produce the money Ralph offered for the seed was not declined, and those farmers who could spare a week or two away from their own farm work earned additional money.

Farmers throughout the county and especially those in Warren Township were paid not only for the good quality seed their grassland yielded; if they had tractors to pull the grass strippers which were trucked up from Iowa, the short seed harvest brought them a few more dollars.

The first time Stewart stopped in Emmis, the day had been unusually warm, the prototype of the days and nights which made the summer of 1936 the hottest season in Minnesota's history. That day, there were few cars on the unpaved streets running east and west through the center of town.

No surprise there. This was a farm town and the farmers, already worried about the lack of rain, were planting corn. Before too long, clover and wild hay would be piled loose in haymows and stacked for winter feed on the higher ground inside the fenced meadows.

Ralph had been a seed buyer long enough to know that his best sources of information about the local farm scene were the bartenders in town, especially on a slow, sunny day such as this.

When he stepped into Pavlik's long, narrow, half dark saloon there were only three or four man gathered at the far end of the bar and one lone figure half hidden in the dusky interior, both elbows on the bar and a ragged felt hat tilted over the top half of his face.

Two bartenders, both of them heavyset and wearing white shirts and aprons, were standing together before the back bar, each had a towel slung over his shoulder. Ralph sat on a stool nearby and ordered a glass of beer.

The taller of the bartenders nudged the other. "You help this one."

Exaggerating the slowness of trade, he said, "I got the guy ordered a beer yesterday."

Ralph laughed. "Slow days? I guess your busy days are the ones when it's too wet to farm."

He shook hands with both men and told them the hot, dry days were in his favor. "I'm looking to buy as much june grass seed as I can get ahold of up here. We've got about fifty grass strippers we can truck up the last week of June, but I need to find the grass and I need to find the tractors to pull the machines. Am I likley to find them around Emmis?"

The bartender who had introduced himself as Gene Coty thought for a few seconds. "Always a lot of june grass around here if we get normal weather, get a little rain when we need it. Not too many tractors...I guess a tractor can pull three machines, I've heard. Hay around here should be cut by then. Come to think about it, there's probably enough guys using tractors now to help you out, I'll bet you can find the power if you go looking for it. Cy Kennedy, west of town, he's got three or four Internationals and the guy who works for Cy, Shorty Brill, he's put together some pretty fair tractors out of car and truck parts. It'll be worth your time to see Cy."

The man sitting alone a few stools away looked up. "Yeah, give old Cy a try! Wavin' a dollar bill in his face is like showin' a cut apple to a hog. He'll go for it!" '

Nettled, the bartender called Clyde answered, "Hank, what's it to you? You don't grow nothin' but thistles and canary grass and you don't need to go on about Cy Kennedy. If it wasn't for him, you and your sorry bunch and your lame cows would be down the road, gone."

Turning back to Ralph, Clyde signaled for him to move a couple of stools further from Hank. Lowering his voice, he said, "That there's the pride of Emmis, the guy we keep waiting for the damn fool catcher to pick up. Name's Hank Kootseema, lives on sixty acres of Cy's. Talk is he hasn't paid rent for years.

"Cy's daughter, one of the twins, runs the newspaper office down the stret half a block. She'll tell you if Cy's around and she knows as much as anybody what's going on around Sutton County."

Ralph paid for his beer, then looking over at Hank, laid a dime beside it, motioning toward Hank.

Clyde pushed the dime back across the bar. "I'd rather not. He don't need any more than he's had already."

Ralph laughed, slipping the coin in his pocket, "I'll be around a few days, down at the hotel. If anybody wants to see me about selling their grass seed or driving tractors or riding the machines, they can look me up."

The small frame building with ADVOCATE printed on a large sign above the door was easy to find, and Ralph stepped inside the screen door. An electric fan pushed air around the office and a clattering sound from the rear of the building could be heard above the noise of the radio standing on a shelf above the big desk near the window.

Auction bills printed on several colors of paper hung around one wall, some of them fluttering in the slight air current caused by the struggling fan. There were at least a dozen farm auctions imminent in the area surrounding Emmis. A much used captain's chair sat near the desk, and behind the desk, a pencil pushed through her hair, another making slashes across the paper spread in front of her, Thea Kennedy didn't raise her eyes as the screen door slammed.

The presence of someone else in the news office was less important, it seemed, than the job at hand.

After a couple of minutes, Ralph lowered himself into the chair and waited. On the radio, someone announced the time: four o'clock.

Thea swore and threw the pencil across the desk, then she looked at Ralph and wiped one hand across her forehead. A faint smudge of ink appeared there and she asked, in a pleasant voice, "Ever spend a day in hell before you even think of dying?"

Ralph laughed.

"I'm not thinking of dying, for sure, and I've seen a lot worse hell than I've seen today. Actually, I just want to buy some june grass seed, rent a few tractors and hire a crew of about twenty or so men to help. Down at the saloon, there, I was told you could put me in touch with your Dad or someone to get things set up to get that seed six weeks from now."

Thea looked at him, pulling the pencil from her hair, pushing her chair back from the desk. "Pavlik's! The magic word on a day like today!"

Ralph looked at her, and she explained, gesturing at the noise and voices from the room beyond her office. "Less noise down there; I'll see you in twenty minutes."

At Pavlik's, when Ralph returned, only Clyde and Gene were there except for Hank, who had moved to a stool near the door, the heels of his worn boots hanging over the rungs of the stool.

No glasses or bottles on the bar, Clyde put a few nickels in the jukebox, the sound turned low. He and Gene would finish their shift at five o'clock, John Pavlik and his daughter were working nights this week.

Thea hurried in and saw Ralph already seated at one of the tables beneath the small windows high on the wall. Gene came to the table with an empty glass and a bottle of wine, something colorless that didn't look appealing to Ralph. When he had poured her wine, Gene looked at Ralph, waiting for him to order.

Thea waited to sip her wine until Ralph's brandy was set before him, she lifted her glass just as Hank stumbled from his stool. Veering close to their table, his hands jammed in the pockets of his ragged overalls, he asked, "How's Cy's little sweetie doin' down there, across from my place, where he's got the papers for my farm tucked away safe and we got nothin'? Wasn't for old Cy, I'd be sittin' purty, same as you."

Before Ralph could stand up. Gene and Clyde were at the table and Thea watched as they shoved Hank out the door.

Through the open door they watched as Hank stood muttering to himself and finally headed for his car parked near the harness shop.

The late afternoon train sped through Emmis, its shrill whistle sounding until it was a mile out of town. Two men came in, laughing, and set their lunch boxes near the wall beneath the Regulator clock high on the wall.

Their drinks on the table almost untouched, Ralph heard Thea's story about a press so old she couldn't find parts for it and her reluctance to replace it when she was thinking of building a larger shop.

He half-listened to the men, who, on their way home from work, laughed about a trick they'd played on a foreman. He saw the bartenders watch the clock, straightening the rows of glasses beneath the mirror on the back bar.

Through the open door of the saloon, cars rattled past and boys on bicycles slowed to glance inside, at forbidden territory.

Ralph hoped his company, searching for sources of grass seed, hadn't made a mistake, sending him to Emmis.

Thea shook her head as Clyde started around the corner of the bar, headed toward their table with the wine bottle. "My fear of Gladdie, our housekeeper, keeps me at a limit of two glasses on a working day", she told Ralph.

John Pavlik came to their table just as they were leaving. "The boys tell me Hank's at it again. Thea, I can have someone throw that damned fool out on the sidewalk every time he walks in if you say the word. I don't let his ma inside. Every barkeeper I know has at least one guy like Hank hanging around, part of the business. What he spends here amounts to nothing, I don't care."

Thea laughed. "Hank's kind of like a pothole in the road, a chair that you know has just three legs. He's just something you try to avoid. I might feel differently if everyone in Emmis didn't know him. Don't feel sorry for me, John, feel sorry for the folks he lives with."

Cy met with Ralph the day after he came to Emmis and asked him to the farm. Cy recommended that his neighbor, Pat Herter, would be the best person to travel through Sutton County, lining up the ground that would yield the most seed. The Advocate would carry an ad all through June, asking for the farmers who were interested in helping in the harvest to notify Pat.

That evening, in the dining room of the Kennedy farm house, Bert spoke about her plans to take some special classes at a nearby State Teachers College, beginning as soon as Emmis High closed for summer.

Ralph said that his daughter, Joan, would be beginning college in the fall and that he was worried that she might be lonely; she'd never spent much time away from her mother.

He saw the questions in the eyes of those sitting around the table. Not someone who usually dodged disclosures about himself, he hesitated to go on.

"My wife and I don't live together, we haven't since our girl was ten. My wife, Ellen, doesn't believe in divorce. She lives with her mother and Joan in the house I bought before we were married."

A minute passed before Bert asked, "What kind of training will Joan look for, in college?"

"I'm not sure; teaching school, I think. Her grandmother has two sisters and two daughters who are nuns but my wife has never pushed her in that direction, I'm pretty sure. My wife's mother has talked about it since Joan was born."

No one responded to the bitterness in Ralph Stewart's voice.

Gladdie said that her cousin was married to a Lutheran minister who wanted his two daughters to be missionaries.

Cy asked, "Do you think they'll be?"

"Not unless they can take their families. One girl's got three kids, the other one, five."

Bert and Thea exchanged grins. Gladdie to the rescue, once again.

Ralph stayed three days in Emmis and called the man in Shenandoah the evening before he left town. "Depending on the weather, once we get started, there should be an awfully lot of bags of seed shipped out of here right before the middle of July."

Emmis

In the last two years, Thea and Ralph met a dozen times in Minneapolis or St. Paul. When he returned to Emmis each June, on business, he was welcome at the farm.

Thea wasn't surprised that Cy didn't question Ralph's personal life; she sensed that Bert was apprehensive about her sister's liaisons. Outwardly, Bert appeared to welcome Ralph each time he came to the farm, but Thea knew that at her twin's core there lay a bevy of questions, centered around the one that Thea considered, too: "How will it end?"

Gladdie gave out few clues of her opinion about Thea's friendship with Ralph but seemed to be uncommonly gracious when Ralph was a guest. Cy thought he knew why both Shorty and Gladdie were reasonably calm about Thea's decision to maintain an interest in a man already married.

He overheard their discussion as they sat on the porch one afternoon.

Gladdie told Shorty, "It ain't like she was chasin' him through the streets, makin' a fool of herself. She's still runnin' the paper and earnin' her keep. We like her, so why shouldn't Ralph feel the same?"

Shorty replied, "Use your head, Gladdie, he don't like her the same way we like her. That's not why he keeps comin' back. He's a level-headed guy, the same as her."

Cy listened long enough to hear their mutual assurance to each other that more than likely, things would work out.

CHAPTER 8

Saturday, usually a bustling day in Emmis, was unusually quiet. This was the first weekend after Lent, and Thea knew there was a wedding dance tonight at the Emmis Ballroom. But most families, having spent as much as they could to celebrate Easter, probably hadn't planned much shopping today. All three of the town's feed mills closed at noon on Saturday, both lumber yards shut their doors an hour later.

Thea had remembered to tell Gladdie not to hold supper for her, she had anticipated a day in the office with few interruptions or distractions, but there were several jobs holding fire. For the past few months, since she'd increased the size of the newspaper by four pages, Thea had been aware that she needed help in the office. She knew too, that she'd be a difficult work mate for anyone who tried to fill the position. She was impatient, scornful, even worse than during her brief teaching career which ended when she admitted to herself that Bert could not be a better teacher; she, herself, could not be worse.

She had nearly asked Bert last week to suggest to one of her better students that she stop at the news office and talk to Thea about working there for at least a few hours every day. But she doubted such an arrangement would work. She had never involved Bert in anything connected to the paper nor had she ever visited the school after she began publishing the Advocate.

By nine-thirty, the only cars on the street were gathered near the two cafes on main street and further down the street and around the corner, at Pavlik's. The ballroom was a mile east of Emmis and she guessed the parking lot was filled by now.

Earlier, Thea had thought she might stop at the saloon for a minute...Cy might be there...but she had changed her mind. When the phone rang as she headed out the back door to her coupe, she almost didn't answer. Charlie Ott, over at the dry goods store saw the lights at the news office, could he drop off an ad for next week's paper? Exhausted and hungry, she hoped Charlie was in a hurry to get home; she took his paperwork at the front door and then locked up.

She walked the length of her building and into the small lot where her car was parked. In the soft glow of the one light that hung above the alley, Thea saw Amelia Kootseema. Clutching her soiled cloth purse in one hand, clad in a dark coat with ripped pockets and no buttons, Thea saw the hem of Amelia's cotton dress hanging unevenly beneath the open coat. Her left arm was extended above her body like a rudder that she counted on to keep her aloft.

She didn't notice Thea standing near the Chrysler, and clutched blindly at the uneven brick wall of the old Ford garage. She leaned heavily against it, twisting slightly as she tried to keep her clumsy, doubtful balance.

Emmis

Thea knew she'd be committing an irresponsible act if she drove away alone; she knew also it would be impossible without help from at least one other person to get Amelia into the car nosed against the wall of the news office. She silently cursed Hank for not hauling his mother home, worse yet, for furnishing the bottle that Thea guessed was the only thing in his mother's old handbag. Blacklisted at Pavlik's, the only store in Emmis that sold whiskey, Amelia depended on Hank to bring her a pint from the side door of the saloon.

Shaking her head, Thea opened her car door; she'd find Jack Nolan, the constable, and let him decide how Amelia could be taken home. Backing from her parking place, she saw Amelia turn and stare, and when the car passed close to her in the pallid gleam of light, Thea saw her staring eyes clouded with fear, suddenly bright with anger.

Thea had seen eyes like these once when Shorty had trapped a wild tomcat that had been killing kittens in the barn. She shuddered slightly as she swung slowly out of the alley to the back street of Emmis, driving slowly past Pavlik's searching for Hank's old Chevrolet or Jack Nolan's Packard. Neither was in sight.

When the sun disappeared earlier, the springtime temperature had dropped and now a chilly dampness crowded in; Thea reached over and turned the knob that would send a bit of heat into the car, then circled the main part of Emmis again. She drove slowly through the alley where she'd last seen Amelia and decided to drive home.

That damned old woman, floundering around in the dark, Thea wondered how long Amelia's luck would hold out.

Amelia, her mind filled with doltish funk and her body with abject tiredness, knew how to escape detection as she charted her return to the farm in darkness. Having evaded all afternoon any serious observation in Emmis as she hid herself and her bottle behind the vacant, fallen down buildings near the track, she believed the way home would be simply a matter of keeping herself upright in the dark.

She had long ago abandoned the most direct route home: the gravel road past Kennedy's and then the curve that led her to Matt's parents' homestead.

No roads.

Amelia feared the speed of the traffic that sprayed gravel as the drivers sped through the dark and she feared more the intentions of those who, sighting her, crept slowly past, drivers and passengers staring through the glass, the sound of noisy gears making her wish she were invisible, sending her scurrying to the edge of the road.

Instead, Amelia, when there was no deep snow, dodged sinkholes in the pastures, straddled barbed wire fences, struggled across plowed fields and took cover in fields of corn. She had overcome her fear of walking among cattle lying peacefully, waiting for the light of dawn. She was able to skirt the stone piles between the Kootseema farm and Emmis.

68

But tonight, cold moisture in the air, through which small cloud-like layers of shadow circled, pressed against her face and tired legs. Her trek to the farm and the familiar comfort of her old bed suddenly seemed impossible as she considered the miles ahead.

"I'll take the road", she thought, "It couldn't be no worse".

Near the edge of Emmis three small houses stood close to the sidewalk; she sat down on the steps of the first and pulled the barn rubbers more securely on her feet by adjusting the rubber jar rings that encircled them.

Wouldn't do to lose your shoes so far from home.

Lifting her purse from the step on which she'd rested, the bottle inside it nearly empty, she pulled herself upright. She wished she had a stick to lean on.

She wished she'd hitched a ride with Hank, but he never told her when he was startin' home, unless she'd forgotten, maybe.

Davis and Bert, returning to the farm, discussed the production of "The Children's Hour" and the darkness of the theme.

She asked, "Did you really enjoy it? I'm a little surprised you'd want to sit through a story about a couple of teachers having such a hard time. Not just hard, but evil!"

Davis laughed. "I didn't know what the play was about until it was half over, I just wanted to spend some time with you."

Bert didn't answer right away; Davis drove faster than she drove, his Studebaker skimming over the tarred roadway, the engine in this car more quiet than the engine in her small Ford.

"Well, I thought it was great! And going back to the auditorium at St. Mary's …I don't know…at first when I'd return for a few hours or a day to the college, I always felt when I returned home that the years Thea and I were there were somehow more important, more filled with promise than the years that followed. I didn't feel that tonight. I actually felt my four years there were just something that got me to where I want to be."

Davis reached across the car seat and held her hand.

"I'd like to think I'm somewhere in all that reasoning, Bert."

Bert smiled.

"I just finished teaching my senior class three weeks worth of Shakespeare's sonnets, but apparently none of the language rubbed off on me. I can only say that it seems you're someone who makes me satisfied."

"Satisfied? Not happy?"

"Should I say I'm happy to be satisfied or satisfied to be happy?"

They laughed, and looking through the side window Bert noticed the rolls of moisture laden whiteness floating above the ground, rising nearly to the tops of the leafless trees that crowded close to the dirt road into which they'd turned a few minutes ago.

Davis had seen it, too, in the headlights, and hoped it was a band of fog they'd pass through quickly. In this area, the moisture from the lowlands produced swaths of vapor that hung unevenly, and they both scanned the road ahead for the lights of other cars.

He asked, "Where did your folks come up with the names they gave you and Thea? Alberta Rose and Althea Summer! If they were going to call you by shorter names, why choose such fancy names?"

"Our mother named us. Dad planned to call their first baby Bridget, if it was a girl and when there were two of us, Gladdie says our mother sprang the names on Daddy and in a state of shock, he agreed. She warned him to not call us anything but the names she gave us but a week after Mother died, when we were five, we were Bert and Thea. Gladdie didn't like it and she didn't stop calling us by our longer names until Dad made her stop, when we went to school."

Davis said, "I always wished I'd been named David, but my mother's family was called Davis, and here I am."

Bert felt the car slowing further and looked through the windshield. No longer finding their way through intermittent bands of fog, she could see clearly only to the radiator cap, then for a few seconds, a few yards ahead of the car's hood. They crept in silence; Bert wished she'd see a mailbox or familiar farm buildings close to the road.

She saw Davis lean suddenly forward, straining to see ahead. Then a layer of fog lifted and there was a dark streak of road before them, the yellow headlights playing with the swirling panorama through which they inched.

"God, Bert! There's no wind out there, but it looks like a bush or something's blown to the road!"

He turned the steering wheel sharply and braked the car; Bert's heart hammered as she cried, "It's someone, a person out there! Davis!"

Shaking, each stepped from the car, unable to see each other until the fog rose slowly, leaving the roadway bathed in bizarre, shifting shades of light to dark, dark to light.

Bert saw Amelia first, in front of the tire on the car's passenger side, her arm lay on the road, her coat bunched up behind the tire, beneath the car.

Stooping low, unable to extricate her body and afraid to move the Studebaker, they heard the sound of a car, headed toward Emmis.

A young man neither of them knew stopped, his headlights strangely meshed with the light from Davis' car. He ran toward them, shouting, "Cy

Kennedy's place, it's right up there!" He pointed to the north and, running back, said, "Kennedy's got a phone! They'll get some help."

He backed carefully around on the road and Bert and Davis stood, not looking at each other.

Forming a circle around Amelia's body, straining to hear the sound of Aubrey's hearse, the small group stood silent. Doc Dennison realized that not once since his own arrival had he heard Davis Mader speak. His eyes cast down, Davis stood five feet from anyone. Bert, when Thea had arrived, burst into muffled sobbing as Thea held her close; then the two of them walked as far as they could and still remain in the circle of light provided by the headlights of the cars gathered there. Now, Bert stood alone, watching as Thea, a flashlight in one hand, picked up the broken bottle that had rolled from Ameliea's coat or purse, one of the mud rubbers that had flown to the edge of the road,

Amelia's old handbag, the clasp mashed into the road, a dirty comb, half the teeth long gone, lay close to where they'd pulled her body from beneath the car.

Cy cleard his throat and everyone looked in his direction. "I think we'd better wait til Aubrey leaves before we run up to Hank's."

Doc said, "Aubrey drove the hearse to St. Cloud this afternoon to get the engine tuned up and a couple of new tires. Edna said as soon as he drives up to the garage door, she'll send him out."

The sound of a heavy car approached and Frank Keefe strode to where the group waited. "Third accident tonight, damn fog. The others, not as bad as this one."

His eyes moved around the small, silent crowd. Last night, doing the crossword puzzle in the paper, he'd been hung up for twenty minutes by the word "surreal". A coincidence, he knew, if he'd ever heard of one. Seven or eight people who knew each other standing around in a circle on a dirt road lit by yellow lights.

A new word, but by God, he'd remember the meaning if it crossed his path again.

In the woods, just inside the fence that ran parallel to the road, an owl hooted. Bert looked at Thea, then Cy, who opened his coat and pulled her to himself. Thea stared at the thick darkness of the woods, the fog now reaching in straight-edged shafts between the nearest trees and when the sound of an owl drifted over the landscape, she felt a compulsive need to answer. Repulsed by the fear that she might laugh, that this indecent absurdity could be entertained for even a split second, she turned away and saw Cy watching her. He winked.

Thea stood straighter and walked to Frank Keefe, who was talking to Davis. "If this is anyone's fault but Amelia's, I'm the guilty one. I saw her getting ready to leave Emmis and I let her go."

The fog lights on each side of Aubrey's hearse shone downward as the machine crept closely toward the cars parked at the side of the narrow road. Aubrey angled the hearse so the spotlight mounted near the driver's door spread light from ditch to ditch.

Shorty and the twins remembered that Cy had been at the Kootseema farm for only a few minutes, to tell Hank and Mabel that Amelia was dead. Frank Keefe had argued with Cy: the visit was unnecessary, it was the duty of the sheriff's office to deliver the facts and answer the questions.

"Hank's not interested in the facts", Cy replied, "and he thinks he already has the answers to any questions. I've learned the pattern of dealing with Hank. I'll go."

As Cy's truck lights crept slowly through the thinning fog toward the Kootseema farm and the others walked toward their own cars, Frank said to Thea, "Whatever the hell Cy thinks is the pattern, it sure isn't leading him to any place sensible with that crew."

Thea didn't answer, and turned to see if Bert was behind her. She saw her sister, hesitant, watching Davis as he walked slowly to his car, his eyes not seeing them, his steps wooden and carefully measured.

Then Bert looked away, and suddenly, had reached Thea's coupe before her sister had opened the driver's door.

"I wonder if Gladdie was wakened by the noise and lights almost in her backyard."

Thea squeezed her hand. "She'll be at the farm tomorrow, Sunday or no Sunday. You know you're the apple of her eye and she'll be there before you wake."

Bert cried loudly, both hands supporting her head as she rocked forward. Bert's tears, Thea knew, were filled with bitter regret and horror and sorrow not only for the end of this life, but for the years, empty of meaning, that preceded Amelia's death.

"Look at me, Bert, it's true, you know. It's not fair; you're the apple kid and I'm just the onion in Gladdie's gizzard. Goes to show, even Gladdie makes mistakes."

Thea stopped the car near the steps and when they entered the kitchen, headed for the pantry and carried Cy's bottle of whiskey to the table. Shorty knocked sharply at the porch door and walked inside. He'd been sleeping until a few minutes ago, "I had this damn neck ache and took a few drinks and a couple aspirins. You shoulda got me!"

Thea, hearing Shorty and Bert on the porch, called "Come on in, Shorty. Dad should be back in a few minutes and we should all be here, waiting. Things might be hard for him, up there."

When Cy arrived a few minutes later he was white-faced and he had no explanation of his encounter with Hank.

It seemed that heaven was making some sort of judgment of events in Sutton Township and the wish of everyone for an early spring was erased by days of clouds and gloom. Shorty was tight lipped about the lateness of grain seeding when suddenly the brilliance of summerlike weather leap-frogged over the drabness of the weeks so hesitant to displace winter.

Above the sound of the small motor that powered the fanning mill which separated the chaff and weed seeds from grain, Cy heard the steady knocking of the screens as they moved back and forth. He stepped up into the granary where Shorty was cleaning the oats that would seed the field behind the woods.

Shorty seldom went into the fields anymore, unless there was a breakdown of machinery that could be repaired without hauling it back to the shop. But he enjoyed seeding the small grains: oats, rye, barley. This year, he planned to seed two weeks earlier than the planting was done in an average year, but, as Gladdie said when she gave him rare sympathy for the bad weather that slowed spring work in Warren Township, "Maybe it was a mistake to cut the trees around here, making fields. But what's done is done."

When abruptly and with no fanfare spring had come, most farmers had cleaned their barn pens and fixed pasture fences, readied their machinery and no matter which direction one drove from Emmis, teams of horses and tractors were visible in the landscape.

Sacking the last bag of seed needed to finish this spring's planting, looping the twine around his fingers and pulling the knot tight, Shorty grinned at Cy.

"Well, next is the cornfields. If we get rain when we need it and the cold don't come back, this could be a pretty fair year."

Cy nodded, distracted somehow, but listening to Shorty. He cleared his throat.

"You didn't look across the field at Hank's place, did you? I hate to think he's not getting his fields worked up."

Shorty, carrying the sack to the doorway, said, over his shoulder, "Now, what do you suppose I'm gonna say about that? You oughta know damn well Hank ain't been near his fields. Hell, you know he ain't got but a dozen discs on his drill. Never picks a stone, hits every rock in the field and I shouldn't wonder he goes back and hits 'em again. I ain't seen a thing of him and I ain't been lookin'."

Cy stood, his hand resting on the top of the fanning mill.

"We could maybe give a couple of whirls around that field next to the road, help him out a little..."

Near the granary door, Shorty turned and stared at Cy. Cy knew what he was thinking.

Neither spoke for a couple of minutes, Cy studying the floor, Shorty studying Cy. Cy cleared his throat again. "I guess you're right. Finish ours and push the drill back in the shed."

He was surprised at the coldness of Shorty's reply: "Don't I always?"

Cy thought he was a double fool; he allowed Hank to stay on Matt's farm and he cared that Hank was an incredibly bad farmer. Last fall, Hank had left three or four acres of oats standing until the grain fell to the ground. The binder with which it should have been cut had been overhauled by Cy's men only two years ago...no cost to Hank...and had never been pulled into the machine shed since. Mabel had finally, last fall, carried the canvases from the rollers to the back porch of Kootseema's house, storing them out of the weather.

Cy had noticed, later, that the pitman that sent the sickle back and forth, cutting the stems close to the ground, had broken; Hank had removed it and thrown the two pieces near the binder. Walking to the house, Cy knew he shouldn't visit his concerns about the Kootseemas on anyone else, especially on Shorty, who had known most of the story since Hank was a child.

"Not the whole story", Cy thought, "but enough of it to know Hank's not going to change."

Overnight, Shorty changed. As soon as he was sure Cy was out of bed and ready to begin the day, Shorty knocked on the kitchen door.

"I sent two of the men up north, there, to Hank's. I told them to finish plowing that twelve acres and disk it down smooth.

"We ain't pickin' stones, though. I ain't askin' them to do that. I cleaned about thirty-five bushels of seed after supper last night. Don't rain, it'll be in tomorrow night."

He stopped for a few seconds. "I know I'm crazy, Cy, and I'm afraid you might be crazier. What the hell kind of a man don't do a damn thing?"

Cy heard the frank appraisal in Shorty's terse message and he knew the criticism wasn't directed only at Hank.

An hour later, Cy walked down to the shop. Shorty was backing the F30 toward the grain drill. He jumped down from the tractor seat and reached for the draw bar on the grain drill.

Cy said, "I figure Hank is kind of spinning yet, his ma hasn't been gone all that long and that might mean more to Hank than anybody figures. He might get his bearings once he's figured out she's gone and won't be back. It's not just Hank up there, Mabel and the girl, they can't live on nothing, either."

Shorty jammed the pin in the draw bar and brushed his hands on the legs of his pants. "Cy, Hank ain't spinnin'. He don't make a move to keep goin' because somebody else moves for him. Don't ask me to do for him any more. If the only way I can be here is to chase behind Hank, scratchin' his back, I won't be here."

He climbed back on the tractor and the engine purred softly as the drill, filled with seed oats, started across the yard.

Rowdy came out of the shop and stood beside Cy, who rubbed the old dog's head, both of them watching Shorty, seated, his back straight, the steering wheel gripped in his gloved hands.

The dog pressed more closely to Cy's leg and Cy reached in his shirt pocket for the makings of a smoke.

"Dog, maybe we'd better straighten up pretty quick or we'll lose our best friend."

Frank Keefe, searching in the tall file near the window of his office, was surprised to see Cy's Terraplane beneath the big elm close to the parish house near St. Mark's.

Inside, waiting for Father McKee's housekeeper to call the priest from the garden, Cy wished he hadn't come. It would have been more wise to talk it over with the twins. He'd seen in last week's Advocate the appeal for funds to replace the roof above the sacristy; he could just write a check and leave.

It would look kind of odd, though. For twenty-five years he'd mailed checks to the church. Damn it, anyway! It never paid to do something that wasn't thought through ahead of time!

Jerome McKee was the oldest priest of the six men who led Catholic parishes in Sutton County, small, wiry, his sad looking eyes behind thick lenses seemed at odds with the smile that seldom was absent from his face when he was not engaged in the most serious duties of his position.

Cy stood as the priest entered the hallway, and followed him into a room where bookshelves covered the walls. Father McKee asked, "Or would you rather sit outside, on the porch?"

Cy hesitated. "I've got some kind of private business, we'd better stay indoors."

His words seemed strange to his own ears, and Cy sat down.

Jerome McKee, when he was a boy living on a Wisconsin farm, dreamed of being anywhere but in a world of barns and cropland, endless work. In the seminary, he dreamed far less, but thought about spending his life in a large city; he was torn sometimes by the idea that perhaps the vocation he'd chosen would not satisfy him any more than his father had been happy to milk cows and plant and harvest.

He had been a priest for three years when he was sent to Emmis to replace Father Cavanaugh. A relatively small parish attended by about half of the people in the immediate area, many of them first generation European immigrants, large families, limited knowledge of the English language, little money to contribute to St. Mark's.

Some of the priests who had been called earlier to Sutton County told Father McKee they envied him; Timothy and Bridget Kennedy were members of St. Mark's and had given almost all the funds necessary to build the church only eight years before father Cavanaugh retired. Most of the other churches, scattered through the county, were in need of serious repair.

The young Father McKee, unlike his predecessor, was regarded not as an aloof, fearful bearer of the scripture but a fair minded, approachable leader of his flock.

Soon, Father McKee wished that a hundred families like Ayma and Cy and their small daughters were strewn among St. Mark's membership. He had no reason to doubt the devotion to the church shown by all the parishioners but there was something so compelling about Ayma's family.

The funeral service, when Ayma died, was more difficult for the priest than any service in which he had participated, ever.

And he felt bereft, betrayed when, after her death, Cy came less often to Mass, never to Communion or Confession. Sometimes he attended Mass alone, sometimes with the twins. Father McKee heard that once in a while the girls went to the Swedish Lutheran Church with Cy's housekeeper.

In 1913, Father McKee and two other priests in Sutton County realized the contributions to these rural parishes were lagging. They considered their obligations to the Church and their obligations to those to whom they ministered.

They decided they would attempt some gentle prodding; each church would list the names of those families who, over a period of time, had made insufficient offerings.

It was unlucky for Father McKee that on a Sunday shortly after St. Mark's list was posted in the vestibule, Cy and the girls came to church. A week before, heavy rain and wind that reached fifty miles an hour had flattened crops and torn buildings apart, cattle had been killed by flying debris and horses, frightened by the storm, had escaped through gates and fences that no longer existed.

Church attendance looked especially good, thought the priest, as he hurried to the church from the parish house. He was met, just as he reached the side door of the church, by Cy and the two little girls who wore ribbons in their hair, their black shoes reflected the sunlight.

The notice, unpinned from the wall and folded several times by Cy, was thrust at Father McKee. "This is a bad time to be doing this. It's not right and I don't want to see this back on the wall."

The priest was stunned, he turned away without speaking and entered the church, the paper clutched in his hand.

The next Sunday, a beautiful day when the sky seemed wider than it could possibly be, Cy and Bert and Thea returned to church. On the previous Monday, Cy had mailed a check to St. Mark's along with a note that said "to catch up on expenses."

Ada McAlister, the sister of the parish housekeeper, asked Cy to introduce her to the girls and Cy looked up and saw the list hanging as it had a week ago.

Everyone on the church steps or in the vestibule, heard him say, "Come on, girls, we'll get away so these folks can get inside."

The three of them left the churchyard in Cy's touring car, the girls with puzzled expressions on their faces, Cy white lipped and staring through the windshield.

Five weeks later, at the end of summer. Father McKee called on Cy one evening. "It was an error of my own. The church should not be made to suffer for my ways. And you've been a Roman Catholic all your life."

Cy looked at him. "You don't know that, do you? I haven't lived all my life just yet."

Always, on the anniversary of Ayma's death, Cy sent a check to St. Mark's, but never returned as a member of the parish. When the girls enrolled at St. Mary's College, Bert became captivated by the history of her mother's faith and returned to St. Mark's when she came back to Emmis.

When the twins were twenty-one, they exchanged birthday gifts. Thea opened her gift first, and found an ornate solid silver cigarette lighter. She hugged Bert, laughing, and handed her a slender box.

Inside was a rosary, more lovely than any Bert had seen. She looked at Thea, "From you? Is this a joke?"

Offended, Thea said, "Of course not! But if you're going to say prayers every morning, say them in style."

No one had approached Cy about his lapsed membership since the day when he and Shorty were beneath a corn shredder, pulling bolts and washers, trying to move immovable shafts and gears with their hands. At the edge of the machine, in the gravel near the machine shop, Shorty saw two shiny black oxfords beneath two beautifully cuffed trouser legs. He nudged Cy.

Cy peered carefully. A large Saxon sedan was parked twenty feet away, he looked carefully at the man standing close, looking uncertainly toward the shredder, and Cy recognized someone who had been a guest at the dedication of St. Mark's new church, years ago.

He slid out on his heels and elbows, a greasy wrench in one hand. He stood beside the man who, startled, asked, "Is this a Catholic home?"

Cy said, "Who the hell wants to know?" As he crawled back under the shredder, Shorty snorted.

Cy didn't think he'd done the right thing, but he never apologized.

Today, sitting in Father McKee's office, Cy wasn't asking, he explained, for spiritual guidance, although he didn't rule out the possibility that he might need it.

"It's my neighbors. Well, actually they're my renters, who live next door on sixty acres I own."

Cy and the priest talked for nearly an hour. There were a few possibilities, said father McKee, all of which would likely be refused by the Kootseemas.

It might be possible to have the care of Glory taken over by one or two groups with which the priest was familiar, but when Cy told him she was nearly an adult it seemed less possible.

Mabel?

Hospitalization of some type, he supposed. What did the welfare office propose?

Then, "Cy, it seems to me you have a long history of culpability here. This is something you might have been able to keep from happening if you'd acted sooner."

Cy reached for his hat lying on the chair next to his. He shook hands and Father McKee walked him to the edge of the porch.

"I'm curious, Cy, about why you sought me out for advice after so many years."

"I figured with your education and being used to the people around Emmis you might see something I appear to be missing."

"I'm afraid not. And I'm sorry, Cy, I really am. For everyone involved in this dilemma."

Cy nodded and Father McKee turned back. "We talked for the best part of an hour and I noticed...you never addressed me as 'Father', not once."

Cy looked perplexed, then grinned."I'm trying to remember, now, but I guess you're right. I appreciate it that you never called me 'son', either."

A smile lit the priest's face and he said, "Bert means a lot to this church, she's one of the brightest people I know."

From the bottom step, Cy smiled back."You mean *I'm* not? The fix I'm in and you don't think I'm bright?"

On Thursday afternoon, three weeks later, the grand jury made it's decision in less than an hour. Business was brisk in Pavlik's and John called upstairs for his wife to help tend bar.

In mid-afternoon Hank Kootseema, in a clean chambray shirt and new bib overalls, worked his way through the crowded bar to where Katie Pavlik was serving. She glanced at him and said, "Hank, I was going through some slips in the drawer and you've got a tab you should have paid two years ago. Seven dollars."

Men at the bar stepped back and Joe hurried to his wife's side. He looked at her, saying smoothly, "I don't think that's necessary."

His wife answered, "Not to you, maybe, but it is to me." Joe pulled a glass of beer for Hank and, leaning close to Katie's ear, said, "We're just barkeepers here, Katie, not God."

Hank had been curiously silent for the most part since Amelia's death and Emmis wasn't surprised that the grand jury's refusal to charge Davis Mader was the blasting cap that ended Hank's reticence.

He had visited both law offices in Emmis the week Amelia was buried and found no comfort in the advice of both attorneys, that it would be a futile measure to attempt a lawsuit against Davis.

Hank told Mabel, "They don't know what they're talking about! Hell, Ma's killed, ain't she? She wouldn't got buried if they didn't kill her, would she? Once you're dead by somebody mowin' you down, there's pay in it some place!"

Whatever he expected when the jury met, it wasn't a verdict finding Davis innocent of Amelia's death.

"How could he not be guilty? They said half her coat was wound around under the damn car! School teacher or not, drivin' a car regular people can't afford, breaking about ten laws, running over people walking on the road. Public road, ain't it?"

Hank, his new bib overalls no longer spotless, called at the school and asked to see Davis. The superintendent's secretary called Frank Keefe, in his office across the street from Emmis High.

A few days later, Hank sat at Pavlik's long bar, talking to himself and gesturing angrily at the empty stool next to his own. John walked around the end of the bar and sat next to Hank.

"Hank, I had a look at those slips and Katie's right. You better pay up before you come back."

When the welfare board penciled out Amelia's name from the list of Sutton County residents entitled to a small amount of money from the general relief fund, Hank went to the courthouse to complain. He slammed the door of the office so hard the glass fell from the transom window above. Tony Katz, the custodian, puttying in a new pane, said, "Small price to pay, if the son of a bitch don't come back."

Cy Kennedy paid the expenses of Amelia's burial, as he had Matt's sixteen years earlier.

"You're a hell of a landlord, Cy," said Eli Kanter, "but it seems the only way you can get loose of your renters is to bury them."

Amelia's obituary notice in the Advocte measured less than three inches. Cy told Thea she should be ashamed of herself and Thea reminded him that she had paid up her debt last winter and owned the paper fair and square, but thanks for his opinion.

A month after the accident and a few weeks before the school year ended, Davis resigned from his position at Emmis High and was shocked that the faculty, the business men in Emmis and many of his students' parents begged him to stay.

He wasn't sure why he'd never called again at the Kennedy farm: Bert was directing the spring class play and he seldom saw her, even in the hallways of the high school.

On his last day in Emmis, he appeared in Thea's office, asking that she include in the next issue of the Advocate his letter of appreciation for the town's support of his work at the school. He called Emmis the best town in which he had ever lived.

Neither he nor Thea spoke Bert's name and neither of them thought of anyone else for the remainder of the day.

CHAPTER 9

Billy Maxwell had no enemies and no close friends with whom he spent much time. The youngest son of a farmer who lived north of Emmis, he wished the best for all in this neighborhood and felt no jealousy toward those who were more successful than himself. In dire emergency and mostly at the prompting of others, Billy was willing to lend a helping hand to someone whose luck went south.

His vague and tenuous attitude toward others was really the only reason he nodded at Hank Kootseema and then straddled the stool next to him in Pavlik's Saloon shortly after noon on the Friday before Decoration Day.

The bartenders there were always cool to Hank, moving to some distant spot behind the bar as soon as he was served. John Pavlik, who knew the success of his bar depended on the goodwill he showed his customers, refrained from exchanging words with Hank. John's wife, since the death of Amelia, ignored the tap of Hank's dime as he waited for another glass of beer.

But Billy's easy grin and frivolous banter made him a man close to the heart of a small town bartender; never insulting nor argumentative, never joining in a fight between those who might sometimes mistake Pavlik's for a boxing ring.

It wasn't long after Billy joined him at the bar that Hank became aware of the bartenders' acceptance of the newcomer and he resented the words and laughter which passed between Billy and the men on the other side of the bar.

But what if the guy was maybe a sop of some kind? Wouldn't hurt none to say a few words.

For an hour or two in the quiet bar the two exchanged brief opinions and talked about the hardships of farming, each boasted a little about how different life would be if milk or hogs or eggs paid out. Cruelly bored at last, Billy was thinking of drifting down the street to the Friends Cafe when, glancing toward the open door, they noticed a small man standing at the off-sale bar close to the door. Not much larger than a boy, clean shaven, dressed neatly in dark trousers and a faded shirt beneath a buttoned vest, a watch chain spanning his narrow chest, he laid a couple of bills on the bar and picked up the change when he was handed a half pint bottle in a paper bag, the top twisted tightly.

He nodded smartly, touched the brim of his felt hat and disappeared through the open door.

Hank asked Billy, "Who the hell is that old jigger, anyhow? Seen him for years. He ain't from around here, is he? I mean like, he never was born to Emmis, right?"

Billy laughed. "Well, he ain't from too far away, I guess you could say. His name is Sandy McDonald, lives down there by the creek at the east edge of town. Where them big trees are. My Pa knew him, he says, since the guy drifted into Emmis from the east coast, somewhere, to help lay the brick of the old Callahan store, there by the bank. Somebody sold him that little strip of ground by those big willows and he stayed on.

"Gets a pension check at the post office, I guess. Goes clear back to the Civil War. Far as I know, got no family, at least not here."

Hank, who had occupied a stool since ten o'clock this morning, stared at his beer glass, nearly empty once more. The bitterness in his voice surprised Billy. "God damn old coot, gettin' bushels of money for something happened nowhere near here. Shoulda stayed east and outa our post office collectin' money. We got none to spare."

Before Billy could respond, Hank sat straighter on his stool; he looked oddly alert. "So what does a worthless cuss like that do with all that money? Got his own house...he can't eat that much, one old man..."

Billy, who had firmly believed all his life that a trouble free life is the best life, wished he had told Hank nothing about Sandy. Probably try to bum a beer off Sandy, next time the old fella showed up.

"If he's got anything left at the end of the month probably drops it in the church plate," he said as he slipped from the stool next to Hank and waved at both bartenders as he left the saloon.

By the time Hank left Pavlik's the streets of Emmis were nearly deserted. The feed mill had shut down at six, the stores locked for the night, the movie at Emmis Theater wouldn't begin for another hour. Women from the nearby farms had stocked up on the needs for their families for the Decoration Day weekend and the evening crowd that would eventually show up at Pavlik's and the town's cafes had not yet arrived.

Hank didn't know why, but he felt a shiver of held-back secrecy run through himself and he hoped no one would see him when he backed his dust coated car away from the curb. Slouching behind the steering wheel, he drove slowly down the main street.

He couldn't get that juggy little McDonald out of his mind. Who the hell did that cocky little runt think he was, anyhow. Slipping that little bottle in his hind pocket when he left Pavlik's, regular like he was a God damn banker or something. Vest, hat on his head, walkin'those quick little steps like he was goin' some place important.

Hank turned west at the bank corner and found himself, a couple of minutes later, reaching the short alley near the creek, where the back of a small building was overhung with the cascading limbs of huge yellow willows that anchored the banks of the creek, their wide trunks four or five feet across.

A little house, a smaller shed and a white painted outhouse were wedged into an area so close to the trees that no vehicle could enter the shared surround. There were no wheel tracks in the alley and Hank stopped short.

Only the west side of the house and a newly spaded garden plot lay in the late sun, all else was dappled by the narrow leaves above, countless as the stars might be in a perfect sky.

Hank stared at the broom-swept yard; he had never seen anything like it. Smoke from the single chimney drifted slowly upward and disappeared in the low hanging willows. A chopping block and a small axe stood near the shed door, a piece of wire was strung from the corner of the house to the shed. Pinned neatly to the wire was a shirt and one towel. On the door of the outhouse a black porcelain knob showed plainly against the white door.

"Old son of a bitch,' muttered Hank. "Got a better doorknob on his shit house than I got on my front door." The white curtains at two small windows that flanked Sandy's doorway were a little high-flaming for an old man, too.

The house nearest this sweet enclave, Sandy's infinitesimal buttress against all but the natural world, was fifty feet away; there was no sound as Hank climbed carefully from the car. Suppertime, he supposed. Good time to look around. Better not slam the car door; he half stumbled over the hard packed earth beneath his broken boots.

Pretty nice little hideaway, when it came right down to it.

Inside, Sandy was cutting a small onion to add to the sliced potato in the frying pan on the wood stove. Listening, he pulled himself tall, carefully setting the knife on the corner of the stove. The pounding of his heart made it difficult to hear. He hadn't been sleeping well and he planned to go to bed soon after supper.

There was no reason to fear the sound outside the walls of his home. But still, a friend who meant well would come to the door, not shuffle softly around the perimeter of the house. He had written his cousin Belle last week, "there's not a menacing soul in Emmis".

Emmis

Sandy pulled the collar of his shirt more tightly to his withered neck. A funny little wind flitted through him, touching, tugging something in his thoughts. He hoped that when he fell asleep tonight he'd sleep until dawn.

Sandy looked across the narrow kitchen at the unshaven, scruffy figure who had lifted the latch and stepped inside. Even in the dimly lit room, it was the lack of light in Hank's eyes that frightened the old man most.

When Sandy was fifteen, In New York State, he and his older brothers had run away from their father's farm on the bank of the Genesee River, hoping to travel with Mr. Lincoln's army. Tom and Will were given rifles; Sandy, so young and frail, became a bugle boy.

Disappointed and resentful, Sandy stayed with the specified, inelegant position until one day a battleworn medic who had endured without sleep for three days and three nights grabbed Sandy's arm and shouted, "Throw that damn horn away and come with me!"

On the battlefields and in the wind torn tents where men were carried to die or to be cut and sewn for further battles, Sandy learned to measure the intent, the hope or hopelessness, the future of the wounded. Everything was always in the eyes. Hollow, pleading, angry, spent.

In his kitchen, Sandy reached for the knife on the stove, knowing the effort was useless. Hank lunged at him, grabbing the old man's wrist and pushing him backward into a kitchen chair that slipped on the floor and nearly tipped. Sandy's heart hammered against the thin little snap purse he carried in his shirt pocket, one gnarled hand reached for the cane hooked on the back of the chair.

Hank kicked the cane across the room, then faced Sandy, his eyes curiously changed, less cold but filled with stunned astonishment, as though he'd momentarily lost some gravely urgent question he had meant to ask someone before this venture, here, began.

Knocked nearly breathless and unable to right himself on the chair seat, Sandy found the strength to say the words which he knew would be his last. Looking upward at Hank, knowing that the purpose of this uninvited guest was as clear as the water that ran in the old Genesee, he set aside the great fear rising in his chest and, gasping for air, said, "You, sir, are a mudlark and I am a better man than you."

Hank stared at him, then cursing, pulled Sandy to his feet. Sandy caught the smell of onion on the knife blade as Hank held it to his face, playing with the old man's fear.

Shadows, some memories as clear as the sun through a spotless window pane, rushed through Sandy's mind. He thought of another spring day, a day in Tennessee, when the air reeked with blood. He'd always told himself that the exorbitance of dread he'd carried home from Shiloh was only a reflection of his beardless innocence among the dying men.

He knew now that he was someone who could simply not lose the dread of massacre and its sweet-sour stench.

The faintness rippling through his veins was suddenly rekindled but he knew it meant nothing, the heart that had carried him away from the cannon fire to Emmis would soon be still, as noiseless as the sunset, as the unfolding of another petal among his mother's roses.

Held upright by Hank's arm, the back of his head pressed tightly to the bib of Hank's stained overalls, Sandy saw the knife being lifted nearer his face. He closed his eyes. Coming westward to be redeemed from the threat of man's evil to man...he wondered if he'd closed the shed door...that swallow, yesterday, she'd fly in, carrying bits of mud in her beak, build her nest in the rafters...

He slipped to the floor, almost able to seize some vague equivalence connecting the endless thundering ranks of ragged men and this small, tidy kitchen where soon morning glories would brush against the window, this room that would in a few weeks grow darker with their bloom and vine.

In five minutes the carnage and wreckage was complete, the pulling apart of boxes and an old leather case from beneath Sandy's small cot and the rapid searching of the ancient warrior's hut yielded small gain for Hank. A few bills pressed together, a few coins, a cheap pocket watch and chain, old trifles in a tin box and a half pint of whiskey didn't amount to much, not even to an ignoble thief whose hope and vision had never ventured far beyond the day he first escaped his mother's womb.

Hank had thought the little purse buttoned inside Sandy's shirt pocket might have more money, but still, it was worth the time, he guessed.

Halfway to the car where the drivers door still hung wide, Hank stopped to look inside the shed. He wondered if the old bugger had hidden something there. Well, he'd better go...only one other house down here, but who knows. Might be somebody nosy.

He grabbed Sandy's single bit axe and flung it inside the car. His own had a split handle. Hank smiled to himself as he eased the car out of the alley. Lucky, he thought, the old man wasn't a squawker. Coulda got nasty.

When he reached the farm, Hank swung his car close to the pump house, behind the sagging machine shed that was barely visible from either the road or the house. He gathered from the seat Sandy's watch and the little leather purse in one blood stained hand and lurched through the door of the small building. Along one wall was a rough shelf which held old tins without

lids, most of them at least half filled with ruined bolts, odd washers, bits of
wire and small pieces of useless metal.

He dumped the contents of one of the cans on the cracked cement
floor and dropped the watch and chain and the empty purse inside, kicking
the scattered bolts and rusty nails beneath a sagging bench. He thrust the can
back on the shelf and tried to pull the door at least halfway shut. Damned
bottom hinge busted, Cy ain't fixed nothin' here don't know when. Door
drags like it weighs a hundred pounds.

Suddenly he remembered the little tin box from beneath Sandy's bed.
He ran to the car and retrieved it, then took a few minutes to paw through
the metal buttons, a G.A.R. pin, a tiny tin stencil with Robert McDonald's
name and the number of his New York regiment. Hank tossed it aside. What
shit.

Christ! Lived almost a hundred years and this is all the old bat had? He
jammed the tin box behind the can he'd just replaced on the shelf, annoyed
that now the can stuck out a little over the edge of the shelf. "What the hell,
nothin' in here but rats, anyhow."

He looked back, worriedly. "Don't know how far a fella can go, doin'
this stuff. Depends if anybody starts lookin'"

Thank God, Mabel and Glory were gone to Loretta's to help plant her
garden. That Loretta, nose like a sheep but she always bought more seed than
she needed and gave what was left over to Mabel. Hank wasn't sure a garden
was really worthwhile, those government guys at the courthouse who handed
out commodities, they always bragged up gardens, but you never saw one of
them with a hoe handle in his paw.

Satisfied there was no one in the farmyard or the house to witness his
return from Emmis, Hank pushed Sandy's half pint of Four Roses into the
space behind the woodbox in the kitchen, then pulled the kitchen door shut
as he left. He hurried to the wash line and grabbed a pair of overalls and a
torn chambray shirt from the line, letting the clothespins drop to the bare
ground beneath. Back in the car, he sped to the most secluded spot he knew
along Stony Brook and stripped in deeply wooded pastureland, wading into
the center of the stream. He was a mile and a half from any decent road. He
bundled everything he'd worn at Sandy's into a burlap bag, and, back home,
doused it with kerosene. Thrown on a pile of long-dried brush near the edge
of a field, in twenty minutes nothing was left but white ashes and smoke
dimmed buttons and suspender hooks from his spattered clothing.

As he kicked the ashes apart, he smiled. He kinda hoped old Cy saw the
smoke and feared the place was burnin'. Get his goat, the old devil.

On the top step of the porch, Hank pulled his boots off and rubbed some axle grease over the leather. In time, the stains would wear away. Not too much time, this pair of boots was done. He knew that Mabel wouldn't ask why he was down to one pair of overalls and one shirt. Teaching her to stay shy of his business was the only outstanding success of Hank's life.

By the time Mabel came home, the sun had set and a breeze from the east moved sweetly across her face as she set a small box of seeds on the porch and bent to pick up the lantern close to the wall of the house. She'd better check on her hens; some had been sitting on eggs for more than two weeks.

She fumbled in the pocket of her old sweater for a match to light the lantern; some of the setting hens were hiding deep in the machine shed. After all these years, she still hated walking here in the dark.

Walked in the dark all the time, on her father's farm.

When the yellow flame spread across the soaked wick, Mabel saw Hank's boots, black and stiff with grease, on the top step. Troubled, she stooped to see them better, and, picking one up by its laces, let it drop. Soaked, she supposed, but God knows where. When she returned to the porch she looked at them again, then blew the flame from the lantern and went inside.

Glory sat at the kitchen in a pool of harsh light that circled a glass bowled lamp pulled close to the magazine she'd borrowed from Loretta's girls. Her mother studied the girl's face for a minute, resenting the sullenness, despising her indolence, lamenting the sight of a face devoid of all dignity, forgiving her everything because Mabel knew in the part of herself still living that the guilt for all these flaws rose out of herself.

Decoration Day, the thirtieth of May, family graves in Sutton County were tended, last year's grass pulled away from the tombstones, fresh flowers laid near the markers of the dead.

In Emmis, it was the goal of most of the town's gardeners to transplant their tomato plants to their vegetable plots on this day. Lyd Murray, who lived in the house nearest Sandy McDonald, no longer started her tomato plants from seed. Her seedlings were never as tall and sturdy as those Sandy grew in the cold frame on the south side of his shed and he charged her only a quarter for a dozen plants, wrapped in a scrap of newspaper, the long threaded roots better than any she might grow.

She was touched and almost ashamed that the plants Sandy reserved for her were always clearly his top plants, better than the ones he carefully hilled into his own plot.

Today, after Lyd came home from tending family graves at St. Mark's Cemetery it was already mid-morning and she spied Scoop in the open doorway of the garage, sharpening the blades of the lawnmower. She yelled from the back step, "Scoop, you hightail it over to Sandy's and get those plants! I got the rows marked yesterday and I'm gonna set 'em in right after we eat."

She thought, as she began cooking lunch, "I hope the clouds stay so the plants don't get scalded before sunset."

Scoop pulled his gloves off and laid them on the lawnmower. Might as well go, although Lyd always told everybody it was *her* danged garden. Today was the last Sunday before he got seriously involved with fishing and he didn't want to spend the day arguing about two-bits worth of tomato plants.

He walked through the short brush that separated Sandy's property from his own. Stepping around perfectly, methodically arranged rows in Sandy's garden, Scoop noticed that the onions and peas were taller than Lyd's. He'd have to point this out when he got home.

Sandy's spade, recently sharpened, and his hoe and rake were hanging beneath the eaves on the north side of the shed, his rubber boots with holes recently vulcanized were laid on their sides beneath the tools.

Scoop knocked lightly on the door of Sandy's house and felt it swing inward a few inches, on well oiled hinges. He called out softly, the old man might be stretched out for a mid-day nap. At last, he pushed the door open more widely and stepped inside.

On the floor between the stove and table, the top part of his body covered with dark blood, Sandy lay with his arms stretched outward, one leg twisted beneath his body.

Lyd, shaking a rug from the bottom step, stared at Scoop as he shouted, from the edge of Sandy's garden, "Call Frank Keefe! Call his house! Ain't nobody at the courthouse on Sunday!"

When Lyd disappeared into the house, Scoop bent forward, a myriad of small red lights dancing behind his closed eyelids.

"Damned good thing I didn't tell her to fetch her own plants."

On the first Thursday in June, Billy Maxwell's father sat at the kitchen table reading the Emmis Advocate. "For God's sake," he called out, "Some son of a bitch killed Sandy McDonald." Billy and his mother listened as the old man read aloud the story in the paper.

Billy was unusually quiet as the three ate their noontime meal. Although he had a history of never volunteering to work or suggesting that any work needed doing, he asked if today wouldn't be a good day to look over the hayslings before they began cutting the meadows. Gratified but somewhat puzzled, his father agreed.

About three o'clock, when most of the ropes had been checked for thin spots and the pulleys oiled, Billy asked suddenly, "Dad, ya know that Hank Kootseema?"

"'Bout as well as I want to", the older man replied.

Billy told the story of his conversation with Hank. He wasn't surprised when his father said, "Tell you what, Billy. You get the hell into Emmis and look up Frank Keefe. You tell him what you told me, although it makes you sound like a nincompoop from hell. After this, flap your ears shut and tie a rock on your tongue when you see Kootseema. He ain't our kind."

CHAPTER 10

There had been almost no rain since the corn planting was finished, and Cy was worried that some of the rows, even some fields might need to be replanted. But two weeks ago the rows had become visible and now they were established with only a few vacant spots.

Cy and two of his hired hands were cleaning and oiling the three corn planters they'd used to check and drill this year's crop when Frank Keefe drove close to the shed where they were working. Frank greeted the men and signaled Cy to get in the car.

"Had a funny little talk with Jack Maxwell's youngest boy. Took me by surprise. It's about Sandy's killing; you know that different folks around saw a couple of tramps that weekend on the tracks and on the back road by the tracks and I'm trying to get a fix on those guys. But this, now, is entirely different." He told Cy what he'd learned from Billy.

Cy thought about Billy's story

"Frank, I hope you don't expect me to go up there with you. I get so damn mad at Hank I'm afraid of what I do or say up there. Try to not bring Mabel into it if you can help it. She's so flighty this summer sometimes I think she'll just lift up and fly."

Frank looked at Cy. "If she had any brains she would, and not come back."

Shortly before supper, Frank was back at Kennedy's. Cy was sitting on the porch steps, waiting to be called to the kitchen table, cooled by the soft wind carried in from the night pasture, over the lawn.

"Well, I guess I'm still hunting for the tramps. Hank claims he was home early afternoon that day and never left. Mabel swears the same, that they were working together."

Cy laughed. "Right away, that's pretty suspicious in my book. That devil ain't worked a half day straight in the last ten years."

He invited Frank to stay for supper, but the sheriff gave Cy a speculative, enigmatic smile and climbed back in his Buick. He waved as he turned to go back to the road that would carry him to Emmis.

When the graveside service for Sandy was finished, Cy walked across the cemetery to where Ayma, Tom and his parents were buried. A few days before Decoration Day, Thea and Bert had hand trimmed the grass that grew near the monuments and enlisted the help of Shorty to scythe the tall grass beneath the nearby trees.

Cy knew he could count on the twins, in a day or two to carry away the vases filled with lilac blooms, already fading, the slight perfume detected by a few fat bees hovering in the warm air.

Cy didn't visit the grave sites often and when he did he no longer left the cemetery filled with agony and that early sense of loss he'd always known had bordered closely to pity for himself.

And he never lingered near the stone on which "Thomas Timothy Kennedy 1885-1909" was sculpted; bits of moss now outlining those common symbols that offered a brief review of his brother's life.

The anger Cy felt toward Tom, dead now for close to thirty years, had diminished little. He was sure his feelings for Tom were well concealed but he recalled when, on the first anniversary of his brother's death, he had sat in the machine shop, smoking a cigarette, angrily throwing it to the floor as Shorty walked by, wrenches in his hand.

Shorty halted close to the bench where Cy looked up. "Buck up, Cy. He's gone. You couldn't change nothin' when he was here and you sure as hell can't now that he's gone."

When Cy was ten, he became aware of the favoritism Bridget showed her younger son. Tom, a month after he was enrolled in the frame school house near St. Mark's, had established himself as the least favorite student of the three women who taught there.

Lydia Meyer, in charge of the school, approached Timothy after Bridget had stormed into the schoolhouse and demanded that Tom be shown more patience and that he not be disciplined in front of his classmates.

"We can't run the school that way, Mr. Kennedy. We can't abide disorder, we're teaching more than one hundred children. Maybe you should keep Thomas at home another year. Seven would not be too late to begin school."

Timothy was adamant. He knew that another year of being cosseted by Bridget would not make Tom a less difficult child.

"Miss Meyer, when Thomas gives you trouble you can't handle, come to me, not to his mother."

Lydia smiled, but shook her head. "That would be quite difficult; Mrs. Kennedy demanded that I report to her."

Timothy stared for a moment at the papers on his desk, then, clearing his throat, said, "As I say, you come to me. I sit at the head of my family."

The request was made with unexpected dignity and as Lydia made her way from Timothy's office back to the school, she wished suddenly that Ben Larson, at the dry goods store, would ask her once again to marry him. This time she might say yes, having faced Bridget Kennedy three times in the last two weeks.

Liz and Stella, who taught with Lydia, laughed when she told them her thoughts.

The night after Tom's teacher visited with Timothy, Cy was asked by Timothy to walk over to the mill with him, after supper

"So, all right, Cy. What's going on with your brother over there at the school? How's Tom fitting in?"

"He fights with everyone, sometimes right in the school. He mocks the boys, sometimes the girls who don't talk English as good as we do. He doesn't do his work. He hit Miss Palmer. One day he locked Mayme Butler in the toilet and she cried."

Timothy stopped on the boardwalk and told Cy, "I'm going to straighten this out. You keep in mind that what he does never makes you look different to me or to the school."

Timothy closed his hand over Cy's, the first and only time the two of them walked together holding hands. When they got to the mill and entered the office, Timothy lit the lamp on his desk and sat down..

He reached behind himself to a shelf filled with pencils and pads of paper and steel measuring tapes. From behind it all, he pulled a bottle and set it on his desk, then took a tin cup from his desk. He looked at Cy and smiled, "Want some?"

Cy smiled, too, and shook his head.

"Good, you might have to lead me home."

Halfway through the night, Cy heard the loud voices of his parents, downstairs in the living room. The next morning Bridget told Cy that doing well in school was not an important achievement.

All day, Cy thought he'd ask his father, tonight, what she meant, but he never did.

His childhood behind him, Tom became one of the boys who ran around Emmis, not occupied in serious employment and Bridget's attempt to protect Tom from the town's censure became her life.

She had seen herself, since the Kennedys arrived in Emmis, as the wife of the wealthiest, most successful man in Sutton County, a man known throughout the Midwest and North America's lumber industry as a wise investor, a builder of new life in the wilderness.

Her increasingly frantic behavior was apparent to her friends in Emmis and secretly enjoyed by those who regarded her a smug and modish woman whose chief accomplishment was a fortunate marriage.

Bridget's refusal to recognize the growing insolence and irresponsibility of young Tom was a matter of bitter disappointment to Timothy. And he rejected full tilt his wife's attempt to blame him for Tom's behavior. He reminded her that Cy had come into the mill when he was twelve, when he was still in school.

"Cy knew I wanted my men treated well and he knew I expected a day's work from everyone, especially him. The men like him. I don't think he likes lumber, but by God, he does the job."

Bridget was suffused with rage when Cy told his parents he was giving up his position at the mill; his father knew he'd been saving his wages and he was aware that Cy was spending time at the Emmis Land Office, that he was more interested in land than lumber.

Fearfully, she imagined that the Kennedy empire, which made her a pivotal force in Emmis, might falter, even disappear. When Cy was gone from the mill, the lumberyard, the woodenware factory, would the town's eyes light on Thomas, handsome and charming when he wanted to be? Or would there be dark, darting glances from which she had to look quickly away?

Two of the three saloons in Emmis refused to allow Tom past their doors. At Martha Osalsky's hotel, he was allowed in the dining room, not in the bar. Martha warned the half dozen girls there, "Don't you girls be fooled by his name, thinkin' la de da and all that."

Most of the girls rented rooms upstairs or at the rear of the shops and stores in Emmis; not all of them listened to Martha. Cy knew that Thomas seldom came home at night.

In 1903, when Cy decided that the six hundred and forty acres he owned near Emmis would be his farmstead, the house and buildings were built in a few months. Timothy often showed up to watch the progress of the dozen men hired by Cy, most of them Timothy's employees who would return to the mill before winter. Bridget refused to come to the farm; Cy asked her just once.

Tom, eighteen, arrived there with two friends on the day Mike Garrity and his sons finished painting the house. Tom told his brother that a house this size, in St. Paul. could house thirty women and make the owner a rich man.

His friends laughed loudly and, looking up, Tom saw Timothy in the doorway of the porch, his hands in his pockets, his eyes squarely on his younger son.

"Pa! Carl and Paul and me are on our way to Emmis, to see you!"

"You've seen me, and I won't be in Emmis today."

Tom turned away uncertainly and climbed back in the buggy he'd rented at the livery barn in Emmis.

Timothy told Cy, "He's mostly in South St. Paul now. A lot of poker playing in the hotels and bars near the stockyards. Your mother has hardly seen you boys this summer."

"I know, Pa. I tried."

"Try harder."

Before Timothy lest the farmyard that day he shook hands with Cy. "You made a good place here, now make some money." Cy grinned. He felt sure he would.

When Cy and Ayma were married two summers later on the last day of September, Tom was not part of the wedding party but he was invited to the wedding at St. Mark's and to the party at the farm, a gathering that would last until dawn.

He didn't come.

Bridget, regal in her satin dress, attended the wedding and then asked Timothy to take her home. Anticipating her request, Timothy had asked Myra Scott, their hired girl, to stay the weekend.

Later, Ayma said, "Your father seemed so happy today, I think he had the best time of anyone."

"I know. He was afraid I'd marry some ugly old woman. Instead I got you; I'm pretty sure Pa's relieved."

Ayma looked at him. "You are such a charming man."

Bridget's silence evoked in Cy a sense of shame, a feeling of regret that something missing in himself caused her to look at him as she might judge a random, unwelcome stranger.

He wondered how much she knew about Tom, who often boarded the afternoon train headed for St. Paul and rarely spoke to anyone in Emmis.

Neither Cy nor Ayma were blind to Timothy's distress and it was obvious that he gained at least small comfort in the hours he spent at the farm. He came alone and no one asked the reason.

Since their marriage they were surprised when Timothy transferred money to them, stocks and cash, funds about which Bridget knew nothing, they were sure. When he asked, his father said, "It's the way I do business; it's for the best."

In their bedroom, in a ledger kept in a bottom drawer, the sums received from the old man were labeled in Cy's careful hand, "from Pa".

In 1907, Cy stopped at his parents' house to tell them Ayma was expecting a baby. Timothy hurried to the pantry and brought to the table a jug of Irish whiskey, motioning for Cy to sit. Smiling broadly, Timothy moved quickly to the cupboard and filled two glasses.

Bridget sat in a small rocking chair, her fingers hovering above the lace she was attaching to a square of linen.

She smiled. "A baby! Maybe Kennedys will still have someone for the church! Your father, here, he never listens when I tell him your brother could have been a wonderful priest, God willing. I told Father Cavanaugh so long ago that someday Thomas would be saying Mass, maybe right here in Emmis."

She shook her head when Timothy offered her a drop of whiskey in the glass he carried to her chair. Dreamily, she said, "You can't do more than give a child to God."

Alarmed, Cy looked at his father, who smiled thinly and shrugged, his smile gone completely in a second.

Just this morning, Cy had gone to the bank in answer to a terse note from Lou Pattock, Timothy's attorney and the vice president of First National. Making no apology for the sudden summons, Lou sat behind his desk and asked Cy to take a chair, motioning for him to first close the office door.

"Cy you need to know some things and I need to say some things.

"Your father...well, he set up this account that I'm in charge of, and I don't like it. It doesn't make any sense, none of it does. I told that to Timothy and it sounds like he's trying to please some whim your mother entertains.

"Your brother writes bad checks and I write checks to make them good; it's like a Goddamn giggy-turner, and some of the checks just plain go against me."

Lou looked at Cy. *"He's your brother and I know you don't see him very often, but the way this thing is set up, I'm in the middle. Tuesday, I got a notice Tom wrote a check to some quack in Minneapolis and he's written a couple before, to the same man. I asked Doc Dennison to check out this doctor named Jeffers. Goddamn butcher, one of those let's-go-in-the-backroom-missy-it-won't-hurt- a-bit-guys. I don't want to tell Timothy."*

Cy stared at the floor. He pictured Tom's enigmatic smile, the slim wrists, the delicate fingers on hands not much larger than a girl's. The auburn hair, fine as silk, his grace and confidence on the dance floor.

It was the smile ...a margin of deceit, of sly beckoning, of the need to be first in all things shared that always invaded Cy's thoughts of Tom.

Lou said, *"I got a letter yesterday, he's coming up here next week. I know damn well he's going to your father, asking for more money. I've been with Timothy since your folks stepped off the train from Ontario but I may have to cut the ties."*

Cy thought for a moment. *"Find out when he's coming to Emmis and I'll pick him up as soon as he gets off the train."*

Lou looked at him. The ticking of the wall clock...the rhythm of the sound made Cy feel that part of him was drifting away from this office, from the town.

"I was wishing, Cy, that you could go down there to talk to Tom where he loses his shirt at a poker table at least once a week."

He shuffled the papers on his desk. *"I've got the address somewhere, I'm damn sure."*

Cy made no response and Lou continued, *"It'll be a lot easier on Timothy. Things can't go on as they've been headed; Tom's been taking a few girls from Emmis down to St. Paul; you know what that means."* Cy never told Lou or Ayma or anyone else what happened in St. Paul. He wondered if Tom contacted Timothy.

When Cy stepped into First National one morning to deposit the money he'd been paid by his renters, Lou Pattock signaled him from the door of his office. Shaking hands with his father's oldest friend, Cy was surprised to see how tired Lou looked today.

As was his custom, the banker came straight to the point.

"This goes beyond what I know about the law and against my friendship with Timothy, but I need to talk to you about the new will your father had me draw up yesterday. Some awfully big changes, I'd say, and I can't make him listen to reason."

Cy stared through the window to the sidewalk outside.

"How bad will I be hurt?"

"I'm not sure what you expect, Cy, but for sure somebody's going to be hurt. I told Timothy to think it over a week or two but he wouldn't agree. If you think you could influence him, I'm willing, God help me for saying this, to tell you the details. A will to replace it might save a lot of grief down the road."

Cy felt neither shock nor dread and little curiosity about his father's will; he stood and reached across Lou's desk to shake his hand.

"I appreciate your telling me this, Lou, but see no cause to stand in my Dad's way."

He saw the wariness in Lou's eyes and said, "I'm not going to bring our talk up with anyone. You did right and I will, too."

Leaving Emmis, Cy stopped at the sawmill office, wondering if he might detect something different in his father's bearing, wondering why there was some sense of new urgency moving around the perimeter of his parents' lives.

Timothy was sitting in the big chair back of his desk but turned toward the window from which he could see the south edge of Emmis, much of it his property. A freight train was stopped near the water tank, it would be heading east in half an hour.

When Timothy heard Cy at the door, he smiled. Cy thought his father looked younger, somehow, than he had for years. He smiled broadly at Cy and said, "I'm glad you stopped. I walked here this morning and I promised your mother I'd be home at noon. I could ask one of the boys to take me but they're busy."

He came around the desk and took his hat from the rack near the door.

"You know, I had a chore to finish, a job I knew I should do, but I kept putting it off. I took care of it a few days ago. It's the first time I did business not just for money. I'm not telling you what I did, just that I did something I should."

Cy turned in the doorway so Timothy would walk down the steps first.

Seated in the buggy, Cy said, "I understand. Yesterday I had a stone in my boot and I could feel it poking and pinching from morning 'til suppertime. I finally pulled my boot off and shook it and the stone fell out. I understand exactly what you're saying."

Timothy looked at him, then looked again.

"Close, Cyrus, but not exactly."

When the buggy stopped in front of his house Timothy climbed out and asked after Ayma's health.

They saw Bridget sitting on the front porch, a shawl pulled about her shoulders. Cy raised his hand to wave and she looked away. Timothy said, "I'll be out there this afternoon to see if Shorty can tighten the spokes in a wheel of my buggy."

· · · · · · · · · ·

97

On an improbably warm day in late autumn, Cy and Ayma were down near the long machine shed where Shorty was painting the trim on a buckboard Cy had bought at an auction sale. Ayma scolded Shorty for working on Sunday and he grinned bashfully. He had painted the buckboard yesterday and today he was painting with great care the trim. "This time of the year, ya gotta paint when there's good sun for dryin'".

Suddenly, on the gravel road beyond the shed there was the sound of horse hooves and, turning to stare, Cy saw Timothy's chestnut saddle horse turn into the driveway. Tom was astride, his white shirt billowing in the wind.

"Brother Cyrus! How the hell are you folks doing? Ma and Pa are in church this morning, so I stopped over at the barn and got old Murph!"

Ayma began walking toward the house and Shorty wiped the paint brush on a tuft of grass and laid the brush across the top of the open paint pail.

Cy stared as Tom slipped to the ground, the horse stepping backward in confusion, then Cy quickly grabbed the reins and tied Murph to the hitching post nearest the shed.

He looked at Tom. "Didn't know if you knew the way to Emmis anymore."

"Hell, yes. Who could forget Emmis? Never did see the town any deader than it is today, though." He looked at Ayma, who had reached the sidewalk leading to the house and said to Cy, "Think I could get a cup of coffee around here?"

He looked at Shorty. "C'mon, Shorty. You could use some coffee, too, workin' out here in the sun."

Shorty said, "I have my coffee at a decent hour and I don't expect anyone else to cook it."

Tom laughed. He stooped to pick up a piece of straw near his feet. He stuck the straw in the corner of his mouth and looked sideway at Cy, his eyes artful, cunning.

"Ma, she wrote you brought them a piece of news a while back. I always wondered, Cy, if you knew what a woman was for. It's a good thing you do, a good looker like Ayma might not hang around waitin'."

They were on the ground beside the path that ran from the shed to the barn. Cy ripped Tom's thin shirt nearly in two, and straddling the smaller man, held his shoulders tightly, pressing his torso against the smooth grass.

Cy felt his own anger thundering as Tom bucked and kicked and then his hands were fastened on Tom's throat, his fingers digging into the soft flesh.

Suddenly Shorty was bending over the struggling men and then Ayma's voice carried above the ringing in Cy's ears.

"Dear God! Get off him! Let him up, let him go!"

Breathing harshly, Cy knelt for a few seconds on one knee and eased slowly to his feet.

His face red and twisted in anger, Shorty fitted his hands beneath Tom's arms and dragged him near the buckboard, and the frightened horse, now nickering and tossing his head, held fast where he was tied.

The smell of blood rose from Tom's limp body and Cy and Shorty pulled him to the shade at the side of the shed and laid him there.

Shorty disappeared to the rooms at the rear of the shop, the snug space which was his home on the Kennedy farm, and Ayma, now, was out of sight.

Cy stared at Tom, not moving, one leg drawn up beneath his body, and smelling the sweat on his own body, seeing the blood on his hands, the sleeve of his shirt pulled loose, he walked to the house.

Inside the screened porch, Ayma watched and then hurried to the kitchen. As Cy washed at the sink he heard her in the pantry, the clink of china, her movements near the stove. Then, wiping the soap and water from his face, he listened to her footsteps going upstairs, the soft creak of bedsprings in their room above the kitchen.

It was the next day before Ayma spoke of the fight between the Kennedy brothers. Cy hoped this would not be one of the quite ordinary Sundays when Timothy drove to the farm, a near-ritual that he and Ayma enjoyed and which left no one wondering about the absence of Bridget on this or any other visit to the farm.

Late in the afternoon, Cy helped Tom button a clean shirt over his bruised body after his head had been doused in the water trough beside the barn.

Tom climbed carefully into the buggy, dragging his body as far from his brother as the seat allowed. No words were exchanged until they reached the depot in Emmis where the southbound train would stop Monday morning. Tom followed Cy inside and heard his brother ask Paul Moore, the station agent, to see that Tom boarded the train that would carry him back to St. Paul. He handed Paul money for the ticket and two dollars for playing watchdog, then turned to Tom, offering him a paper bag containing something from Ayma's pantry. Tom pushed the sack away angrily but took the five dollars Cy thrust at him.

Looking back when he got to the door of the depot, Cy saw Tom lying on his back on the narrow bench, staring at the smoke stained ceiling above him.

Out on the platform, Cy hesitated. Should he remind Paul again that he expected Tom to be on that southbound train?

Instead, he allowed the horse hitched to the buggy to travel so slowly that the trip home could have been not two miles, but a dozen. Ayma was on the step when he reached home, she told him supper was ready and that Shorty would join them.

Cy had noticed as he drove past the shed that the trim on the buckboard was finished.

Cy never knew if Tom came back to Emmis to visit Timothy and Bridget that fall or during the winter. But, a week after his encounter with his brother he received an envelope from Tom which included a letter which Bridget had mailed her younger son, a carping diatribe describing her contempt for Cy and Ayma. Cy dropped the letter in the wood stove and watched it, thoughtfully, as it turned to ash. He burned also the boast *written by his brother, that Timothy and Bridget would be grandparents soon of his own child who would be born perhaps earlier than Cy's, and whose mother was not such a bitch as Ayma. He read Tom's description of the girl who carried his child and, glad that Ayma was upstairs, sleeping, Cy went to the shop in search of Shorty.*

"I don't suppose there's any of that whiskey I left out here last week?"

Shorty grinned. "Ain't taken the cork out yet. Had no call for it."

Cy leaned against the bench where Shorty's tools were laid. "I think the call's coming through, right now."

In March, when their parents died, Tom was not among the several hundred people who witnessed twelve longtime employees of Kennedy Sawmill and Lumber Works who carried the couple to the cemetery behind St. Mark's Church.

Timothy, who had spent decades minimizing his place in the world of finance, would have been paralyzed by the eulogies, the dozens of ostentatious funeral wreaths that were evidence of his influence among lumbermen, railroad men as far away as San Francisco and New York.

In the church, Cy whispered to Ayma, "He would have hated this!"

She nudged his arm. "Not so your mother."

An observer, sitting nearby, might have wondered why a man, at his parents' funeral, might suddenly smile.

Two days after the funeral, George Mayer, head cashier at First National, knocked on the farm house door as Cy was finishing his breakfast. George refused to sit and seemed to be searching for words.

"It's Lou, at the bank. This morning Tom came in on the train, went to Lou's house, wants to see your dad's papers. You know, the will. They're at the bank now, both of them, and Lou wants you to come."

Cy looked at Ayma and quickly back at George. "I'll be there in twenty minutes."

Tom looked even thinner than he had last fall, the red cast in his hair was more pronounced, his beard two or three days old, his clothing was wrinkled, his hands so fragile looking Cy was suddenly moved.

Tom said nothing to Cy, who pulled a chair next to the one where his brother was seated. They both watched Lou, who stood behind his desk, a folder of papers in one hand. He reached forward, extending his free hand to each brother and said he was shocked and grieved to lose his best friend and that his sisters would miss their friend, Bridget. Cy held Lou's hand for a few seconds and Tom ignored Lou's gesture, crossing his legs and pointing to the folder.

"Let's get it done."

Lou stared at Cy, looking for direction, then lowered himself to the chair at his desk. He drew several papers from the folder and laid them carefully on the blotter.

"It's not a very complicated will; it's the joint will of your parents, each of whom signed the will and understood the terms. The provisions for your mother are nullified by her death, of course. The problem will be in selling the property and converting it to currency to fulfill the gifts designated by your parents."

Tom snorted and Cy asked, "Maybe, Lou, we'd better hear the exact terms of the will."

Lou cleared his throat. "You're both free to examine everything here", indicating the papers, "but, yes. I can explain to you everything that's written."

He looked at both men and, folding his hands, spoke slowly.

"Your parents' entire estate is divided four ways, with varying amounts designated for each. Your mother had no immediate living family but her sons. Timothy's three sisters and their offspring, all of them believed to live in Ireland, shall share twenty percent of the estate. Anyone who worked for your father at the time of your father's death and has been so employed at least five years will share an amount equal to twenty percent of the value of the Kennedy estate. Timothy and Bridget's son, Cyrus, will inherit with his wife, Ayma, half the value of his parents' bounty. Their younger son, Thomas, will receive ten percent of the amount of his parents' estate.

"A further stipulation is that neither son shall have any access to the funds of this estate until two years after both parents are dead."

Later, everyone who was in the First National Bank agreed that the man who ran blindly through the bank lobby and headed down the early morning street that led to the railroad tracks that ran through Emmis looked like someone they'd known in the past.

Three weeks later, Cy and Shorty sat at the kitchen table, deciding if it would be wise to plant more oats and cut back on the acres given to barley. Lou Pattock drove near the house and Cy, looking out the window, said, "For God's sake, what now?"

He found out; Lou wasted no time.

"Cy, I'm on my way into Emmis and I'd like you to stop in my office this morning. A few more letters to sign and yesterday I got a letter from an attorney in St. Paul. You'd better get some of this business behind you."

Cy was certain the letter from St. Paul would have a connection to Tom and he listened carefully as Lou read the request by his brother that part of his inheritance might be advanced immediately, allowing him to invest in a business recently offered for sale.

Lou was adamant. "I warned Timothy that it could come to this but he wanted the will written in such a way that Thomas would have to wait. I'm not sure it would hold up in court, but anyhow, we have no figures yet to work with. I've had some offers for most of the property but this estate is a long way from being settled. You and I agree that the last *offer for your folks' house is fair, but that's just a small start. I say this letter is irregular and to hell with it."*

He passed the letter to Cy who didn't bother to look at it. He was thinking, *"Why can't Tom just ask about this himself? Hire a lawyer to talk to his brother?"*

Since he'd known about his father's plan to delay the settling of his sons' inheritance, Cy had understood the gifts of money given him before his parents' death, and he wondered if Timothy's obvious denouncement of Tom was fair.

Lou sat back in his chair, his eyes on Cy. They sat in silence, then Cy laid the letter back on the desk. *"Write back, ask how much money Tom's asking for. And tell him I want a letter from Tom, direct. He knows my address."*

Ten days later, Ayma found an envelope in the mailbox, postmarked South St. Paul. She felt uneasy, knowing nothing about the letter that had come to Lou and wondered what kind of turmoil was bringing this letter to the farm. When Cy saw it, close to his place at the table, he stuck it in his shirt pocket, unopened.

Later that day, Lou tried to talk Cy out of his decision to loan his brother fifty thousand dollars, charging one percent interest.

"A saloon almost at the gate of the damn stockyards! Tom doesn't know anything about running a business! If you're willing to lose fifty thousand dollars, at least get someone to appraise the damn thing! I'm telling you, Cy, this is no good for you and no better for Tom."

Cy folded Tom's letter and put it back in the pocket of his bib overalls. *"Draw up the papers, Lou, and I'll be here in the morning. And don't say anything to Ayma."*

CHAPTER II

On the first day of June, Ayma gave birth to twin girls. The only address Cy had for Tom was the street on which the Golden Star Saloon was located, and he wrote once to tell Tom the news and promised that he'd write again when he knew when the girls would be baptized.

Cy would rather have called Tom; Emmis was now connected to the world by the Maple Leaf Telephone Company; its office above the feed store. He wanted to hear Tom's voice, to be assured that his brother would have something to say to him, too.

Payments on the loan were seldom on time and were always mailed in envelopes addressed in Tom's almost illegible scrawl. But on the envelopes Tom had written both their names, the names of the Kennedy brothers, and Cy kept them all. He didn't know why.

Lacking the courage to call Tom, Cy mailed the letter announcing the birth of Alberta Rose and Althea Summer, knowing there would be no response.

On the 4th of July, when the twins were five years old, they stood with Cy and Shorty on the corner near the Emmis village hall, watching the parade in which three hired hands who worked on the Kennedy farm were driving Cy's finest teams.

Cy saw Paul Moore cut across the parade route, heading his way.

The telegram was brief, a few words and a telephone number.

The crackling line, the sound of the parade passing slowly on the dirt road that ran through Emmis were less audible to Cy than the waves of anger and regret that coursed through his head as he listened to the voice of a stranger.

A rancher from Montana who delivered a carload of steers to the yards and a buyer for a commission house had sparred back and forth for hours, ending in a fight that sent glassware and furniture through the Golden Star Saloon. Tom Kennedy, proprietor, had suffered a smashed skull when he tried to end the battle.

Ayma stood next to Cy as Tom's casket was lowered into a grave next to Timothy and Bridget. His hand, just above her elbow, was steady, but she felt a tremor pass through his fingers as the priest began his last prayer.

Looking up at Cy's profile, she saw his steady gaze as he listened to the words floating past Tom's casket.

Today, in the church and in the cemetery, Cy had only half listened to the words spoken above the woefully breached body of a decent old man whom he'd barely known.

He studied the inscription on Tom's tombstone and, with his penknife, scraped away the moss from his brother's name.

The next morning Cy drove into the Kootseema farmyard; he'd noticed Hank's old Chevrolet sputtering past on the way to Emmis and he wanted to talk to Mabel, alone. Glory came to the screen door and Mabel was just a few steps behind her. Cy asked if he could come inside and Glory blurted, "Hank, he's gone. He's got things to do, he said. And we don't let nobody in, 'count of different stuff."

Mabel pushed her aside. Raking her fingers through her hair, she tried to smile at Cy. "You come on in the house, here, such as it is. I was just settin' to put some wash on the line but it can wait."

Glory moved across the kitchen, staring at Cy and Mabel; the defiance in her eyes bright and filled with spite, the malicious scorn directed toward her mother.

It was plain to see that in this house, Mabel stood alone.

"Mabel, I was checking yesterday at the produce plant in Emmis on the price of old hens; Gladdie's getting rid of hers in a couple of weeks. Good birds, but you know Gladdie, she wants to start every fall with pullets. I can let you have the hens, about thirty or so I guess, should be pretty fair layers through next winter."

Mabel looked at the floor. "I never started chicks this summer, my hens is gettin' past their time. That would be some nice birds Gladdie has. I don't have a lot of feed, nothin'..."

Glory, in a voice suddenly coarsened, spat, "You don't be doin' no business less Hank says okay. Loretta, she gives us chickens two or three at a time, don't forget!"

Mabel, her shoulders slumped, said to Cy, "Here, you set down, I never thought to tell you when you come through the door."

She swung toward Glory, "I don't need you telling me my business. You get up there and pull those sheets off the bed for the wash, and pump water for them cows."

Glory didn't move and Mabel looked at her. "I don't mean some other time, I mean now."

Glory walked slowly to the door leading to the rooms above the kitchen and Cy realized he'd been holding his breath.

Mabel sat across from Cy, looking at the stained oilcloth covering the table. "Now that she ain't in school no more, I don't know what I'm sposed to do with her. It's all sass and mean, everything she does. Sides with Hank, like he's so much." She suddenly looked up.

"I don't mean there's nothin wrong with Hank, but some times we see things diffrunt. Little things, mostly".

Apologetically, she pulled at the handle of an empty cup on the table. Cy watched her.

"Mabel, Hank's around Emmis a lot; you don't suppose he knows who killed Sandy McDonald, do you? Just maybe too stubborn to tell the sheriff what he maybe overheard or saw?"

"Oh, Hank, he'd never hold back on something like that! We got our share of bad luck but we ain't the kind, specially Hank, we wouldn't want old Sandy hurt!"

Glory came down the steps into the kitchen, a trail of bed sheets and clothing behind her. She slammed out the back door where a wash tub stood on a block of wood.

She disappeared, then Cy heard the rhythmic sound of the pump handle lifting and falling, the soft cry of an old cat pressed against the screen door, waiting for a handout.

He stood, and Mabel moved toward the door.

"About those hens, Mabel, I'd rather you than the produce plant made use of them. I'll have the boys crate them up and you can look them over; if there's some reason you don't want them, I'll send them to Emmis."

He'd never shaken Mabel's hand, but he reached for it today. Surprised, she thrust her rough, gnarled hand into his, and Cy, hurrying from the porch, stumbled as his boots hit the ground. On the way to his car he took his glasses off and ran his shirtsleeve across his eyes.

God, but it seemed hot out here today! He hoped Gladdie'd be a good sport about sending her hens to Kootseema's.

Cy drove to Frank's office and told him it would be hard to find anyone on the Kootseema farm that didn't back up Hank's claim that he was home when Sandy died..

Frank said, "I wish I knew what somebody took from Sandy's house, what I could maybe look for. The talk about a couple of tramps didn't pan out; Alfred Hehn brought his boys in that afternoon to catch the freight to the harvest fields in Dakota. I talked to Alfred, myself. I'd never bet Hank did the killing, though. I never saw that side to him. He's sly and he's mean but he must know the price he'd pay for something like killing a person."

Shorty ate supper with the Kennedys that night, and Cy talked about his visit to Kootseemas. Bert said, "My Lord, there are certainly some complicated people up there!"

Gladdie, carrying a bowl to the table, stopped in mid-stride. "Complicated! Don't that mean hard to see through? That bunch is as complicated as a rat chewing the head off a dead chicken!"

Thea looked up and laughed. "Gladdie, I hope we're not having chicken for supper."

Shorty half turned in his chair, looking out the window as though he saw something there of uncommon interest.

Cy said, "Gladys Olson, is that what you Lutherans call loving your neighbors?"

Flustered, Gladdie took her place at the table.

"There's neighbors, then there's neighbors."

Cy continued, "I'm going to tell you something, Gladdie, while we have witnesses. I don't want to be found like old Sandy, killed in my own house."

He paused, everyone's eyes on him. "I told Mabel she can have your year-old hens."

Now everyone looked at Gladdie. "It's not the dumbest thing you ever done, Cy. Not by a long shot. And, anyhow, why should I care what happens to a few dozen wore out chickens?"

Beneath the table, Cy felt movement as Thea gently kicked Bert's foot and was astounded that Shorty, looking down at his plate, nudged Cy's.

Seemingly unaware of everyone's reaction to her loss of thirty nice Leghorn hens, Gladdie smiled as she sliced the chocolate layer cake, Shorty's favorite.

When Gladdie Olson walked in and sat near Thea's desk, one of the first things she spotted was a picture of herself taken with the twins when they were small.

"So, why is that stupid thing sitting here in plain sight?"

Thea looked at her. "Gladdie, I've asked you a thousand times to come in here and see where I work and the first time you do you pick on me. Why?"

"I wouldn't call it pickin' on you, just maybe settin' you straight."

About what?"

"About havin' dumb pictures where anybody can see them. Things like that."

Thea laughed. "Okay, Gladdie. I'm set straight. What are you doing in Emmis, anyhow?"

"No need to get mean. It ain't like I go to town every day. I come in with your dad. He's gettin' a haircut. I came to see you about Bert."

Suddenly, they were serious. "I know, Gladdie. I wish she'd gone ahead and taken those classes over at the college. I've asked her to come here a couple days a week, I could really use her; if she'd go with me, I'd take a few days off and we could do a little traveling."

Gladdie broke in; "Her and Shorty was talkin' the other day, her car needs fixin' they said. Well, Shorty, he said she needs a new car, better in the snow, one where the motor starts up better..."

She looked so earnest that Thea had a hard time to not laugh.

"Gladdie, I have to see Shorty about putting an awning over this sidewalk, anyhow. I'll see what he says about Bert's car. Right now, I'm thinking about walking down to Pavlik's saloon. How about you? We could stop at the barbershop and tell Dad."

"Althea Summer, how old you gotta get before you act like a lady?"

When Cy Kennedy told Shorty Brill, in 1922, that he was sending him to Sweeney Automobile and tractor School in Kansas City, Missouri, Shorty told him to go to hell.

Cy didn't go to hell, but Shorty did go to Missouri.

Cy frequently said that the education of Shorty had been his best investment in farming. The Kennedy farm was the first in Emmis County to rely on tractor power although, in deference to some of the farm's hired help, there were always at least two teams of work horses for certain jobs.

By 1930, it was Shorty's opinion that horses were for ridin' and tractors were for workin', but Cy, a man who respected good horseflesh, sided with the men who preferred to work with horses.

"It don't make sense, Cy, keepin' that old horse machinery around."

"Hide it behind the shed if you want, Shorty, but it stays."

When Thea stopped at the shop to see Shorty, he was welding something in the far end of the building. He noticed her and waved her back. "Ruin your eyesight, you dummy!"

Thea laughed. "First Gladdie gives me hell, now you! Why am I suddenly the bad kid?"

Shorty took his gloves and helmet off and walked with her to the open door. They stood in the shade of the shed.

"You were never a bad kid, Thea. Reckless, but not bad."

His seriousness touched her. "Shorty, you must see how Bert's hunkered down here this summer, feeling bad. You've been talking to her about her car...what do you really think?"

"Well, I think she's drivin' a piece of tin and loose bolts, for sure. Shakes. Too cold in the winter. Don't start easy. If it's a new car she wants, in Emmis it'll be a Ford or a Chevy. Wants to do better, she's gotta go somewhere else."

"How, better? Like what?"

"Well, you sure did better with that Chrysler you got, although why you got stuck with one that's got that yellow color I don't figure out."

"I didn't get stuck, Shorty! The next car I buy could be even more yellow, or brighter, or something."

Shorty laughed. "I guess its okay for women to drive, but they ain't much, pickin' out their cars."

Thea grinned. "What do you think, really, for Bert?"

"Leonard Sensa, man I met in Kansas City, he sells Packards, just north of Minneapolis. I see him once or twice a year, stops here when he's going up to the lake."

"Talk to Bert, Shorty. She'll listen. Mostly, she needs something to think about right now."

Shorty's eyes clouded over. "She'd have something to think about if that damn fool didn't take off like he did." He thought for moment. "And that damn Amelia, she was as guilty dyin' as livin'".

Two days later, Cy was leaving Pavlik's when Thea walked in the door. He asked, "Got your work done for today?"

"Yep. But come on, sit a minute."

Cy waited.

"Shorty and Bert and I are going down toward the Cities tomorrow. Shorty's going to help her pick out a new car...I'll drive down and drive Bert home and he'll bring the new car."

She waited.

"Yeah, Shorty told me this morning. But thanks for the tip."

Thea hit his arm and they left Pavlik's together, both smiling.

When Gladdie saw Bert's new car, she told her, "Now you gotta take me to St. Cloud sometimes, shoppin'."

Thea asked,"Why don't you ask *me* to take you shopping?"

Gladdie didn't answer and Cy looked up from the newspaper. He thought, "Well, the year was off to a hell of a start, but it'll be all right now."

CHAPTER 12

Glory hated the way Mabel watched her all the time. Almost as tall as Mabel, she didn't know why she couldn't do anything she wanted; the truth was, there wasn't that much work needed doing and her mother didn't want her helping in the garden, anyhow.

That's one thing that wasn't her fault, keeping weeds sorted out from the stuff Mama planted, well, nobody told her the difference. Mama said she did, but that was last year. That's the kind of stuff that's easy to forget.

She hated how, when lying on her bed, she'd look up and there Mama was in the doorway, not talking, just looking. Same way she did in the sheds, just looking like there was anything to see on this old farm. Today, Hank had asked, his voice good as gold, if she'd sort out the gunny sacks that didn't have holes, the feed mill would pay him a dime for every one. The two of them were in the back bin, looking, when Mama came in, mad.

Hank and Mama, they yelled and Mama's arm got cut on the hook beside the door when she got pushed. And then the same as always, she run off.

And Hank, he grabbed the four sacks sorted out and here she was, alone. There were more fights this summer than before, it seemed the older she gets, the more mad everybody was at each other.

It was better when she was a little kid.

Glory stayed outside.

She'd felt lately like she was floating through an unknown country where even these shabby buildings, the ancient elms in the meadow, the manure piles beside the barn, never more than half hauled to the fields, were almost invisible.

She wished her mother would let her take the chair with a broken back to the space beneath the plum trees back of the house. The trees were not very tall and many of the branches devoid of leaves. In the shade beneath them, bees worked at the rotted plums that fell in late July, wrens scolded the sparrows, Monarch butterflies were spied at the edge of the high grass beyond the trees.

She'd heard it on the radio; something about drifting and dreaming. Glory wondered how old you'd have to be to drift and dream.

Wanda, her cousin and Loretta's youngest girl, had a little building at the edge of Loretta's garden. A door she could hook from the inside, two windows, a table, a couple of chairs and an old humpback trunk. Cast off dishes, a few books with pictures, not like school books.

It was difficult for Glory to be envious of anyone else, that their lives were better, because she really had no life at all. But she noticed sometimes little things and she wished she had some place like Wanda's hideaway.

Back of the barn, where the ground slanted toward the old hog pen, was a small shed built above the well that used to supply water for the livestock. It was the least interesting to Glory of all the buildings on the farm.

The barn well went dry and Cy Kennedy, he had a pipe run from the well up by the house to the cow tank. Nobody went in the pump house now, Mabel said it was a junk shop.

Glory stood at the corner of the barn. Hank wouldn't be back very soon, Mabel had been working all week making a quilt out of some wool pieces Loretta brought over.

What would it hurt if she kind of pushed all those old cans and leaky buckets and jug things to one end of the pump house, quiet like, just for some place to be sometimes, not on purpose hiding, just being away?

She circled the building and stood before the closed door.

Nah, what's the use. It would never be anything like Wanda's, not nearly.

She wondered, suddenly, if the yellow cat whose kittens had disappeared from the porch, up at the house, had hauled her babies down here. That wide crack beside the door, an old cat could squeeze in there easy.

Grunting as she shoved, Glory doubted she could push the door wide enough to enter. "Something's busted", she thought.

But suddenly the bottom corner of the door was scraping and scratching on the broken floor and it opened wide enough to accommodate Glory's entrance to the rank air, the murky floor, the rusted tools and tall bolts and broken files protruding from the open tops of dented cans, most of them missing half their paint. A few cans had lids intact.

Forgetting to search for the kittens, Glory began backing out the doorway. She'd better not be snooping around here, she'd better not be caught. One of her bare feet already on the ground outside the door, she noticed one can, cleaner than most of the others, pulled to the front of the shelf. Something or someone had wiped away some of the film of dirt and oil so evident on the others, wiped it enough that she could sound out the word "*Velvet*".

Velvet. That sounded kinda nice, like something maybe a real nice person would say. Reaching for it, she felt something shift inside the can as she lifted it in both hands; the lid was pried off easily. On the cracked concrete floor, Glory's breath caught in her throat as she tipped a man's watch from the can. A piece of chain, the tiny links slipping smoothly through Glory's hand, was attached to the watch. The hands of the watch stood still; Glory bet that someone could get them circling the numbers again, and then she saw the tiny pocket book with the worn catch, the leather soft but cracked in places. Her shoulders slumped as she twisted the catch and found the purse was empty.

Not as nice as that little beaded coin purse Bert Kennedy had given her last summer, but the mystery of its discovery in this old shed...well, she'd keep it out of sight, up in her room. To look at.

With unsteady hands, Glory carefully put the tobacco can back on the shelf and gave it a little push so it would sit even with the rest. It wouldn't slide and she reached behind it, her hand closing over a small dented box, black, with gold lines on the lid.

Now, here was a surprise, for sure! Inside, a piece of tin, thin almost as paper with letters and numbers punched out; buttons, some ivory colored, some metal, holes through some, some with a steel shank. They was sure cut off something neat like. And the short little ribbon, faded bad, but another mystery, G.A.R.

Glory divided everything between the two pockets of Mabel's old apron, her's now since Loretta sewed Mama new ones.

With the small black can tucked safe behind the tobacco tin, everything looked good as new.

The door was pulled shut and Glory couldn't stop smiling as she started across the yard. She hoped Mama wasn't in the kitchen, Glory had forgotten to bring in a pail of kindling wood this morning and she couldn't do it right now.

She passed through the kitchen unobserved and quietly opened the door that led upstairs. She pulled from her dresser a flat pasteboard box Bert had given her, it smelled like the Kennedy girls and Glory had read a hundred times what it said. Max Factor.

She carefully sorted her treasures and laid them in the box, then pushed it far beneath her dresser.

Flinging herself on her unmade cot, Glory still smiled, even more broadly than when she had sneaked across the yard.

Everything was safe, everything that was just hers. Some day she might show it all to Wanda.

· · · · · · · · · ·

"Glory? You up there? You get down here right now, Hank'll be home for supper pretty quick."

Glory sat for a minute, then half-slid down the steps, her bare feet quick and nimble. Standing near the stove, a spoon in one hand, Mabel stared as Glory grabbed the kindling pail near the door, and kicking the screen door wide, jumped from the porch to the hard-packed, bare path.

Midge, at school, had considered Glory a tuneless wonder and seldom allowed her to participate in the District 9 chorus, but today almost anyone could tell what song Glory hummed as she gathered up the kindling.

Drifting and Dreaming, that was what it was called.

The creamery board meeting had begun at nine this morning and dragged on until almost noon. Cy told Gladdie he would eat his noon meal in town and Thea asked Gladdie to not fix a meal for her, either. Bert and two other women who taught at Emmis High were in St. Cloud, shopping.

At a few minutes before twelve, Cy stopped at the news office and asked Thea to walk across the street to the Friends Cafe for lunch. He was in a good mood, there had been some talk that Emil Vondra, the Emmis buttermaker who had won several butter making prizes, would soon leave Emmis for a better paying position in Minneapolis.

Not one board member disagreed today when Cy proposed a pay increase for all the creamery employees and the man in charge of making butter and managing the creamery was the most handsomely rewarded. At the close of the meeting, Vondra shook hands with all the members and smiled at Cy.

Thea's morning had begun less well, the company from whom she ordered newsprint sent a representative to tell her that the cost of the paper would increase unless she ordered larger shipments. The only storage area in the Advocate building was located in the shallow basement area and she had no intention of storing paper there.

All morning she and her crew had shifted almost everything in the press room to make room for more storage. The air in the windowless area was filled with dust and now, three hours later, Thea, back at her desk, ignored the ringing of the phone as she clipped a thumbnail broken in the morning fracas.

The phone continued to ring and Thea laughed when she heard Ralph's voice. They'd not met since the end of june grass season a month ago but called each other often.

"Listen, Thea. A guy told me this morning that at the Iowa State Fair in late August there's going to be a hell of a deal…"

Thea broke in. "I don't do well at state fairs, Ralph. Ask Bert. Ask Gladdie. When Bert and I were in 4-H, I exhibited a jar of pickles with a dead bee floating in the brine and an apron with a pocket that opened from the bottom…"

"Thea, hold on, now. I'm in a hurry. This is something I want to see, and I know damn well you'll like it, too. On the racetrack there, they won't have any restriction on engine size and some of the drivers are putting airplane engines under the hood. Talk is, a hundred and twenty miles an hour."

Flipping the pages on the calendar that hung near her desk, Thea asked, "How about a deal? On August tenth I'm going to Brainerd for a Minnesota Editorial Association meeting and banquet. Bert decided to attend the second session of summer school over at the college, and I hate going to the meeting alone. Deal?"

"I'll call you Sunday night, Thea. And, hey,wait…did you ever win a prize?"

"You, Ralph. Just you."

In the back booth at the cafe, Cy and Thea talked about Bert.

"I think your sister's doing better now, at least she's trying like hell. In ordinary times I doubt she would have bought that car, and taking classes now, I'm a little surprised. Tougher than I thought she'd be."

Thea nodded. "It'll be hard to go back teaching and having someone there in place of Davis. But listen… I know you don't want to hear this, but what about Hank, up there? God, when he walks past my window and looks at me sitting at my desk, well, you know how I feel. Sometimes I wonder if he'd ever do something to hurt Bert. Have you ever thought about that?"

Cy looked at her. "Not really. He's gutless, underneath. If I thought he might, I'd nail the son of a bitch to the side of a boxcar and send him to the west coast. I have to go see him again, though. Shorty says when the boys were picking up that second crop of clover up there by the line, Hank was shooting in their direction with that old shotgun. Shorty walked over and Hank said he was after pheasants. Shorty told him season doesn't open for two months and Hank said he doesn't have a calendar."

They sat quietly for a moment, then Thea said, "Loretta said the other day that Bud wouldn't loan Hank his bull again to breed those seven or eight cows and he offered Hank a hundred dollars for the herd. Now Bud's afraid Hank might have a mortgage on them, that they don't really belong to Hank."

Cy smiled, and didn't look at Thea. "Bud's right. I've held the paper for five, six years. If Bud thinks he can make anything, buying the cows, he's welcome."

Thea began to protest and Cy said, "You have to remember, Hank's not your average neighbor.

"And speaking of one person beating another, seems like I forgot my pocketbook. You don't mind paying, do you?"

Thea saw clearly the outline of his wallet in the pocket of his bib overalls.

Cy, pulling his hat from the corner post of their booth, said, "See, that's how it goes. Hank beats me so I beat the next person in line. Today, that's you."

On the sidewalk, Thea was surprised to hear Cy promise, "Hank's out of there by freeze-up this fall, so help me God. There has to be a better place for Mabel and her girl. I feel lately like Hank just stole into my life without me knowing what was going on and things went from bad to worse. I was warned, but let the whole thing slide. It did Hank no good, either." He stopped to roll a cigarette.

"Well, Thea, you better get back to work. One of us had better keep track of why we're here on earth."

That afternoon Thea reflected on their conversation several times, feeling more sad each time she ran the words through her mind.

A week later, Shorty told Cy he'd seen a stock truck up at Kootseemas, loading up the cows and it looked like last year's calves, too. "The whole bunch all together, so thin they could have been hauled in a wheelbarrow."

Cy told them he supposed the herd would end up at Bud Swanson's, and mentioned the price Bud might have paid Hank.

Shorty said, "Good cows are a nickel a pound, who'd give two cents for those cripples of Hank's?"

Cy asked, "So, Shorty, you figure every guy that's dead broke should stay dead broke?"

"Not every guy...just Hank."

Cy, his chair tilted back against the porch rail, answered, "Shorty, go count bolts or pound iron or something. I think I need a nap."

Saturday morning, the stillness of the farmyard was astonishing. Shorty had granted the three men who worked around the barns and the fenced areas that included the night pasture an unprecedented dispensation. All young, none of them twenty-one, they were fast friends and had never made it difficult for Shorty to divide the chores among them.

Ervin, Ira and Ted had headed north in Shorty's Chevrolet, twelve-foot bamboo poles strapped to the side of the car, the back seat and trunk filled with what each believed necessities. Halfway through the haying season, when Shorty told them Cy had agreed to turn them loose for ten days before grain cutting began, he had unknowingly interrupted their combined plans to join the U.S. Navy in late summer.

The three lived in a small building built for the purpose of housing hired help, located at the south edge of the orchard. Over the years dozens of men had come and gone; these three, Cy told the twins, were mechanically inclined and he hoped they'd stay.

Today, with only himself and Shorty and one high school boy hired for the summer near the barns, Cy felt an unanticipated reconnection to the land.

Inside the horse barn he rested his elbows on the ledge of the half-cut door overlooking his herd of Shorthorns and his fields which lay to the south and east of the barn. Swallows circled and dived through the morning air, guarding their nesting spots in the eaves of the long barn where a second hatch of the sleek winged birds would soon emerge.

The sun which had risen only an hour ago backlit sixty acres of oats, slate green and unchurned by high winds, the field unblemished by anything foreign to itself. In the night pasture the cows were gathered close to the post and wire gate which kept them out of the lane leading to the big pasture; nearly every cow had a calf nearby.

The dew on the grass would not be burned off for another hour or two.

Behind Cy, two teams in their stalls were snorting softly, moving gently as they reached for the feed Cy had poured in their boxes. Turned out of the barn in late May when corn planting ended, Buster, Prince, Bird and Lady had returned to their stalls yesterday; the man who trimmed hooves in Sutton County would arrive at the Kennedy farm on Monday.

Their hooves stirring slightly on the cement floor, the sound of their chewing and the soft creak of their bridles was so familiar to Cy that he had, for a moment, the unwitting notion that nothing in his life had changed in the years since he had first built this farm.

Glancing down the dirt trail that led to Gladdie's house, Cy grinned when he saw her hurrying toward the farmyard. In a few minutes she would unlatch the garden gate at the rear of the house and enter the farm kitchen. Wood smoke would soon lift from the kitchen chimney; Gladdie would not be persuaded by himself or the twins to cook breakfast on the gas range.

"I need this kitchen warmed up in the morning, it sure don't pay to run two stoves, does it?"

The sun was streaked with red as it climbed higher in the sky. Cy, in the doorway of the barn, had just rolled and lit a cigarette and he reached for the iron hook near his knee, swung the door wide and stepped into the barnyard. The cows turned to look at him as he walked nearer the gate, and the straying calves gamboled to the herd, sliding along the anxious cattle pressed close to the fence.

When he dragged the gate back to let the silent animals pass Cy looked back at the house and saw Bert hurrying to the shed where she kept her car. Shorty was right, Bert had perked up a little in the past week or so.

Last night, at supper time, Cy heard her telling Thea that today she had an appointment at the Model Beauty Shop where a Croquinole Wave cost just two dollars. Neither of the girls had seemed to notice Gladdie's glance of disapproval.

Now, Bert waved at her father and as he tossed his half-smoked cigarette to the dust near his boots, he smiled and waved back.

He watched the cows and calves as they wended their way through the narrows that led to the big pasture, then turned toward the house.

At the edge of the lawn a redwinged blackbird was dancing on tiny feet, spreading his wings, begging for the open-eyed regard of his dull-coated mate. In his black soldier coat, the scarlet epaulets shone brightly as the pair flew off to the meadowland beyond Gladdie's garden.

Well, Cy thought, he might as well face the music. When he'd wakened a few times in the dark, last night, he'd thought of reasons he might postpone driving up to Kootseemas, but the reasons seemed unfounded in the light of day.

He could ask Frank Keefe to talk to Hank or at least to accompany him when he confronted the damn fool.

Gladdie poured Cy's coffee. "Shorty, lettin' all the men off work at the same time, now you got the chores to do!"

Cy smiled at her and the sternness of her face ebbed when he said, "It's okay, Gladdie. Shorty promised me a raise this fall. A fellow could do worse than taking orders from you and Shorty; I think the two of you treat me pretty well. A trifle bossy sometimes, maybe."

. . . .

When the twins were small, Cy believed that Gladdie had a full day's work caring for them and taking care of the house, especially since she refused housekeeping help from anyone. Shorty and the men who worked for him ate their meals in one of the three rooms attached to the machine shop. As well equipped as it needed to be for the preparation of simple meals, the stove and washing machine were tended mostly by Adam Mattson, a gentleman as old as Shorty and Cy.

In 1922, Adam's sister, Laura, attempted to have him committed to an institution, citing his changed behavior after his return from Belgium at the end of the war. Doc Dennison, who had known Adam all his life, spoke to Cy.

"Adam doesn't talk. He never said much, but now he seems to have nothing to say. My testimony won't be worth one damn thing, I'm not a head doctor, but Laura's kids are bound that Adam's silence is hard on their mother."

Cy knew Doc had stopped for something more than a casual visit.

Now, Adam slept in the bunk house, located fifty feet from the shop. All the hired help but Shorty slept there and over the years, the jobs of a half dozen men had been abruptly terminated by Shorty for their reluctance to accept Adam as a key employee of the Kennedy farm.

Now that Thea and Bert were grown, Gladdie's workload had considerably lessened and Cy asked her if it was okay if Shorty took some of his meals with the family.

Gladdie surprised Cy by asking if perhaps Adam would like to come to the house occasionally.

He was asked frequently, and refused each time. Today, Cy sat on the step leading to the front porch, watching Adam mowing the lawn. The grass had been cut earlier this week and now almost no hint of green fell, severed, to the ground.

When the girls began driving, Adam didn't refuse a ride through the countryside now and then, and every few weeks Cy took him to Laura's house, where she fussed over her younger brother and thanked Cy for bringing him to visit.

Farmers who knew Cy had told him often something that he knew was true; Shorty's talents were paramount on the six hundred and forty acres where the Kenendys lived.

Cy knew also that none of Shorty's talents identified the nature of Elwood "Shorty" Brill as explicitly as his unsaid compassion for the man Cy watched now, Adam's arms guiding the revolving blades across the lawn, his eyes gazing straight ahead, his voice unwilling to put into words the things he had seen, so far from Emmis.

Above the sound of the gently turning blades, the meagre wind in the bushes near the step where he sat, Cy heard the snap of the screen door at the side of the house. Not noticing Cy, Gladdie came from the kitchen, headed for the steel lawn chairs near the washline. Cy watched her set a pitcher and two empty glasses on the table near the chairs, then walked toward Adam. She smiled and touched his arm, pointing at the chairs. He pushed the mower to the fence and leaned the handle upright against a post.

Adam wiped the sweat from his neck and forehead with his gloves, then dropped them on the grass near his feet as he sat across from Gladdie.

When their glasses were half empty, Cy heard the screech of a blue jay, pursued by a dozen sparrows flying angrily toward the pines behind the barn.

Gladdie gestured toward the racing birds and Adam smiled, tilting his glass to empty it. She reached for the pitcher and he smiled. Their glasses filled, Gladdie, her ankles crossed, her hands in her lap, said something and Adam laughed out loud.

Cy told himself he was not spying, he was taking stock of the things located on this side of the fence that ran between his place and the Kootseema farm. It had become essential, now, to tabulate, to weigh and measure and compare the acts and affairs of Matt's family and himself, to establish once and for all time the truth that no one or no deed could improve the lives of Hank and his family.

Last week, Cy had asked Eli Kanter if it would be sound, in Eli's opinion, to meet with Hank at the abstract office in Emmis and simply give him the sixty acres.

Eli stared at Cy. "Every time you bring up Hank's name you seem to take a closer step to the bughouse. We've all got at least one thorn in our shoe but you seem to think you have to carry Hank in both your boots. Get the hell out of here so I can work at things that make sense."

CHAPTER 13

In reality, Eli Kanter, although he shook his head when hearing of some of Cy Kennedy's business decisions knew that Cy was more adept at caring for his own financial security than anyone he'd known. Eli thought often of the times, beginning in 1927, when Cy had stopped in the bank president's office to discuss and question the trend of the economy, especially as it related to American farmers.

Eli knew that First National of Emmis was not a key player in the major investments held by Cy, but Cy was a member of the bank's board. Somehow, Eli felt honored when Cy would sit across from him and express minor trepidation about the direction of banking in America.

Late in the fall of '27, Cy disappeared from Emmis for two months. Rumors flew; one of the twins was in serious trouble, Cy was seriously pursuing a new love, his health was in grave danger. Just before Christmas that year, Eli attended a national meeting of rural bankers in St. Louis and learned, in barroom gossip, that Cy had liquidated many of his stocks and bonds.

When Cy returned to Emmis at Christmas time, Eli waited for him to stop at the bank.

He learned later that Cy installed in the small room on the south side of his farm house a modern safe, that the room's single window was now part of the wall, and the floor beneath the safe was reinforced, the door of the room securely locked.

In 1928, he withdrew two-thirds of his money in the National bank and, in the fall of 1929, Cy Kennedy lost little as the stock market collapsed.

Eli, nine years later, knew little about the state of Cy's affairs and as a banker, he thought Cy had lost a small fortune by losing, all these years, the interest his money might have earned.

He also thought he'd be a fool to pry in Cy's life, or offer his old friend advice. Eli had no doubt that wherever Cy's money was held, it was safe.

Sitting quietly, his cigarette crushed beneath his boot so the smell of it wouldn't reach Gladdie and Adam, Cy thought about how often, this summer, he had reflected on the people who had framed his life. He knew that without his father's fortune he would have shared the struggles of his neighbors, without Ayma's place in his life he might have never known the unequivocal love that sustained him twenty-five years after her death, and that without Bert and Thea, he would not have any real claim to the

119

unmitigated pride their presence allowed him to carry as a shield against his wrongful judgments, plaguing him day and night.

He thought often, this summer, of the Sunday afternoon when Timothy had come to the farm alone, as he nearly always came, and seated in the screened porch with Cy and Ayma had spoken of the lack of peace he felt.

"*I never thought and still don't think there's anything wrong in chasing the dollar. When I left Ontario I was already a rich man. I wanted to be richer. I made good money in lumber, I made more in building railroads, I made more even in lucky investments.*

"*I never cheated my men by underpaying or overworking them, so help me God. That's the one thing I wanted you and Tom to know, that having money is having command, and the really great command is not using money to hurt somebody or to stab someone's dreams like nobody's dreams but your own matter.*

"*But all the benefits of having money are not as powerful as what you will find is true about money, sadly true. Nothing can change this one very bad thing about the human circumstance: in a business or in a house, the person with the least good intentions or who is the least noble rules everything.*

"*It's a kind of hell when you live in the shadow of such a person's nature. We can laugh, we can sing, we can look away, but the dark stain reaches us.*

"*Trying to move where the stain can't reach us changes who we are, changes everything.*"

Cy and Ayma knew Timothy had been talking about his own life with Bridget, and as they lay in the dark that night, Ayma asked, "When you were young, were your folks critical of each other, like your father spoke today?"

Cy thought for a moment. "No, never. Sometimes my mother thought everyone but herself was too stiff with Tom, but I always thought that most of what they said was said when they were alone.

"And today, Dad wasn't critical. He was just talking himself to an answer."

Cy stood and opened the porch door soundlessly. He hung his straw hat on the hook inside the door and took his felt hat from the shelf above.

He once believed that time, on its reasonably benevolent course, would intervene in his favor and Hank Kootseema, yet a young man, would seek some kind of paradise far from where he'd come with Amelia to the Kootseema farm.

The course of time had frequently favored Cy but it was obvious that Hank had no concept of paradise, at least none that included his removal from the sixty acres homesteaded by Gottfried and Annie Kootseema.

Cy backed his pickup from the shed.

As he drove slowly past the lawn Gladdie was gathering the glasses and the pitcher, straightening the skirt of her apron as she stood to say something more to Adam. Hearing the passing Terraplane she pointed toward Cy, and Adam, pulling on his gloves, lifted one arm in an old-fashioned salute.

Timothy had waved like that; Ayma told Cy once that the gesture was sweeter than a kiss, it "comes from so close to the heart".

Cy took his time; he stopped at the mailbox although he knew that both girls would likely do so, also.

Since sunup the soft late summer winds had been shifting from east to west in that strange show of dichotomous restlessness peculiar to the days when the seasons are considering change. Even the fireball in the sky, wholly committed to summer, seemed uncertain.

There had been dry spells this summer, but nothing like the drought of recent years and in this month enough rain had fallen to give a hosanna feel to every field, every pasture, even the ditches and swamplands.

For a man who owned more than one thousand acres, the Kootseema sixty was a plague, but the grief of it would soon end. When Amelia was buried, he should have thrown the lot of them off the place, Hank, Mabel and that born to be pitied Glory. Good God, what a bunch.

When he coasted into Hank's driveway, Cy was startled to see Frank Keefe's Buick Special parked close to the barn and Loretta Swanson's old Plymouth coupe near the woodpile. An accident? Mabel?

His heart pounding, his legs slightly unsteady, Cy parked near Frank's car and sat there a minute. He heard voices from the barn, Hank's the loudest, ranting in high pitched denial. The sheriff and Hank stood just a few feet apart in the open doorway and Mabel and Loretta stood with Glory and a smaller girl near the steps that led upstairs to the haymow.

Mabel was crying, Loretta's face filled with rage. Approaching slowly, Cy was stuck by the suddenly silent, energy charged group that turned to stare at him; they stood frozen for a few seconds, as though he had interrupted them in the midst of committing an unspeakable act.

Cy wasn't surprised when Hank broke the silence. "What the hell's he doin' up here, nosy old son of a bitch, never thought I had no rights on this place, waitin' for the chance to run me down like a dog or chase me off a bridge somewhere."

He ran toward Cy, and Frank reached over, grabbed Hank by one arm, pushed him headfirst into a stall where the gutter was filled with dried manure. "You just lay there, boy, I'm about to bust your neck, anyhow."

He told the women to take the girls up to the house, he'd be there in a little while.

Hank rolled over on his back, his legs drawn up to his chest, his face covered with blood.

Frank signalled for Cy to follow him outside.

"Loretta came tearing into Emmis about noon. She was taking Mabel over to the canning company's pea viner, set up in Murray's field, to buy a bushel of peas. Hank was gone and Loretta left her girl, Wanda, with Glory.

"Goddamned Hank came home, the girls were in the haymow looking at a mess of kittens and he climbed up there and pulled his damn britches down. Loretta's girl, she tried to skinny down the steps and he caught her, she was screaming and carrying on when Loretta drove in."

Cy shook his head, leaned against the barn wall. The hide on his face looked like it had been whipped by a high wind and his chest was rising and falling like the flanks of a tortured animal. Frank reached over and grabbed Cy by the arm.

"Cy! Let's go sit down a minute. Hank's not going anyplace. Here, let's go up and talk to Loretta and Mabel."

Frank opened the door of his car and reached inside. He walked back to the barn, stood in the doorway and showed Hank the Smith and Wesson revolver he held high in one hand. "Six inch barrel; I'm a hell of a shot. 32.20, and you'd make a good target. Just stay still."

Glory, sullen and silent, sat in the old car seat on the porch, she refused to look at Cy and Frank as they walked past. Mabel was seated at the table and Loretta, her eyes red and the skin on her face puffed, looked miserable, her usually buoyant spirit gone, and Wanda, twelve years old, her dress torn, her hair escaping from a wide ribbon, studied the toes of her shoes.

Frank pulled a chair close to Mabel. "Did you have any idea Hank was doing this kind of thing? How about with Glory? Ever make you worry? You ever see anything made you think he might be headed this way?"

Mabel was terrified.

Cy pulled a backless chair close. "Mabel, this is not your doing. Nobody thinks it's your fault. But you know what Hank did is dead wrong and he can't be doing this sort of thing. Glory doesn't deserve it, you know he'll start in on her, sure as hell. Hank's got to be locked up, you know it."

"How?"

Frank looked at Cy, then at Mabel.

"What do you mean, how? In jail, Mabel. How else are we going to handle this?"

"Yeah, but how? Who's gonna say what he did and all that? Glory won't, I tell you right now."

Loretta stirred and looked searchingly at Frank. "You mean Wanda, here? Gotta get up in a room full of people and say what she saw? Bud's never going to make her do that."

Then, "I got a better idea. We ain't none of us comin' back here, not ever, or lettin' that bastard near our kids."

She walked over to Mabel. "Mabel, I told you a hundred times to get away from that good for nothin' piece of shit, you never had the spunk. Well, you can keep on having no spunk. And anyhow, I 'bout figured out even before today, no more Glory around my girls. Bud been noticing a lotta stuff lately. He ain't wrong, Bud."

Mabel began to weep as though she stood on a small island and the last-ever ship that could possibly pass was leaving her behind. Almost soundless, the effort of her crying grew louder, almost filling the kitchen. Cy noticed that the fly paper streamers spiraling from the ceiling were completely filled with dead flies, the battered alarm clock on the window sill was nearly two hours behind, the curtains at the three windows were all sewed of different fabric.

He shuddered, and Frank looked at him.

Loretta took Wanda's hand and led her outside to the car.

On the porch, Glory sat on the car seat, one bare, dirty foot swinging slowly, a strand of hair pulled tightly to one corner of her mouth.

The two men walked to their cars and Cy was going to speak when Frank suddenly strode toward the barn door. He looked inside. Hank lay twisted on the cement. Frank assumed a shooter's stance, his hat pushed back, his spine as straight as a yardstick, and Cy heard three rapid shots.

He ran to where Frank stood and saw Hank sitting up, wild eyed and staring. Frank pointed to the top of the old manger. "I put them about an inch apart, a little wood flew, that's all."

Then he grinned and offered the revolver to Cy. "Three more shells. Try your luck?"

Cy looked at him but couldn't match Frank's grin.

"What's going to happen, now?"

"Well, tonight I'll drive up to Bud Swanson's, make sure Loretta told him about this. I'll see what he thinks."

Then, as an afterthought, "You want to ride along?"

Now Cy could smile. "With a Goddamn cowboy? Better not."

Then he remembered. "The reason I came up here today was to tell

Hank he's got to move. Say, Frank...what would happen if I offered Bud a thousand dollars to go after Hank, put him in jail?"

Frank considered for a few seconds. "Probably Hank would be let go and you and me would be pounding rocks."

Cy was surprised to see it was only three-thirty when he walked in the house. He laid the mail on the hall table and asked Gladdie if it would mess up her plans if he took her and the girls and Shorty to the old hotel in St. Cloud for supper.

Gladdie was surprised; she hadn't been there since her last birthday and she said she'd better go home and get dolled up if she was going to be seen with the twins.

Cy told Shorty to change his clothes and shave and he told Gladdie the girls would pick her up at her house about six.

He called Thea and told her that he and Shorty would be at the hotel, in the bar.

"What's up?"

"I never thought I'd say this and I know I'll feel different tomorrow, but right now, I'd like to leave Sutton County behind me."

A week later, Shorty and Cy were looking over the two grain binders the men would use to cut and bundle the oat crop. Cy had rounded up extra help to shock the grain and now their great hope was for two or three weeks of dry weather to get the oats safely stored in the granaries.

Cy suddenly remembered the broken pitman up at Kootseema's, the reason Hank had never finished harvesting the grain last fall.

"Damn it, I knew I should have brought that busted thing down here for welding!"

Shorty looked at him. Last summer the binder he was working on today had not tied the bundles evenly and Shorty had declared he wasn't sending it back to the fields until he'd figured out the problem. "You talked me into seeding for that son of a bitch; don't think I'm going back up there. He can cut it with his pocketknife for all I care."

They worked in silence. The oat fields Shorty had seeded for Kootseemas were as good as any of Cy's, and they both knew Mabel needed the grain for her hens.

Before they quit at noon, Shorty said, "If you can get your hands on that pitman, bring the damn thing down. Whether or not Hank can get the binder put back together, that's another thing. And whether that poor team can haul the damn binder, that's one more thing. Grass fed, old, they don't look like they got the power to walk across the pasture."

Wiping his hands on a rag, Cy replied, "I thought you hated horses."

"Not as much as I hate those that got 'em and don't feed "em."

The following afternoon, Cy drove past Pavlik's to see if Hank's car was there. When he saw it he hurried to Kootseema's. He hadn't seen any of them since Frank had been there last week. Mabel walked tentatively toward him and he forced himself to smile.

Cy knew that someone from the county welfare office had been to see Mabel, along with the County Attorney and Frank. Hank had been warned he was just a step away from lockup; Mabel, Frank reported, begged for mercy for Hank. Today, Mabel's older hens and Gladdie's were pecking in the knotweed and purslane near the henhouse. Glory, a pail in one hand, walked toward Cy and her mother, picking her way through a patch of stinging nettles. Ignoring Cy, she called out, "No eggs out here, Mama. They must not be layin' nowhere."

Mabel said, "I run short a feed, I thought we'd do okay til threshing when we sold them cows, but Bud he never paid but half out front, and now, I don't know. Loretta, she don't stop by."

Cy saw the pitman, still against the shed wall. He sounded to himself like he was talking to one of the twins, twenty years ago. "Don't fret, now. You've got some good oats out there and we'll get that binder put together. The hens, once they're back on their feed, will be okay."

He thought to himself, "I should have taken that revolver Frank offered, and shot lower than he did."

Shorty looked at the pitman, the iron parts skinned up, the wood, split. "Crazy fool, he musta took this out with a post maul. I'll get to it, but it's gonna take time."

Cy knew that if he asked Shorty to have the crew cut Hank's crop, shock and thresh it, he and Shorty would lose something they'd always had. And he might lose Shorty. Goddamn Hank!

The next morning Cy was up early and asked Thea to keep an eye out for Hank's car on the streets in Emmis. "Call Gladdie, she'll let me know what's going on."

Then he went to the granary where oats from a year ago were stored, and filled a dozen sacks. Shorty stuck his head in the doorway. "What the hell? The boys will sweep all these oats in one bin and the new crop'll go in the rest."

He saw the discomfort on Cy's face as he started loading the sacks in the pickup, backed up to the granary.

Gladdie walked half way across the yard and shouted, "Thea says Hank Kootseema's in town! She says be careful if you're thinkin' of goin' up there!"

Shorty watched Gladdie hurrying back to the house, her apron flapping in the small wind that blew across the garden.

"Cy, if ever that famous damn fool catcher comes around Emmis, you'll be the first guy he picks up."

When Cy got in the truck, Shorty opened the other door and jumped in, eyeing Cy stubbornly. "Two damn fools can do this easier than one."

Rowdy had been sleeping in the shop and came out to watch as the Terraplane drove slowly to the road.

"You think we can order out a new pitman for that binder or what the hell?"

Shorty snorted. "An old binder like Hank's ain't been made for thirty years. His oats were put in last, we'll get ours and then worry about Hank's. And, by the way, have Kootseemas ever paid a threshing bill since Matt died?"

"Why would they? I never sent a bill."

Glory and Mabel walked down to the old granary when Cy backed up to the door and Shorty jumped in the bed of the truck to unload the sacks. The bin nearest the door would hold most of the oats and he began untying the sacks and letting the oats pour inside.

Glory stood back as Mabel, fidgety and stepping from one foot to the other, peered inside. "You don't hafta do this. Hank, he'll holler when he sees what you done."

Leaning against the truck, Cy lit a cigarette and looked past Mabel. "This is not for Hank. It's for you and your hens, and Gladdie expects you to pay up by coming down after the first hard frost and helping her clean up the garden."

He saw Shorty looking at two sacks that had been loaded earlier, before Shorty had come to the granary to help. "That's laying mash, there. We'll leave it in the sacks, Mabel."

She said to Shorty, "If you could drop them two sacks there by the house I can pail the feed into a feed box I got so the rats don't take it."

Driving home, Shorty said, "First killin' frost, Gladdie's gonna knock you alongside the head with a broomstick."

Cy tossed the butt of his cigarette from the open window.
"I expect you've got that right."

Bert and Gladdie were canning tomatoes when Thea came home
at noon. Shorty had walked up to the house with Cy, and then, seeing the
kettles and canning jars and the baskets of ripe tomatoes, he backed onto the
porch. He grinned. "More peaceful like down at the shop. I think Adam's got
some soup to heat up."

Thea grabbed her purse from the table. "Enough for me, too?"

Bert laughed and Gladdie turned from the sink, a paring knife in one
hand, a tomato in the other. Cy said, "I wish there was something I could do
to help you girls."

Gladdie pointed the knife blade at two wooden fruit crates filled with
the jars that had been canned yesterday. "They can be took down and put on
the shelf in the cellar."

As Cy started down the steps with the first crate, Gladdie nudged Bert.

"Fixed him that time", she whispered.

CHAPTER 14

Thea walked the three blocks to the courthouse to pick up the list of fall jurors and to ask about the progress of a couple of WPA projects begun in the past few weeks. She stopped at the sheriff's office and Frank was there, alone. He didn't see her until she was in the office and she watched him as she sat in the chair near his desk. Looking up, he barely smiled.

"I think that look is called 'brooding'", she said. "Hard day?"

"Hard life, more like it. That damn thing with Sandy, I just can't get a grip on anything...no money that anybody ever knew about, nobody saw a damn thing, there wasn't but two or three letters from some cousin or somebody like that, everything just left like he was hardly ever here or hardly gone, for that matter.

"One thing, though, he picked up a half pint of Four Roses down at Pavlik's, should have lasted a month by his history and it didn't turn up when we looked around. Scoop, next door, says Sandy always washed out his bottles and cans and took a sackful to the town dump every spring and again just before winter. Scoop's wife says Sandy hauled them out just the week before he was killed. Not a bottle stuck anywhere."

Thea asked, "You're not thinking he was killed for about a cupful of cheap whiskey?"

"I don't know. I always thought if Emmis ever had a murder I'd put cuffs on some sorry devil and get my name in the paper." He smiled. "It's not that easy, I guess. And I was thinking of asking for a raise this fall. If it was that damn Hank and I could prove it I'd kill a lot of birds with one stone."

Thea stood. "Well, that's true enough, but I don't see Mabel as a liar. Hank's got to be the worst thing that ever happened to her, why would she want him around if she knew how crazy he's become?"

"Scared enough, I guess anybody'd lie. Thea, I think you might feel good about something Cy said the other day. He told me, 'My folks gave me no trouble, my wife gave me no trouble, my girls gave me no trouble, it takes my neighbor to make me see that side of the world.' I can't get it out of my mind, Cy saying that."

Thea's eyesight was blurred and when she got to the front door of the courthouse, someone opened the door for her and as she stepped onto the sidewalk she realized she hadn't noticed who let her pass first. Worse yet, she hadn't thanked anyone for the courtesy.

. . . .

While Thea was at the courthouse Hank walked past her office window and peered inside. Nobody there. Well, he'd better get home and get that danged old binder pulled up to the shed. Mabel hadn't told him Cy had taken the pitman and he hadn't noticed its absence. Wished he had a better team to pull the damn thing. Really wished he had a tractor. Bud Swanson last year took an old truck chassis and a car body, made a pretty fair tractor. Son of a bitch never offered to make one for him, now that big-mouth kid, Wanda, she got him cut off from everybody, seemed like.

He never woulda hurt her. Glory, she never said it hurt none just to look, like. Whole world was standin' to the other side from where he was. Old Matt, even, was like that, fussy about doin' nothin' might get called bad. Well, if Ma coulda kept goin', the chickens and milkin' and all, he never shoulda got set up with Mabel. Havin' a kid and all is just plain hell.

He wished he could get a straight answer about some kinda job, next winter. Shoulda stayed with the road job, never nothin' but hurry, hurry.

All them jiggery crooks up to the courthouse, they'd like to see him starve. Ma's money, they shoulda kept it on, not shut it off when she was killed on a public road.

Hank stopped at Val's Service Station and bought three gallons of gas. Damn near half a dollar. How's a guy supposed to make it?

An hour after Mabel and Glory had eaten their noon meal, Hank's car bounced into the yard, stopping a few feet from the battered porch. He stumbled,nearly falling, as he slammed the car door and climbed the steps to the porch. In the kitchen, Mable was scraping the food from an enamel plate into a pail where she kept scraps for her chickens.

"What kinda endless fool leaves a couple sacks of feed outside when it's gonna rain tonight? Whinin' your damn chickens is starvin'; where'd you get them sacks, anyhow?"

Turning her back on him, Mabel slipped the plate into a pan of water at the end of the table.

"Cy Kennedy. He said he had extra, threshing time comin', he cleaned up his bins for new oats. This was leftover. I never ast him nothin'".

Hank circled the table until he stood in front of Mabel, grabbing her arm and breathing hard in her face.

"What the hell does that old son of a bitch want, thinkin' he's gotta feed your hens, the hens he give you. There's no way in hell that's all he wants, snoopin, the same as always, I guarantee you that." He dropped her arm and looked out the window, a cunning look twisting his lean face.

"He ain't up here harpin' on the rent, is he? Never brings that up to me, he knows what I'd tell him. Shoulda been my Ma's place, that's what I'd say, and then mine, by law."

Suddenly, his high pitched laugh filled the kitchen. "He ain't tryin' to collect the rent from you, is he, some other way?"

Mabel backed away, as if she'd been pushed. "More fool him", he laughed. "Even old Cy don't deserve a bag of nothin' like you."

Glory wandered into the kitchen. Mabel turned, saying, "I'm done in here, Glory, til suppertime. You take your love book and go upstairs til I call you."

Hank turned to the silent girl and asked, "If you was here, what do you think old Cy was huntin' for? Was he wearin' his pants the whole time he was talkin' to you girly-girls?"

Glory looked from one to the other, thinking before she answered. "Well, when Shorty he was unloadin' the sacks Cy ast me just about little stuff. He said no rain today, maybe a little tonight. He said that Sandy, he got blood all over himself and his watch got lost and his purse."

The defiance in her eyes startled Hank. What else had Cy said? Hank looked at the girl, then Mabel. "Why the hell is that old crackpot comin' here and talkin' about that stupid stuff? None of us is who did that damage to any old man!"

He sat down and studied Mabel's face, flushed and quivering. His folded fists together on the table, he stared at his wife. "What all was he sayin', anyhow? Like it's our fault old Sandy McDonald got put down that way?"

Confused, Mabel said, "No, he never said no such thing. He put a little oats in the granary, him and Shorty, then he sat these sacks where I could get the ground feed under cover, than we talked a few words, then he went."

"Well, what did he want to know about us seein' Sandy? You told him we never seen him on this place, didn't you?"

"He never said much about Sandy hisself except he was hurt bad. He ast did I ever notice the little purse he had in his pocket and did I hear Sandy's watch went missin' when he got killed. I told him I never seen the purse since we never done no business together but everybody seen the watch when they seen Sandy."

"Son of a bitch! I seen Cy and Frank Keefe hunched up at Pavlik's. Mighta known they was gonna point my way if they could, last thing they ever did."

Usually, when Hank had been drinking, he would sit at the table, slumped over and half asleep, his unshaven face pressed against the oilcloth, spit running from the corner of his mouth. Today, he was strangely energized, and it frightened Mabel. He swung his head toward her. "Get that damned feed put away. Old Cy might be wrong about the rain, but get it taken care of. If it don't rain, won't be the first thing that fool guessed wrong."

Pulling his hat off the nail next to the door, he nearly collided with Mabel as she hurried to empty the sacks of feed into pails she could carry to the feed box. He wasn't in the habit of telling her where he was going, but now he said, "I gotta check if those bolts in the pump house is long enough to fix the binder."

Just as she tipped the last bit of feed into the feed box and looked toward the house, Hank, in a curious frenzy, was beside her, twisting her arm and pushing her against the box.

"You stupid bitch! Are you blind, or just a damn liar? Cy was down to the pump house and I got you to thank for it."

He pushed her so hard she felt the pain in her arms reach her ears, her eyes could barely focus on his face, not three inches from her own. "Any bad comes to me, you'll damn soon know and the bad you're gonna get won't shake loose this side of hell."

Hank ran for his car and Mabel stumbled past the pail she'd flung to the ground when he grabbed her. Standing in the upstairs window, Glory stood silently, watching as Hank's car shot gravel from the driveway, then disappeared behind a wall of dust.

She smoothed a spot on her unmade bed to arrange her small treasures. Oddly, Glory had little doubt where this small bit of plunder had originated, but once the old man was gone, why care who's got his little doo-dads?

She was glad she'd decided to not show them to Wanda. Wanda gets everybody in trouble, anyhow.

Gladdie loved the month of August. When the twins were small, she enjoyed watching their excitement as the school year approached, by the end of August most of her garden work had ended and almost always, she won ribbons at the Sutton County Fair for the bit of canned goods she displayed, for at least one of her pies and for her needlework, usually an intricate piece of Swedish embroidery.

She liked the excitement of the grain harvest on the Kennedy farm, the endless wagons of golden grain, the neighbors who crowded around the table in the dining room, and mostly she liked the generous praise of the men for whom she cooked. For twenty years, Bert had been her best support in the preparation of morning coffee, dinner at noon, afternoon coffee, then supper.

This year, instead of being first on the threshing ring, Cy had scheduled his oats threshing to be last. Bert and two other teachers at Emmis High, Theresa and Jessie, were going to the Black Hills in late July, driving there in Bert's new car.

Cy cautioned Bert to not try to drive too far in one day, Shorty taught her how to change a tire, Gladdie reminded her to not drive like Thea, with one arm out the window or she'd have a sunburned arm and have to wear long sleeved dresses before winter. Thea told her sister to not pick up any hitchhikers who weren't good looking men and if they were really good looking, don't turn them loose.

Secretly, Cy worried that his oats would be rained on in the shocks, awaiting threshing, or rained on before they were cut, with wet fields taking their toll before harvest.

The twins were right, Cy was born to worry.

Worrying about the weather was the easy part.

Shorty pulled the big Red River Special threshing rig from its own shed on the first day of August. The newest threshing machine in Warren Township, it separated the grain from the straw for about sixteen farms, not including Cy's.

Perfect harvest weather dawned day after day, and six farmers had their oats in their granaries before Cy turned part of his crew loose with tractors and binders to cut and shock his own crop.

Several times in the past decade some of the farmers had not had grain enough to harvest and had turned their cattle into the dried-out fields to salvage anything there.

Everyone expected to pay three cents a bushel to thresh, but Cy, in a spate of gratitude for the sweet harvest this year, lowered his price to a penny and a half.

Herman Borcha told John Pavlik, "Last year he forgave me half my rent because me and my boys built a lean-to on the barn with lumber he bought. This year he threshed me out half rate. Hell, I couldn't afford to own my farm."

John said, "I've heard that about Cy. He's never owed me anything, but on the other hand, he's one of my few regulars that almost never buys a drink for anybody but himself. Tight, that way. Probably thinks oats is more important than whiskey."

. . . .

On the Kennedy farm, one hundred and twenty-eight acres of oats were in neat seven-bundle shocks by the time Bert was home and the rest of the neighborhood had the year's grain under a roof. Gladdie won five blue ribbons at the fair and had her picture on the front page of the Advocate. Her protests seemed hollow when she asked Thea to bring home some extra copies of the paper so she could prove to her sister and her cousins that there's no fool like an old fool.

Saturday morning, Cy saw Hank drive past on his way to Emmis and walked down to the shop to see Shorty. "That busted pitman holding together now?"

Shorty laughed, "Probably turn out to be the only part of the binder that still works. I'd offer to put it in for him, but you know how that sort of thing works out."

He hesitated. "Hell, Cy, Hank's oats are just turning now. Both of our binders are still outa the shed, I could send Ted and one of the others up there when we're threshed and cut the damn things. Mabel needs those oats. You don't figure that damned idiot would shoot the boys if they showed up?"

Cy cleared his throat. "Well, whatever the county decides to do about the business with Loretta's girl, I still intend to have him off there the first of the year. And he can shock the oats himself, for God's sake. God, I hate to go up there again!"

Shorty grabbed the pitman, leaning against the bench, and started outside. "Let's go up and see Hank. That's a hell of a nice field of oats to waste. Betcha them oats'll go 80 bushels, easy."

Hank's car was gone. Mabel stood on the porch, her arms wrapped in the skirt of her apron, pulled around her skinny body. "He lit out soon as it was light. Mad, the bank ain't open Saturdays. He got this letter yesterday...", she opened the screen door and Cy followed her inside.

"The mailman brought this yesterday, Glory, she had to sign a paper when she took it."

The envelope had been mailed by Ernest Swanson, the letter was certified mail. "Glory was at the box when the mail come and she had to write down her name to get the letter."

"Hank, he was tickled pink, I tell you. Bud, he mailed a check for the fifty dollars he still owed on the cows we sold. With the bank locked today, I don't see how Hank can get money today, but maybe, he said."

She looked past Cy. Almost whispering, she said, "We sure do need it, the money."

Cy pointed toward the shed where he had parked the pickup, where Shorty had leaned the pitman against the wall facing the driveway. "You tell Hank, Mabel, that if he can't get that binder running smooth, my boys will cut that field of oats and he can shock it. We're threshing next week, we'll pound out yours as soon as Hank's ready."

Mabel stood beside him, her eyes on the toes of her broken shoes.

"My Dad, he said when we was kids it's good to have nice neighbors. It's true, Cy. You don't see my feelings about stuff, but," giving a small, self-conscious laugh, "I do feel stuff."

Cy turned and walked away, having felt the sharp bones of her spine as he patted her back. Beneath his breath he said, "I've seen and heard what you feel a thousand times."

In the truck, Shorty asked, "Everything okay?"

"Hell, no. How could it be?"

In Emmis, Hank was inflamed by his inability to exchange Bud's check for cash. The bank's doors had been open until eight o'clock on Friday evening, locked tight now until Monday morning.

He approached John Pavlik, who agreed with great reluctance to give Hank five dollars, then hold the check until Monday morning when he and Hank would walk down to the bank. But then John noticed that Mabel's name was on the check, making her a payee, also. When he pointed this out to Hank, "the damn fool nearly collapsed, he waved the check like it was on fire and ran out the door."

Enraged, when Hank returned home he bolted from the car and screamed for Mabel. She was sweeping the open porch, hopeful that Bud's check might mean that Loretta might stop in sometime soon.

Hank threw her from the porch to the bare, hard-packed strip of dirt below and jumped beside her before she could stand up. "You lettin' on them cows was yours, you bitch? Ain't one damn thing on this place that's yours, Cy Kennedy goin' on about *your* hens, *your* eggs, he's as stupid as you. Everthing on this place is mine and your name don't mean shit. Far as I know, you can't *write* your name!"

He held the check high, as though someone might snatch it. Mabel tried to scramble away as he swung one boot, knocking her nearer the porch. She reached up one hand to grasp the edge of the step and he kicked at her hand. The screen door opened and Glory appeared.

"You get that paper all dirty ain't gonna get no money for it, you can't get it all bent up and messed!"

Hank charged up the steps to the kitchen and laid the check beside the envelope on the table. Glory came in and sat in Amelia's old rocker, staring at Hank who was at the water pail, the dipper raised to his lips.

"Goddamn it, Glory, I got no say!"

Breathing heavily, adjusting his suspenders with one thumb, he peered out the window. "Where the hell did she go?"

Mabel was nowhere in sight and the screen door snapped shut as Hank ran from the house. He kicked wildly at a white hen who flew into the forest of pigweed and burdock near the outdoor toilet.

She musta been hurt some, enough to slow her down for much of a hike. He quickly searched the sheds and ran into the barn. Outside the barn, his team had come up from the pasture for water, he hoped there was a few inches in the bottom of the tank. Otherwise, they'd lean on that damn fence til they pushed it over.

He wouldn't call for Mabel, she was too tricky to answer. She'd pulled this stunt before and maybe still had the scars to prove it. Just so she didn't get out on the road and get that damn sheriff out here again.

Hank raced back to the house and folded the check carefully, pushing it deeply into the pocket in the bib of his overalls. The snap still works, nothin' should come loose so's anything could get lost.

He was on the bottom step when he stopped, climbed back to the porch and reached up to where his shotgun hung just below the roof. He wouldn't want to kill her but he might get the chance to scare the hell out of the silly bitch.

He searched behind the barn. Old fool probably hit for the pasture where there was good footing, horses eating most of the weeds up there.

He shoulda dragged her in the house, too much place to hide out here. Anyhow, what was the use? He couldn't teach her nothin' anyhow.

Beyond the field where the oats were ripening, the best field of grain Hank had ever seen, a few acres of rough grazing land lay in the scrub woodland which extended to the fence that separated this farm from Cy Kennedy's largest field where grain shocks stood like confident, unworried sentinels in the haze of a late summer morning.

Hank scanned the brush line a few feet from the intermittent creek which ran through bent and stunted willows, its scant flow of brown cast water barely trickling to the shallow, eroded banks where faint hoof prints left by his water-searching team were pressed into the silt.

How could that stupid bitch just up and disappear? She'd probably slid and sneaked her way through the space between the granary and the barn's lean-to, but he knew she never woulda circled back to the house. She wasn't *that* stupid.

There weren't that many hiding places up here and she knew by now he'd find her, anyhow. Suddenly, Hank spotted Mabel struggling through half-dead weeds and a small patch of canary grass almost higher than her head. Shit, she was headed for that ditch that ran beside the road,

Starting across the space between himself and Mabel, he hesitated for a moment, wondering what would be the best route to head her off.

On the road, coming up from the south, he saw dust flying behind a car and when the small car came into view, Hank knew he'd have to finish up with Mabel later. He watched as she climbed into the little Ford that was driven by Midge Corrigan, Glory's schoolteacher, then saw it turn carefully into his own driveway.

Hurrying back to the edge of the barnyard, Hank saw both women emerge from Midge's car and walk toward the porch where Glory sat on the top step.

When the screen door had closed behind the three of them, Hank leaned against the corner post of the vacant hog pen, lighting a cigarette and then smiling for a second or two. If he didn't need a place to hang his own hat, he'd burn the house to the ground. And them three sly bitches with it.

Mabel, no better than a crippled sow, Glory seemin' lately like she's gettin' ready to spring a few secrets, Midge, yammering about school, school, school, like it mattered.

The shotgun in his hand, Hank opened the rear door of his car and threw it on the seat. He wasn't goin' near the house until that old schoolteacher was gone.

That noon, Cy was lost in thought and an unexpected silence settled over the kitchen until, halfway through their meal, Gladdie announced that last night, in her mail box, she'd found a note from her sister.

"Her girl, Bernice, she's got a baby boy. One of you girls could maybe mail out a little package I tied up to send. She named him Donald. Everybody's forgot the old names."

Bert said she was driving to Emmis later today, she'd be glad to mail Gladdie's gift. Then, absently, she said, "Sometimes I wonder what our brother would have been called if he'd lived."

She glanced at Cy, who seemed to be startled; his cup, as he sat it down, rang against the saucer. They all looked at him and then they heard Gladdie. "Timothy Cyrus if a boy, if a girl, Augusta Gladys."

Cy stared at her and no one moved. Gladdie dropped her hands to her lap and looked from one person to the next. She stared back at Cy.

"She never told you? She told me that last night before it all happened, when I put her to bed. You never knew?"

"I told her to make up her mind, but I guess she figured there was time to talk about it."

Both girls were silent; they'd never heard an exchange like this between Cy and Gladdie.

Then Cy grinned and the twins sat back in their chairs.

"Gladdie, you make me feel like a million dollars, I was always afraid she might have named him Cozack, after that damn French mailman we had at the time."

Everyone laughed and Gladdie, going to the stove for the coffee pot, lifted the skirt of her apron to wipe her eyes.

Barney and Jim, brothers who ran the Tydol station on the east side of Emmis, had a bitter argument that afternoon when Barney saw, in the cash register, the folded check written to Hank Kootseema and Mabel Kootsema.

"What the heck is this in here for?"

"Kootseema, he got the check when the bank ain't open and he needs a little cash so I gave him 40 bucks and when he comes in Monday we'll cash it and I get 50 bucks back."

"For God's sake, Jim, we ain't set up to do bankin' here. Come Monday, I'll go to the bank with that fool. We don't need to be doin' favors for somebody can't do nothin' for us."

Alice, the filling station's bookkeeper and Barney's wife, was working at the cramped desk behind the counter. "As the bookkeeper here, I should be the one to go but you can bet your socks I *ain't* goin'. Not with Hank!"

Clyde, tending bar during the afternoon and evening, told John, "I made the sale of the twentieth century. Just sold Hank Kootseema a quart of the cheap stuff."

John Pavlik was alarmed. "Paper money? Not coins? Did it look like good money?"

Clyde laughed. "Good as Hank, himself. Does that make you feel safer?"

John grinned. It was nearly three in the afternoon and not too many at the bar. Lots of folks rounding up a week of threshing. Busy tonight, more than likely.

CHAPTER 15

When supper was finished and Gladdie and Bert were clearing the table, Cy, tired and restless, announced that he was going to Emmis. Farmers from all over Sutton County were finished or nearly finished with the harvest of small grain, and Cy wondered what was being said about the yields.

His own threshing would begin on Monday, as soon as the dew had lifted and his neighbors had gathered in the fields. He had no doubt he'd have the best crop in years; the market price had actually fallen in recent weeks but he wasn't worried. He could sell any surplus to his neighbors before the next harvest rolled around.

The boys would go up to Hank's when they'd finished here; a long half-day would finish Hank's field and then the season would be over.

And then, the high water mark he could no longer ignore. He'd made up his mind to find some type of accommodation for Glory. And, somewhere, there had to be a small house where Mabel could exist in peace and Cy had decided he'd find that house. Eli Kanter had shook his head when Cy said, "It's not going to bust me to give her a hand".

And Hank. Hank was beyond any help Cy could give him. As Shorty said, "A guy can succeed at bein' nothin' if he's lazy or if he's mean or if he's stupid. Hank's got everything it takes."

Thea said, "Shorty studies Hank like John D. Rockefeller studies the stock market."

Leaving the house, Cy paused on the step and called back through the screen door, "Gladdie, I'll give you a ride if you're ready to hit for home!"

Gladdie came to the doorway to peer out at him. "No, it's so pretty out here, the fields all cut, easy walkin'. I plan to traipse off on my own. Come next week, threshing, I won't be sayin' no to a lift."

Thea called from the dining room, "Gladdie, Rowdy and I will walk you home. I've hardly seen anything outside the office all summer. That rotten old Bert gets the summer off, but I'm just a poor working girl."

When she walked through the kitchen Bert snapped her with a dish towel and Thea jumped from her reach. Gladdie was gathering up her apron and a jar of flowers she'd picked in the garden before supper.

"I'll be home before dark," Thea told Bert.

"Bert, I wish you were teaching in another town so the two of us could go to Emmis and have a drink once in awhile. I feel like going in tonight, but I know you'd bawl, being left alone. What a stupid rule! The banker, the doctor...what's wrong with a teacher having a drink in public?"

"Terrible things," laughed Bert. "Once, I heard, a schoolteacher who took a drink told her class the next day that women should have the same rights as men."

Gladdie stood by the door and told Thea, "You don't be draggin' your sister away at night when she's been workin' all day. You keep your spunky ways to yourself."

Thea stuck her tongue out at Bert. "See you in awhile."

She carried the jar of flowers and shortened her stride to Gladdie's and listened to Gladdie's chatter about how she and Ayma had taken care of the house, the garden, the girls, long ago. When they reached Gladdie's she knew she was expected to step into the house for a few minutes.

Thea was surprised when Gladdie told her, "Sit by the table, I'll be right back."

Gladdie came from the pantry with a tall bottle and set it on the cupboard near the sink. She turned to Thea, a sly grin on her face. "Rhubarb. Rhubarb wine. Gus, he always liked it. I don't say nothin' but I still make it. I have a little, now and then, sittin' here."

The liquid in Thea's glass was the color of a wild rose and perfectly clear. "Gladdie! I always wanted to meet a moonshiner and here you are, right in our own family!"

Gladdie sat across from her, her own glass untasted. "Keep this to yourself, Thea, I ain't even told my sister."

"Yeah, Gladdie, I'd hate for you to lose your reputation over a bottle of booze."

The sound of Gladdie's laugh echoed in the little house. "Thea, that's the best laugh you ever give me. Now don't step in a gopher hole on your way home. The way Cy thinks of you girls, he would toss me out if I hurt you any way at all."

When she opened the door into the near dark, Thea said, "You know, don't you, Gladdie...you know you've never hurt Ayma's twins in any way." She held Gladdie close in her arms and realized she couldn't remember having done it before.

Gladdie watched her walk away and closed the door. As she wiped her eyes, she thought, "I hope that wasn't just the wine talkin'".

Bert turned off the lights in the dining room and settled herself at the kitchen table, a pad of paper before her. She and Gladdie had made a list of the groceries needed to feed the threshers next week, and she had to remind Cy to bring home a few cases of beer. Gladdie's birthday next week, too.

The sound of an engine came suddenly through the screen door. Surging and sputtering, it wasn't Cy's truck, Bert was sure. And anyhow, Cy never parked so close to the house. Bert sat quietly, listening; she wished Shorty hadn't gone to Emmis for a haircut tonight.

The motor died and Bert crossed to the door and looked out. She turned on the light above the door and saw no one, just the shadow of a car.

Then Hank Kootseema was on the walk, looking up at her. His dark hair grew over the collar of his shirt and he hadn't shaved for at least a week. He looked thinner than Bert had ever seen him, the leather strap of his belt overlapping the worn buckle by six or eight inches.

There was no mistaking the bitter malice in Hank's voice.

"Kennedy home?"

"I'm sorry, Hank, but my father's not here just now. You might find him in town or you could stop in later, or come back in the morning."

Hank stared at her.

"You can tell him for me, since you're so good with words. You can tell him keep his sorry ass off my place and don't worry if my oats is cut. Don't be botherin' Mabel about if her chickens is doin' okay. My oats is cut when I cut 'em and he better not be up there."

Bert felt weak and reached up to latch the screen door. She saw in the light a film of sweat on his forehead and cheeks. Hank made a half turn on the cement walk and looked toward the road, toward Emmis. He was breathing heavily, his shoulders moved back and forth as though he had been running a great distance.

Bert felt ashamed to be reminded of a mad dog Cy had shot not far from the house long ago, she and Thea frightened by the quivering old hound, unsteady on his feet.

She felt a tremor an her legs now as she closed the wooden door, then leaned against it briefly. "God," she thought, "I wonder if Mabel is more afraid when the sun comes up or when the sun goes down."

Holding her breath, she heard the car door slam and the grinding of the starter, then the soft crackle of gravel beneath the slow moving wheels of Hank's old car.

Bert reached for the phone on the wall. If Thea was still at Gladdie's, she'd better not start home in the dark....but then, Gladdie might be upset... what was Pavlik's number...the sharp trill of the phone seemed to explode in the kitchen.

Jack Kraemer, the auctioneer in Emmis, was calling to speak to Thea. The sound of his voice, so normal, so unhurried, calmed the beating of Bert's heart.

She said, "Jack, Thea should be home in a half hour or so, I'll have her call you then."

"Just tell her I found out ten minutes ago that Otto Lund's auction bill Thea printed has the wrong date listed for the sale. I got my kid out, ripping them down. Tell Thea I need a correction quick, I hope on Monday."

"I'll tell her, Jack. I don't see why she made that error."

"She didn't", he snorted. "I'm a damn fool, can't read a calendar."

Bert laughed and she was still smiling as she went to the door and let the night air come again through the screen.

Thea, with Rowdy beside her, walked through the dusk. She wondered why she so often neglected night-roaming in these fields, something she and Bert had done often when they were younger. Only an hour had passed since the sun had blazed across the harvest fields and now the air felt cool and charged with a quality of dampness common to the early dark at summer's end. A veiled moon urged itself to take over the sky as it rose further from the horizon; the trees at the edge of the field were black with shadow.

Looking over her shoulder, Thea saw faint light in the distance, a fine haze defining the town of Emmis. Here and there, the yellow of headlights moved on the roadway running past the farm.

There would be a mist riding above the grain shocks at dawn, burned off by noon.

Harvest time. Although she wasn't at the farm as the harvest was completed except to join the crew at the supper table now and then, the process of the growing piles of straw, the filled grain bins moved her as nothing else in farming now or in her earlier years.

Next week she'd be working longer days than usual, clearing things up at the paper so she'd be able to meet Ralph for a few days at the fair in Des Moines. She'd probably leave late Wednesday.

By the time he'd driven to the end of Cy's driveway Hank was feeling sick. A guy should never drink that much without eatin'. He sat there a minute, wondering if he should go into Emmis and find Cy.

Tellin' Mabel don't worry, we'll get them oats in the granary. Like the only way was if him and probably that stupid Shorty figured it all out.

He opened the car door and turned in the seat. God, he felt sick! He stood beside the car, and then heard the yipping of a dog, sounded close to Cy's house.

Like hell Cy's in Emmis! That dog's tied up every night in the shop, everybody knows that! Cy ain't gone, havin' a smoke with Shorty, most likely, laughin' when that Bert lied for him.

Well, two can play bein' sneaky.

Hank climbed back in the car and found the reverse gear, his foot pressed lightly on the gas pedal. When he drove to the space in front of Cy's barn, he turned the key and sat there. He'd been holding his breath, the driveway was a straight shot but a person could veer off in the dark, with no lights. He pushed down on the door's latch and stepped out silently, then quickly sat down again and reached over the back of the seat for the shotgun.

He let the door hang open and stood quietly, listening for the dog. He felt scared, even with the gun. Wouldn't come to using it, anyhow, but old Cy might perk up his ears better if he knew a guy wasn't foolin.

Hank still felt sick and maybe he'd better go home. He couldn't see in the shed if Cy's truck was gone, what if he was and he come home right about now?

Approaching the circle of buildings, Thea was aware of the lights in the house, at least in the kitchen. She heard, west of the house, horses stepping on stones, nickering, rubbing against each other inside the night pasture. She saw the hen house door closed against marauders from the fields and ditches.

She paused briefly as she traveled the last few rods of the lane between Gladdie's and the Kennedy house, noticing the fragile wind in the maples at the edge of the lawn, hearing its faintness in the highest of the trees, moving in and out of the green, green leaves.

Rowdy ignored the clicking of the latch when Thea swung the gate open; if he was lucky he might catch at least one field mouse tonight.

Hank heard the metal on metal sound of the gate being opened. He hadn't thought of it before, but old Cy probably went over to that Gladdie's pretty regular like. Wonder how many in Emmis knows that?

Suddenly the lights of a slow moving car moved up the driveway, back of the house; Thea recognized the sound of Shorty's car. She smiled; haircut and not more than two drinks at Pavlik's. Good going, Shorty!

Hank saw the lights, too. What the hell! Gangin' up on him, boxin' him in, he can't just run and leave his car!

Suddenly he was filled with rage. Bert standin' there, lockin' that screen door like he was a peddler, Cy Kennedy sneakin' around in the dark with an old dog for protection! Thea, the one at the paper, well, they ain't got a chance to call Frank Keefe this time, shots goin' past a guy's head.

With both hands on the shotgun, Hank stumbled to the corner of the porch and rested the barrel against the house at the level of his shoulder. He hoped the damned dog didn't sniff him out. He was lucky he caught the sound of Cy out there in the dark. His breath was ragged but his mind was suddenly enraptured by an impassioned power that stilled the trembling of his finger as it stroked the worn trigger; the moonlight was enough to catch Cy, easy.

From the corner of his eye, Hank saw a car park near his and heard, almost at the same time, the sound of hurrying feet on the sidewalk leading to the house.

Bert, in the kitchen, heard something, too. A cow in the night yard, brushing against the gate, moving the latch? Rowdy, home before Thea, nosing his tin dish against his bucket of water beside the step?.

Bert was stunned for a single heartbeat as the sound of a sharp blast cut through the walls of the house and a dull thud followed as something was flung against the cellar door beneath the kitchen window.

She flipped the light switch as she ran from the kitchen, the backyard and the edge of the garden were flooded with pale light. A row of red zinnias stood half in shadow, the top half of each plant caught in the sudden light.

Her view of the convulsive movements of Thea was blocked by Shorty's frame as he knelt beside the wounded body lying across the flat wooden cellar door. Bert fell to her knees beside Thea, her stricken eyes taking in the shattered face and the blood soaked chest of her sister, her twin. She heard the fluttering moans, the faint whistling of Thea's breath, she smelled the warmness of the blood.

Shorty stumbled to his feet and began to run toward the sound of a car's frantic whine, the sound of wild despair and fear lifting out of the gears as the car half stalled, then sped west, its single headlight bouncing against the dark.

There was another sound and Bert moved her head slightly to one side, straining to know it.

The sound was herself, no voice, no cry, no plea, a frenzied tone that went back further than any link between her own life and the barely moving limbs of Thea.

The light above was encircled by moths oblivious to everything but their own motion, and when Shorty returned to Bert's side she looked at him.

"You called for help?"

"I couldn't get through to Pavlik's but the operator, she's gettin' Doc Dennison. She'll send somebody to Pavlik's if the line's still busy".

Cy and Frank Keefe were standing at the long bar in Pavlik's when young Buddy Lease, a wild look on his face, raced through the door and up to Cy. "Hank, he took off from your place like he was on a racetrack and nearly took me sideways. Something musta happened and Hank was headed home but he never coulda got there in one piece."

Frank's Buick swept out of Emmis as though it was carried by a tornadic gale. When they flew into the Kennedy yard Cy had his door open before Frank killed the engine and then both men were running to the side of the house that was bathed in light.

Cy fell to his knees beside both girls and looked in horror at the scene. Frank, one hand on Shorty's sleeve, said, "I'm going up there after that son of a bitch. You stay put, I don't want anybody seein' the law in action in Sutton County."

"Hold on!" Cy called as Frank ran to his car. As he stood, Cy pulled Bert to her feet. He reached out with one arm, drawing her close. "Tell me, Alberta."

Before she could reply, the two of them stepped apart, allowing the doctor to kneel near Thea. Margaret Dennison, Doc's daughter, had gone to school in Emmis with the twins and had been one of their best friends at St.Mary's. She set her father's bag near him and embraced Bert.

Cy had seen at once that Thea was dead, and he called to Frank, who was getting into his car, "Just wait, Frank. Hank's not going far; give me a minute."

In the shadow of the wooden fence that surrounded an oval bed of flowers, Shorty was wiping his mouth with his blue bandanna handker- chief. His eyes, red-rimmed, were on Cy. In one hand a small rifle was gripped, balanced horizontally, the barrel gleaming in the light from the bulb high on the wall of the house.

Frank walked behind Cy and then stepped quickly to Shorty's side. "The Lease boy saw the son of a bitch tear out of here, he's not coming back. Set the rifle down, Shorty, set yourself down. Cy's bound he's going with me but you stay here til we get back."

Shorty didn't answer and stuffed the handkerchief into his hind pocket.

Frank touched Shorty's arm and, then, looking at both men, he said, "I can't have anybody here doing something that'll bring any more regret to this place."

They watched Doc and Bert and Margaret near the cellar door, an oddly minimal panorama. Doc had gone into the house five minutes ago. Frank wanted Cy out of there before Aubrey arrived in the hearse.

Cy, looking at the ground near Shorty's boots, began to speak and lost his voice. He tried again, standing straight and looking Shorty in the eye.

"Just the other day, Thea told me that when she was a kid, she figured she had two fathers, one a tiresome and bossy old coot and the other, Shorty."

The rifle fell from Shorty's hand and his knees began to buckle, his shoulders shaking inside the chambray shirt.

Frank picked up the gun and put it on safe, then emptied the shells into his hand.

Frank didn't hear the short conversation between Bert and Cy, but he heard Cy tell Doc and Aubrey, "You fellows do this thing right, from start to finish. I'm riding up to Hank's with Frank and we'll see you back here pretty quick."

He said to Doc, "I'm hoping Margaret can maybe stay the night, if that's what Bert wants."

He walked over to where Thea was wrapped in a sheet, the back door of the hearse standing wide. "I'll lift her in, myself", Shorty told Cy.

"I wonder, Shorty, if you'd run down to Gladdie's. Don't scare her, she pulls the window shades at dark and doesn't know anything that's happening."

Shorty knew he was being asked to do a job that Cy couldn't bear to do, himself.

As Frank wheeled the car past Aubrey's hearse, Cy whipped off his felt hat, half closing his eyes but staring at the knees of his faded overalls. Frank reached under the seat and pulled out his revolver, wrapped in a square of old leather. He laid it on the seat between them.

A couple of rods past Cy's mailbox, Frank swerved when Rowdy climbed out of the grass filled ditch and ran toward the Kennedy driveway. Seeing him, Cy said, "Hid out, poor old devil. Scared of guns. Always was."

Frank heard him sob softly as the car turned north, to Hank Kootseema's place.

It was going to rain, after all.

Lightning sprinted boldly across the western horizon, the line between earth and sky now mostly obscured by darkness. As they drew closer to

Hank's place, ragged bolts of gold descended from the sky above the sagging barn.

In the barnyard, Hank's old team of horses crowded near the sagging wire gate, startled and frightened by the sounds and the nighttime movement in the dim light.

Just before Frank stopped the car, both men saw Mable emerging from the shadows of the old machine shed and they saw nearby the shape of Hank's Chevrolet. Mabel, rain drenched in her sagging cotton dress, stopped suddenly in the bright light of Frank's headlights.

As Frank and Cy approached her, she suddenly stood taller. She pointed vaguely toward the spot next to the shed where Shorty had leaned the pitman at noon. Frank stepped toward her and she began to speak before he could say anything. "Hank, he fell right there."

Frank swore softly and pushed past Cy. Kneeling, he saw beneath a wet and tangled quilt, Hank's bloodied face and one arm, flung to the side. The bib of his faded overalls and ragged shirt were covered with bright blood.

Mabel said, as though she was reporting a casual event, "He drove up right there and never shut down the motor and that one crooked car light showed up against the shed. I come down to see if he was comin' in, the rain was just a drizzle but gettin' dark, out here. He just looked up from the dirt where he fell, drunk like, and he said, 'I'm off the place, at last. I just shot old Cy. I'm after Glory and she can be all the house woman I need.' I reached in the car door, still open, and turned off the key.

"Glory, she stood on the porch with the lantern. The headlights was goin' dark but I seen this binder thing in the gleam. I took it by the wood part and two-handed Hank hard on his arm when he tried to get up, and then his head. After, I pulled this quilt off the wash line here and covered him up,"

Mabel pointed toward the house. "You can see Glory still on the porch. She never come near or seen the whole thing in the dark."

The sheriff stared at Mabel and reached toward her as he began to speak. Cy moved closer, too, and shook his head at Frank. The rain seemed little more now than a shower, and Cy put one hand on Mabel's shoulder, steering her toward the Buick, its engine murmuring, its lights continuing to bathe the small yard in yellow light.

Cy walked Mabel past the old quilt, rain soaked and outlining the body beneath it where blood, mingled with the yard's fine dust, ran in pink rivulets toward the barn.

"Do you want anything from the house" Cy asked her.

Mabel hesitated. "No, I left my life between them walls. I can't get it back, and nothing else matters."

Suddenly, she shook off his hand and looked directly at Cy. "Hank said he left you dead. Why would he say such a thing?"

"He maybe thought it was me, but it was Thea he killed, in the side yard." Mabel spun, clawing at the side of Hank's car, her legs failing to hold her upright. Kneeling, she threw back her head and screamed.

"Innocent souls, he never showed no care for innocent souls!"

Frank helped Cy lift her back to her feet.

Both men were aware that four or five cars had driven slowly into Hank's yard, stopping near the ditch. The occupants stood before their dark cars; two or three were talking softly, and when Cy turned to look at them, he was surprised that they looked like neighbors at a country auction or a church gathering. They stood alert and listening.

He knew they guessed who lay beneath the sodden quilt a few yards from where they waited, and no one seemed to be shocked that Hank was dead.

Glory, when Mabel screamed, disappeared into the house and now lunged from the porch, the lantern hitting against her leg and she carried close to her body a smooth cardbox. She set the lantern on the ground near Frank and opened the box.

She pulled Sandy McDonald's watch and a stiff, small leather purse from the box. "I got stuff here. Mama, she never seen me put it in the house. I kept it just for lookin' at, that's all."

She looked at Frank when he tried to see inside the box and pushed it at him. Mabel's wailing began again and Glory, startled, asked, "Who hurt Mama? Who made Mama cry? She never done it! It's me took it!"

Frank, grim faced and angry, took the box from Glory and slid it in the back seat of the car.

Liz McGuire approached Frank and asked if she could take Mabel to the house and help her get cleaned up. Cy said, "Frank, we need to look Hank over for a minute or two." Dismayed, Frank followed him. He'd told the Lease kid fifteen minutes ago to go find Aubrey, where was that damn hearse?

Frank's boots were planted firmly beneath him as he crouched low; he rocked slightly as Cy began to pull the quilt aside once more.

Was Cy seeing something more than the smashed head of a man for whom no decent person would wish mercy?

The blood from Hank's wounds, still mingling with the slight rain falling in the dark, gathered on the gravel in small pools, and Frank knew that the knees of Cy's overalls, buried slightly in the wet ground, would be soaked through.

"Hanging over him." thought Frank, "Like he's not quite sure it's Hank!"

He said, "For God's sake, Cy, get yourself out of the mud!"

Cy righted himself slowly and stood with his hands in his overalls pocket, still looking at Hank's face.

Frank said, "That old Sid Jako, he sure comes to mind when you see Hank. They both had that sly look about them."

Cy stared at the sheriff. "He always looked a lot like Sid, you're right. But the same blood that ran in him runs in me."

Frank held his breath and raised his arm as though he was reaching for Cy. Cy was silent, he hesitated, choosing the words he knew he must say. "You're looking at my brother's woods colt, there, Frank. Tom knew it. It's my great sin that I knew it, too.

He stooped and pulled the quilt over Hank's face.

Frank's arm fell to his side and he turned when Liz McGuire asked if her boy could run home quickly, find something of Liz' Mabel could wear. Frank nodded and motioned for Cy to get in the car.

"Tom and I got in a hell of a fight one Sunday when Ayma was carrying the twins. If Shorty hadn't been there I might have killed Tom, it got that bad. He went back to St. Paul and a week later he wrote and said that if our folks were so damn proud Ayma was having a kid, how would they feel if they knew he was in the race, too, and did I want to tell them that his kid's other grandfather was Sid Jako?

"He wrote that he'd been staying in Amelias's room for about six weeks whenever he was in Emmis. He said she was so damn dumb she'd never figure out whose baby she had...she had a dozen names to pick from. He said he knew he was the one but she'd never get her arithmetic figured out."

Frank stared out the windshield at the small rivulets of water sliding downward, remembering how Tom, his best friend, had become someone he didn't know.

Cy went on, "I'm not so sure why it was so important to hold it secret. When Tom heard how things were divided when the folks were killed, I expected him to spring out in the open, to name another Kennedy in line for something, but he never said a thing. I thought at the time it was just his way of not having to say what a rounder he was but I know now that he never gave Amelia another thought. He just forgot the whole thing."

Frank stirred uneasily, watching for Liz to bring Mabel back to the car.

"Cy, nobody can fault you for the way you put up with the Kootseema mess. Money wouldn't have done Hank or his ma any real good, and Good Christ, you didn't need them any closer than they were."

"I wasn't so much those two that made me feel wrong. It was Matt! It ended up with Matt and Mabel and Glory taking the load on this place!"

Staring out the window beside him, at the rainswept, desolate farmyard, Cy said, "Old Gottfried and Anna! God damn it, Frank, look at this place!"

Liz was helping Mabel down the porch steps and Frank turned to Cy. "What are you going to tell Bert?"

Cy sat, slumped forward, his eyes cast downward, the fingers of one hand splayed across his forehead.

"What would you have me tell her? That my pride, my shame, my silence killed her sister?"

Bill and Mae Henry had been the first neighbors to arrive after Cy and Frank had come to Kootseema's. Now Mae ran toward Glory, grabbing her arm and setting the lantern to the side. No one could hear what she told Glory, who stared at the scene lit by Frank's headlights.

Frank helped Cy put Mabel in the front seat of the Buick, where she fell sideways across the seat, her head beneath the steering wheel. Cy closed the door as Frank went to the driver's side. He turned to Mae. "Can you keep the girl until tomorrow?"

Mae stepped forward. "I can do that. I knew her from a baby on and we never had no trouble gettin' on."

Cy came close to Mae. "Don't try to explain to her who hurt Mabel or made her cry. The list is too long for one person to figure out."

Cy stood, frowning, for a few seconds near Mabel's window. Then. with his knuckles, he tapped on the rain streaked window. Mabel jerked, alert, her breath uneven and she looked at Frank, beside her, then at Cy.

Cy bent to speak to her when Frank reached across and rolled down the window. "Hank...it was Hank, wasn't it, last spring over at Sandy's?"

Mabel straightened in the seat, sighing loudly and rubbing her forehead as though she just might be able to bring some order, something true to this wild day. Her voice was strong and Cy listened, rain dripping from the brim of his hat, his hand gripping the half raised window between them.

"I figured so, maybe, but when Frank come after he saw Sandy dead, I told him what Hank told me. I always did."

Turning to Frank, she said, "You never ast me but the once. I thought maybe you'd stop by sometime when Hank was gone."

She dipped her head, her eyes closed. "But I expect I woulda said the same, anyhow."

It was nearly ten, and once again the rain was falling. The lightning and thunder that had marked the rain's beginning had faded away and as Frank drove toward Cy's place to see his best, his most trusted friend home, he wondered if Cy noticed the damage this moisture visited upon his oats, acres and acres of oats in rounded shocks.

Loose thoughts, he knew. Cy was thinking of his daughters, of Ayma, of the high cost of being a Kennedy, just west of Emmis.

Next to Frank, Mabel huddled loosely on the seat, her thin legs stretched against the sill of the passenger door. She had not spoken a word since Cy climbed in the back seat after questioning her about Sandy's death. The sheriff dreaded locking her in a cell tonight. He had a deputy but Frank wouldn't bother him tonight; he guessed he'd better sleep at the desk in the jail, himself.

He thought he'd stop off at his house and pick up a couple of blankets. The thin cotton dress Liz had given her was probably the best piece of clothing Mabel had ever worn, but small protection from the night's chill.

Frank pulled the car close to the front porch at Kennedy's farm, and glanced over his shoulder at Cy, who looked at the sheriff a couple of seconds, then opened the back door of the Buick and stepped out. Halfway up the steps, Cy raised his hand and pushed up the brim of his hat, staring at Frank briefly.

Frank guessed it was some kind of a salute, and he was glad he'd waited to see it.

In the kitchen, Gladdie and Bert sat at the table; Gladdie half stood when Cy walked in, then sank back into her chair. He took his hat off, held it by the brim and looked at the two women. Then Gladdie stood and walked quickly to his side.

"Cy Kennedy, I take this for a day I cannot abide. My heart ain't twisted sideways like other times. It's gone."

She wept quietly, his arms around her shoulders.

Bert moved closely to them both, and when Margaret Dennison appeared from the pantry with cups and saucers, Bert and Gladdie and Cy stood together, each enfolded in the arms of the others.

Shorty had seen Cy's return and he came through the door quietly, setting a bottle of Wilkens Family whiskey on the table. Bert told Cy that

Margaret would stay until morning and Shorty told Gladdie he'd drive her home when she was ready to go.

The next morning Cy and Bert met with Aubry at the funeral home. Gladdie declined the suggestion that she come, too. "I'll be here. Shorty, he can't do everything that needs doin' on the place." Little was said at the table that noon.

Davis Mader doubted he'd be welcomed by anyone in Emmis and as the barns of the Kennedy farm came into view he wished he hadn't read of Thea's murder in the morning paper.

The farmyard was strangely quiet and he was glad when Shorty came out of the machine shop; he felt a stab of gratitude as Shorty recognized him and raised an arm in greeting.

They walked together to the house, where Shorty stopped and said, "There's an awful lot of tender feelings goin' on in there, and there's no quick mend in sight. They'll be glad you come. I got some fixin' in the shop so I'll leave you now."

When Cy opened the door, Davis looked past him to the kitchen where Gladdie and Bert sat at the table.

Cy said, "We were just sitting down to coffee. I'll get another cup."

On Monday afternoon, fewer than a dozen people attended Hank's funeral. The new minister at the Redeemer Church agreed to give the sermon at the Emmis Funeral Home and his wife was seated at the ancient pump organ from which lugubrious tones settled over the nearly empty room.

At noon, Cy had decided to attend. Frank had been to the farm earlier in the day and hadn't asked Cy his plans but he wasn't surprised as he sat alone in the last row of folding chairs, to see Cy walk in and several pairs of eyes turn to stare.

Frank moved from the aisle chair to make room for Cy. But both were surprised a few minutes later when Bert bent close to the two of them and whispered "May I?"

Settled between the men, she stared ahead at the casket which she knew Cy had purchased, her hands tightly on the black handbag on her lap.

Frank was sure neither of the Kennedys joined in the silent prayer the minister asked be given for Hank, but Bert's voice was clearly heard as the last hymn was sung.

The sheriff was alone in the country cemetery, then, except for the minister and the six casket bearers, who at Cy's request, John Pavlik had recruited from regulars at the saloon.

This morning, Frank had asked Mabel if she'd like to attend the service. She thought for a moment and said, "It's enough for me, I don't have to see him no more."

Bert asked Cy the day after Thea was killed if she could arrange with Father McKee to have Thea buried from St. Mark's. "Why ever not?"

Two days after Hank's funeral the doors of every business place in Emmis were closed between the hours of one o'clock and three. Shorty Brill, Davis Mader, Gladdie's nephew, Anton, one bartender from Pavlik's and two men from the Advocate carried Thea's casket to the plot where the gravestones of Timothy, Bridget, Tom and Ayma were grouped near the circular drive that led through St. Mark's cemetery.

CHAPTER 16

As soon as Frank got to the outskirts of Emmis, he tossed his hat beside him on the seat. The early autumn wind sailed through the open windows and lifted his hair, played across the back of his hand resting on the steering wheel.

Cy had called him last night, asking him to stop out to the sixty where Hank and Mabel had lived, but a couple of mortgage foreclosure sales on the other end of Sutton County had taken most of the sheriff's day.

September had never been the good part of the year for Frank and this year, he felt melancholy and privately defeated. Indian summer might be in the wings, but the summer of 1938 had disappeared.

After a week of rain in August the hot dry winds had moved in and given the countryside the feel of fall.

He noticed more traffic than usual on the road west of Emmis and he recognized most of the cars. An accident? An auction he'd forgotten about?

When he was a half-mile from the old Kootseema farm he saw a whirlblast of dust where the buildings had stood side by side. Jim Vort, whose small road building crew had built nearly every county and township road near Emmis, was in the seat of a Caterpillar tractor moving in a cloud of dried clay and particles of topsoil, the dirt in the air obscuring the autumn sun.

Cy stood at the edge of a rough, pushed-together pile of rubble, boards and shingles, cement, rusty stanchions, woven and barbed wire.

His checkbook protruded from his shirt pocket, his eyeglasses were covered with a film of dust.

"What I was wondering, Frank, maybe tomorrow you could watch traffic off the road here so I can torch this pile. Burn what'll burn, Jim will haul the rest off and bury it. Wind supposed to be from the east, the radio said at noon. But the smoke's gotta go somewhere."

Cy looked at Frank. "It always does, doesn't it?"

Two strings of early mallards flew overhead in a perfect V, toward the cattail slough. Passing above the foundered ruins of Kootseema's farmyard and through the dust ascending from the relentless surge and gashing of the Cat, some of the ducks drifted sideways, as though they had known all along that flying in a feathered regiment gave them no immunity from anything above or below the pattern of their flight.